UNEXPECTEDLY RUINED

IRENE BAHRD

To my readers who wished the Indiana Jones trilogy was smuttier...

You're welcome.

AUTHOR NOTE

For the best reading experience, read Jack and Amanda's prequel novella *Maybe in Fifty* before diving into *Unexpectedly Ruined*. It shows their amazing night in New York that you will only get glimpses of here.

Unexpectedly Ruined can be read as the first in the series, after *Maybe in Fifty*, but contains spoilers for *A Voice Without Reason* (Becca's story) and *Not Her Villain* (Layla's story).

Jack's chapters are written in British English, Amanda's are not. You will find an extra "u" and a lack of "z" in his point of view. **<u>This is intentional.</u>**

Finally, please be safe and talk to your doctor about what works best for you and/or your sexual partners regarding birth control and STI protection. There is very little discussion about contraception in this book. Jack and Amanda are fictional, you are not.

PROLOGUE
JACK

Please read author note
prior to starting this book.

"What's a pretty lass like yourself doing in a place like this?"

The gorgeous, blonde woman on the barstool to my right sighs and rolls her eyes. "Is that the best you've got?"

"I've watched you brush off no less than six other men tonight. For you to turn down these sharp suited stock-monkeys, you must be heartbroken and drowning your sorrows. Or you haven't found the right man... _yet._"

I thoroughly enjoy people watching in hotel bars. There are rarely regulars in places like this, most people coming and going, and every so often, there's one full of intriguing stories. Today is no exception. In fact, from observing this lass for the past hour, she's one of the most intimidating and fiery women I've encountered.

"And you think you're the right man?" she chuckles. "Don't think you can tempt me with that hot accent of yours. It would take at least three more whiskey sours for me to consider a man who wears a leather jacket in the middle of summer."

Shite, she's feisty. I take a sip of my drink. "Oh, she's a wee spitfire. Well, I don't need my accent to seduce you; I'll simply ignore you until you're desperate to talk to me."

"You'd never ignore me," she insists, lightly licking the corner of her lip in an attempt to hide her smile. She knows I've got her. We both do.

My new drinking companion finally looks over and… *fuck me.* She's not just pretty, she's fucking stunning. While I was previously making conversation to pass the time, I realise I'm a bit out of my league flirting with her. She has to be nearly a decade younger than me, with ocean blue eyes, dark crimson lips practically begging me to kiss her, and honey blonde hair cascading over her shoulders. It's the perfect length to wrap around my hand while I…

I shake the thought away, clear my throat, and introduce myself, "I'm—"

"No names. No jobs. It's easier when I disappear into the night."

"Well, well, sprite, it sounds like you're suggesting you want to spend the rest of the evening together," I chuckle softly and take a long drink of my whisky.

Just as I think I've lost her interest, she replies, "My place or yours?"

I nearly spit out my drink in shock. She can't be serious. *Can she?* Absolutely not. Surely, someone like her would never consider a night with me.

I'm in New York for the week to solicit donors for a big archaeological dig I'm proposing and don't need the distraction of a sinfully gorgeous woman. I also don't need her to find out I'm related to my wealthy cousin. He's supposed to be coming to America soon, with a stop in New York, and I'll be damned if he sets his eyes on her for one of his many PR stunts.

"Neither."

"Should've guessed you're just a big flirt," she laughs. "Well, I best be off. Long morning of writ—I mean, work. Lots of work. The workiest work. I—"

"No names. No jobs," I remind her, my words coming out like a purr.

Our eyes lock, then hers dip to my lips for a brief moment. "I should go," she sighs, almost disappointed —a stark contrast to the edge she's had since I sat down.

There's something about her; I don't want to let her get away just yet. "Stay." Her dark blue eyes dart between mine in question. "Let me buy you a drink. I don't want to take you upstairs, spitfire. Let's spend one night where I'm not—" The blue nearly disappears from her irises; she narrows her eyes. "Right, no names. How about I'm not me and you're not you?"

A small smile tugs at her lips. "I'm not an escort, you know."

"It never occurred to me that you could be," I laugh. "If you were, you would've left with one of the last four investment bankers flirting with you."

She eyes me suspiciously. "So, if you don't want to take me upstairs, what do you want?"

"Let's hit the town. See where the night takes us. Leave the baggage at the door."

She chews on her lip. "A night together? But then I might start to like you."

"We can't have that, can we, my wee spitfire?" I lean in and whisper, "Too late for me, though."

She brings the glass to her lips, pauses, then sets it down. "Alright, hot Scot, what do you have in mind?"

1

AMANDA

FOUR MONTHS LATER

I'm not a great writer; but I know how to tell a hell of a story that will keep a reader on their toes.

While I specialize in romantic suspense, after watching my friends find success and happiness writing outside their typical genres, I'm excited to start a new work in progress today.

~~The Hot Scot.~~ Too on the nose.

~~Adventures in Scotland.~~ Sounds like a travel book.

The ~~Wee~~ Spitfire. I can't help my smile.

Most of my friends who are authors pick their titles last, after their book is written. Not me; the title is where I draw all my inspiration from. I get a book idea, work-shop a title, and even go so far as creating mock-ups of cover ideas for my graphic designer. Then, I'll do the actual writing. After publishing independently for years,

I recently took the leap and became traditionally published with a publishing house—they hate my chaos.

My critique partners, Becca and Layla, will probably roll their eyes when I pitch them my idea. They're used to my rapid release schedule and unhinged book ideas, but this is unlike anything I've written before. In the meantime, I'll enjoy the bliss of believing my idea isn't absolute shit.

I'm not writing about *him*, per se, but I thought it would be fun to write an age gap romance with a hot Scot with golden retriever-energy. The man will spend an evening wooing the heroine, and just when she thinks he's going to leave her high and dry, he hauls her upstairs to fuck her on every surface of his hotel room.

Fuck, that night was amazing.

Waking up to find him gone had squeezed my heart more than I expected it to. I was looking for a fun night, but found someone I had a real connection with. We never exchanged names or contact information; he didn't know who I was and I had no way of finding him. Even four months later, it stings to know I'll never see him again.

Especially with the note…

MY WEE SPITFIRE, THANK YOU FOR THE BEST
NIGHT OF MY LIFE.
-J

PLAYLIST

Promiscuous [feat. Timbaland] — Nelly Furtado
When Love Sucks [feat. Dido] — Jason Derulo
Maroon — Taylor Swift
Suit & Tie — Justin Timberlake
Greedy — Tate McRae
Bad Idea Right? — Olivia Rodrigo
Lose Control — Teddy Swims
SOS — Rhianna
Shut Up and Dance — Walk The Moon
Until I found You — Stephen Sanchez
Like I'm Gonna Lose You — Meghan Trainor
Electric Love — BØRNS

CONTENT WARNINGS

By reading this book, there is a good chance you will experience the following side effects:

- Wet panties.
- Considering owning a bullwhip.
- Sudden interest in archaeology.
- Desire to move to Scotland in hopes of finding your own Jack.

You're welcome.

All jokes aside, this is a super **instalove**, **medium-spice romantic comedy** novel with a healthy dose of on-page explicit content. It is intended for mature audiences. Also, it's a quick novel, so only expect to use your buzz buzz a few times before it's over.

Additionally, there are scenes with:

- Oral sexytime — it's an Irene Bahrd trademark, you knew it was coming
- Mild edging — don't worry he'll let her come
- Mild masochism — just a little biting/marking
- Mild cum play — mostly bonus epilogue, super brief in a few other scenes
- Butt stuff — bonus epilogue only
- Mild bondage — bonus epilogue only

Ok, fine, this is a shopping list and not warnings…

If you are triggered by anything in this book, do us both a favor and don't read anything else in my backlist. The rest of my books are equally unhinged.

Jason, Jacob, Jeff, Jameson... there's no way I'd narrow it down.

Best night of his life? Fuck, it was certainly mine. Hopefully, writing this book will get him out of my system.

Comfortable silences.

Ripped clothes discarded on the floor.

Kisses I felt all the way to my toes.

His strong hands gripping my thighs as I rode his face.

The heavy feel of his cock on my tongue as he fucked my mouth.

His thrusts, hard and deep, but never fast.

Coming harder than I had in my life... seven times.

Watching the sunrise together.

Wrapping me in his arms after a night, and morning, of bliss.

Him whispering, "You ruined me, spitfire."

All it took was an unexpected night for him to *ruin* me. I haven't stopped thinking about him for months, and every man I date doesn't compare to how comfortable I felt that night. I haven't even been able to sleep with anyone else.

I snap out of my daydream and begin writing.

"Where should we head first?" he asks, taking my hand.

I glance down at our interlocked fingers and back at him, meeting his bright green eyes that crinkle in the corner when he smiles. "You're the one who wanted a night out. You decide."

"You're the local, what would you suggest?" he counters.

"Are you hungry?" I hope he says yes. My stomach is on the verge of growling and I would love a bagel with cream cheese and lox from the bakery down the street.

His eyes darken. I should've been more careful with my word choice. "Aye, but what I'm hungry for will need to wait until later."

Even though I saw it coming a mile away, his low timbre coupled with his piercing gaze are more than I can handle with this flirting. Time to shut it down with salmon and a mouth full of gluten. "Right, well, are you ready for the unsex-iest food you can eat?"

I lead the way to the bakery and...

Fuck. This reads like a damn diary entry. I'm trying to write something new and unique, not just a retelling of our night. I rip an inch of the pages from my mono-grammed notebook, but stop.

I can't destroy our story. If it's meant to be a journal for now, then so be it.

The last week has been rough. Most of my author friends are planners—outlining their books prior to diving in. I prefer freewriting, letting the book guide me as I tell my characters' story, but this time I've been stumped. The catalyst for me is always the character names; only once I've found the right ones do the words flow. I've sworn off 'J' names—though I've considered Jeremy and Jeffrey. Nothing seems to fit the character I want to write.

A change of scenery is necessary. There's an adorable little coffee shop a few blocks from my apartment that should help spark inspiration. They call out dozens of names as they hand out drinks, maybe one will fit my hot Scot.

A small bell chimes as I enter the coffee shop and, before I've made it to the register, my usual barista greets me, "Well, if it isn't my smut peddling queen, Amanda Storm. What can I get for you today?"

I curtsy with an invisible skirt and a teasing smile. When I right myself, I reply, "Why, Sir Jackson, my dashing knight, I'd love a soy chai latte. *Extra spicy.*" I throw in a wink to accompany my atrocious British accent, making him chuckle.

Jackson. Hmm… That could work for my book.

I gasp. It actually fits. A forty-year-old, ruggedly handsome Scottish man who gives hand necklaces while telling his woman how extraordinary she is. He probably wrestles those weird cow-sheep things in Scotland for fun.

It's the perfect name.

I'm lost in thought when Sir Jackson addresses me. "Queen Amanda?"

"Sorry," I laugh. "Inspiration hit."

"Well, if it's as good as *Maybe in Fifty*, there will be a line around the block for a signing." Jackson begins steaming the soy milk to my preferred 125°F—I like to chug my first mug and savor the second one steamed a little warmer. Ever since the night I met my mystery man, my heart squeezes when I hear the title of my book. I wonder if he ever finished it, or worse, if he read the release after it that brought me to the bar where I met him in the first place.

"I can only hope! It's not a suspense this time." I wince. "It's a borderline romantic comedy." He stops steaming my latte and stares at me with wide eyes. "I know, I know. Trust me on this one. He'll have quite a bit of mystery around him."

Jackson offers a wide smile and continues making my drink. "I have no doubt. When will it be available?"

"For you? I'll make sure you get an early copy."

"There better be"—he lowers his voice—"*you know.*"

"Butt stuff in the epilogue?" I ask quietly. "When have I ever let you down?"

He laughs as he finishes making my drink, insisting it's 'on the house.' I refuse at first, but I'm anxious to get to my book and don't want to argue with him. I toss $30 in the tip jar for him and the staff—they don't get paid nearly enough to deal with me several times a week. It's the least I can do.

I find a comfortable leather chair to settle into. Like clockwork, I finish my latte in under a minute and Jackson replaces it before I can ask for seconds. It reminds me of those wizard and witch movies where the cup magically refills itself, making me want to read a cozy romantic fantasy book, like the ones Layla writes. It's a terrible idea; reading other books while I'm writing actually makes my creative experience more difficult, so I try to avoid it whenever possible. When I finished another friend's novel—which was sad as fuck—I found myself writing a depressing book right after. I usually have to read a smutty book or get laid to shake off the melancholy vibes and shift the energy.

When was the last time I had sex… other than my vibrator?

Four months.

Fuck, that's sad. The last time I had actual sex was my hot Scot.

Am I ever going to have amazing sex with another man after him? Not just any mediocre orgasm. Earth-shattering sex that makes me question my existence.

Am I ever going to have sex again… ever?

I fucking hope so. But, it wasn't just sex with him. It was as if two lost souls found each other…

Oh, that's good. I should put that in my book.

I retrieve my notebook from my bag and dive in, writing a star-crossed lovers cliché trope where they miss one another over and over; as if fate thinks it's a cute joke.

I've wondered so many times what might have happened if my hot Scot lived here. It would probably be the worst idea, seeing as I can't even walk past my favorite kosher bakery without thinking of him. I've turned street corners and breathed in wafts of his woodsy cologne on other men, or saw someone with the same build and man-bun walking down Canal Street while I'm picking up dinner. I would have to move.

What if it was him? What are the odds I'll see him again?

Does he think about me, too?

Does he even remember me?

I blink away the thought and write what would've happened if *Jackson* didn't leave a note, and instead stayed until morning. A few pages in, I have an incoming text from Becca.

BECCA

Layla's being wooed by a billionaire.

Good for her.

Come to Seattle and help me shut it down?

Layla was planning on writing a billionaire romance. Maybe she's going for an immersive writing experience. Let her live her best life!

Please? Julian can fly you in.

With a defeated sigh, I cave and agree to fly across the country to be the ultimate cockblock. The things I do for my friends...

2

JACK

On the balcony, looking out onto the city, I find my spitfire and wrap my arms around her from behind. Fuck, she fits perfectly; I never want to let go. The sun peeks over the horizon, painting the dark blue sky light orange and yellow. She sighs against me as I press a single kiss to her neck.

"Night's almost up," she whispers, her voice laced with disappointment.

"I have a meeting in a few hours. You?"

"No meetings." She turns in my arms, wrapping hers around my neck. A small smirk tugs at her lips, but I kiss it away.

"Night isn't over until one of us has to leave, spitfire."

An ache coils around my heart; I only have the morning with her. It's not enough. I bend to grip her thighs, wrap her legs around me, and—

My eyes flutter open to the sound of my brother knocking on my door.

"Mornin', Jack." Cameron leans against the frame, crossing his arms. "We need to get an early start today. Toby is making beans on toast; better move quickly or the bastard will eat it all himself." I rub my hands up and down my face to wake up. "She's still haunting you, isn't she?"

"Every day for nearly four months." I shake my head, resting my elbows on my knees as I sit up at the edge of the bed. *When will it stop?* My dreams have become a constant playback of the hours I spent with her. I blow out a long breath and ask, "What's on the agenda today?"

"Another dead end. I think you're right, the Black family left nothing here. I know you're worried about funding, but maybe Ben can——"

"You know we can't. It'll ruin everything we've done if we attach the Turner name to this dig any more than we already have. And before you suggest it, Julian has invested far too much already. Ben is in Seattle and heading to New York, maybe they know someone who can help." *Other than my ex-wife.*

"They're fucking billionaires, Jack. We have money from an anonymous investor, but it's not enough. Let them help; we're running out of time. If we want to turn Swarthmore Castle into a museum by the end of the year, we'll need more money."

I rub the back of my neck and concede, "I'll ask, but I make no promises."

The anonymous investor is my ex-wife, but I can't bring myself to tell Cam. I don't want to add a new investor into the mix while I'm dealing with her weaselling her way into my excavation and renovation.

"Well, for now, let's catalogue everything," he suggests, pushing off the door and leaving. He calls over his shoulder, "And maybe take care of that sword in your pants."

I fall back onto the bed with a groan, glancing to my side table, where a small bouquet of fresh thistles tortures me daily.

The morning I left, I had a meeting with Julian. I returned to the hotel room afterward, in hopes she might still be there. She was not. Thistles are the only thing I have to remind me of her, other than her last unspoken words I keep folded in my wallet. I take out the small note written on hotel stationery that she left me; the paper soft from being reread so many times.

MAYBE IN FIFTY, WE'LL FIND EACH OTHER AGAIN.
XO, YOUR WEE SPITFIRE

If only.

For the last year, I've been busy securing donors for an upcoming archaeological excavation in Isle of Skye. As it all seemed to fall into place, an anonymous donor funded the majority of my research. I assumed it was my cousin, Ben, or even his mum, but it turned out to be none other than my ex-wife, Blair. I should've known she would try to attach herself to my work.

Ben has offered to subsidise the project a thousand times, but I can't include the Turner name on it. Too many academic journal publications have been swallowed by his publishing company; listing him as a donor would tarnish my reputation and the credibility of the project.

Now, I'm stuck with Blair, who insists she needs to be on-site for the dig. She's not an archaeologist, or even an anthropologist, she's a fucking psychology professor. The excavation project doesn't require her expertise. What does she plan to do? Analyse me? Obviously, it worked out great for our marriage.

I was an eejit for marrying her in the first place; she never loved me and only stayed with me because of my family. Now, I'm stuck with her for the foreseeable future —until my research is complete.

If my research is complete.

Our marriage was short lived, only five years, and I never remarried. Blair came from money. It didn't take long for it to become painfully obvious that she only wanted to be married to me for a piece of my cousin's billion-dollar fortune. Whenever money was brought up, or we had a tight month, she would insist I should contact Ben for money, even when I was comfortable living within my means. We were two broke academics, it wasn't enough for her.

I want nothing to do with her, despite her continued advances after the divorce. How could I, when I haven't stopped thinking about my spitfire in New York? It was just one night, but that one night changed me. Why would I want to rekindle an old flame when there was a fiery vixen somewhere out there who made me feel more in one evening than I've felt in the last decade?

That night was beyond anything I could've imagined. We only spent hours together, but it felt like I'd known her my whole life. Something about her called to me, and months later, I still can't shake her. I should've found a way to find her. Instead, I was a fucking coward, leaving only a note.

Biggest regret of my life.

3

AMANDA

After a bit of internet sleuthing, I discover that Layla is being pursued by Julian's obscenely rich, book daddy friend. This Ben guy is in Seattle, swallowing up my publisher, and has set his eyes on Layla. Julian and Becca have offered me a boatload of money to help stop it. I declined—I'm a lady, after all, and don't need to be bought off—but I did ask that they cover the rent on my New York apartment while I'm gone. My apartment is rent controlled; I don't know how long this babysitting task could last, and I don't want to lose it.

Layla is the epitome of a sunshine character in a grumpy-sunshine trope—the girl is borderline cartoon princess. The last thing she needs in her life is a bosshole billionaire. So, here I am in Seattle, ready to make sure my friend isn't falling for a man she shouldn't. She was supposed to interview him for her upcoming billionaire romance but apparently it's more than that.

Becca picked me up from the airport—or rather she met me at the airport with a driver. I would've been fine taking a taxi but I'm not calling the shots here. We arrive at Layla's, and since Becca has a key, we sneak into her apartment like the stealthy creeps we are. Becca turns on a couple lights, and I immediately zero in on Layla's fancy coffee maker and begin brewing some of the most delicious smelling coffee I've experienced in my life. If I have to deal with this ridiculousness, I may as well enjoy some of the best coffee the Pacific Northwest has to offer.

A few minutes later, Layla emerges from her bedroom with a baseball bat, wearing black and white buffalo plaid pajama pants… in the middle of summer. What is it with people wearing inappropriate attire for the season? I should be shocked, but I don't blame her; living the single life for too long will make anyone resort to all sorts of odd behaviors.

"What are you two doing here?" Layla asks. "Amanda, I thought I wasn't going to see you until Harriet's wedding."

"Hey, bitch," I call over my shoulder, pouring three cups of coffee for us. "Julian flew me in last night. Something about keeping you away from some hot as fuck billion-aire. What is it with you two? And where can I get one of my own?"

Becca smacks my arm. She is living her own real-life billionaire romance with Julian. I'm not jealous, I just… *Ok, I'm a little jealous.* Not because of the money, but the way that man is head-over-heels obsessed with my friend.

"It's not to keep her away from him," Becca insists. "It's to keep her busy so she isn't tempted by a charming man who is only here for a few months and way too into her."

"Same fucking thing, Becs." *Why am I Layla's keeper, again?* "Anyway, put some real clothes on. We're going out today," I command.

Layla checks her phone, and after a minute, finally replies, "Sure."

Layla's disappointment is painted all over her face. She sucks at hiding it and attempts a smile that looks more like a grimace. As she saunters off to her bedroom, Becca and I sit in comfortable silence at the kitchen table, enjoying some of the most delicious coffee I've had in years. When Layla finally returns to the kitchen, this time wearing respectable clothes, I'm scrolling my phone and come across an email from Turner Publishing.

Looks like Benedict Turner moves fast and he's every bit the asshole Julian warned us he was. "Did you get an email from our new publishing giant?"

Oh did I...

I summarize the email I received for Layla and Becca. "They're making major cuts. They fired everyone on my team and said they won't be publishing any new titles.

Fuck!" I toss my phone onto the counter, praying it will shatter so I don't have to read that again in the near future. *I'm a goddamn top three romance novelist, why the actual fuck would this guy rip up my contract?* "They cut a ton of romance, fantasy, and young adult. Becs, maybe going the indie route was the right move. You're saved from this shitshow."

"YA and fantasy? Shit! I need to check with Harriet and see if her books are safe." Becca texts our friend, Harriet, I hope she wasn't on the list. With her wedding a month away, she doesn't need the added stress.

Layla doesn't appear as upset as I am; there's a good chance her contract is intact with our new book daddy. She continues checking her phone, avoiding my gaze, but then my cinnamon roll friend suddenly looks a little perturbed. *She knows something.* I'll need to get it out of her, and the only way to do that is a spa day, with tacos and margaritas. Lots and lots of margaritas.

Becca left for Portland with Julian this morning after coffee, so I'm treating Layla to mani-pedis. I need to loosen her up if I want to find out what's going on between her and this guy who is so into her that his own friend has enlisted me to be a buffer.

Layla and I spent a lot of time together at Julian's home in Temecula a few years ago. This is the first time it's just been the two of us since then, so while I'm supposed to keep an eye on things, I'm actually loving spending time with her.

If I know my girl, and I know I do, tacos and margaritas will have her singing like a songbird for me. It definitely helps that the guacamole on the west coast is superior to New York's—we've ordered three refills already, but I don't think I could get enough.

Or maybe it's the heavy-pour margaritas that are making me extra hungry.

An idea strikes me. "Hand me your phone," I demand between bites. She passes it to me. It's brand new without a single scratch. I turn it over. "Holy shit! This model isn't even out yet. How did you get one?" She tries to respond but I steamroll over her, "How do you even unlock it?"

Layla unlocks it, hands it back to me, and with a furrowed brow, "What are you up to?"

"Nothing," I lie and begin texting her new beau.

> If you are still up for an interview, would you meet me for a drink?

BEN'S A DICK
> Of course. What time?

Damn, he's eager.

> Now?

> My darling Layla, I didn't take you as a day drinker.

Look at this guy with his flirty response. This should be fun.

Layla snatches the phone back and reads the thread between the two of them. "Damn it! What did you do? Becca said you're supposed to be helping but—"

"What? I wanted to meet this guy who pissed you off so much that you didn't even enjoy an hour-long massage from a hot Swedish man. Love that he's in your phone as Ben's A Dick, by the way."

I did my research on this guy, like a good girl. Benedict Turner is a deliciously attractive publishing tycoon who dates models, probably just to keep the media off his ass, since he's never seen with the same woman twice. I'm curious what he wants with Layla, a romance author who doesn't do flings.

Layla's phone vibrates with an incoming call from Ben. "Do I answer it?" she asks, wide-eyed.

"Fuck yes, you do! Use a sexy phone voice. Make it all breathy. 'Oh, Ben, I missed you.'"

Layla tries to maintain her composure and answers, "Hello?" Whatever he says makes her redder than a bloody mary. "Don't mind the texts, my friend sent them."

Bitch.

"Yes. I mean, yes, I can meet you," she says, a little too happily.

Attagirl, go out with the hot billionaire, so I can find out what the fuck he's up to. Wait, why am I encouraging her to possibly date him? I'm supposed to be a cockblock.

He agrees to meet us in fifteen minutes, giving me ample time to help Layla revise her interview questions... and for me to suggest a few additional ones.

Layla is sipping her third margarita when Ben comes up behind her. "Hello, sunshine." Fuck, his accent is tastier than the guacamole! No wonder she's into him.

There's something familiar about him, but I can't place it...

"Holy shit. You didn't tell me he was hot!" I fib. I knew that, obviously, but he is definitely hotter in person. As I drink him in, Ben reminds me a little of the hot Scot I hooked up with. Maybe all the men across the pond are hot as fuck?

Shit, I really should've rummaged through the Scot's wallet for his name so I could internet stalk him.

Ben pulls up a seat next to Layla. "You didn't tell her how incredibly handsome I am? Such a shame, considering I have no issue telling anyone that you're the most beautiful woman I've ever met."

I roll my eyes. Who falls for this kind of over the top romantic shit?

Layla lets out a little snort and tells him, "Yeah, ok."

Apparently, she does...

Who am I kidding? If he was my hot Scot, I totally would've fallen for it.

I interrupt their vomit-inducing moment. "So, publishing daddy, thanks for releasing me from my contract. Love that so fucking much."

Embarrassed, Layla looks everywhere but at Ben. He addresses me, not taking his eyes off her, "It's Amanda Storm, isn't it?"

"That's me!" I sneer and raise my glass in the most insincere toast in the history of time.

"Check your email, Ms. Storm." He still doesn't look away from Layla, so I check my phone.

Layla breaks her silence and asks, "What did you—"

"What needed to be done, darling."

Well, I'll be damned. It looks like he reinstated my contract. I stop my scroll. Did he just say darling? "I'm sorry, what's happening? Why are you calling her... oh. Oh! Ok, I should head out and leave you two to eyefuck. Or fuck-fuck. You know, the whole, spread her out right here on the table, and feast on her thing. Could be hot. Could get you arrested."

My hot Scot would do it...

Layla's about to defend herself, but Ben beats her to it. "That won't be necessary, Ms. Storm. Please stay, my feasting will have to wait. I'm headed to an appointment shortly. I'd like to think I'll be able to join you right after, but this one can be unpredictable. We might need to push out your questioning to this evening, sunshine."

I rest my chin on my fists in anticipation. "Ok, but now you have to tell us what the hell this appointment is. A tattoo? A mole removed? One of those water spas? A drug deal?"

"A piercing," he replies matter-of-factly.

Oh shit! I didn't expect that!

"What kind of pier— Nevermind, it's none of my business," Layla says sheepishly.

Ben leans in and whispers something that makes her shiver, then kisses her temple as he stands. "Enjoy the rest of your meal." Without another word, he walks away, stopping at the host stand for just a moment to hand them something.

Layla is lost in thought, most likely on the verge of freaking out, so I tease, "He's totally getting his dick pierced. What do you think? A Jacob's ladder? Or maybe a Prince Albert?"

Please tell me it's a Jacob's ladder…

"I… I don't know."

Since we are nearly done with our dinner, we ask the server for our check, but she insists that someone already paid for everything. She hands Layla an envelope. Inside is a note reading:

SUNSHINE,

I KNOW YOU'RE WONDERING, SO HERE'S A HINT:

ONLY WAY I COULD GUARANTEE I WOULDN'T TRY

TO FUCK YOU ON A SECOND DATE.

SEE YOU TONIGHT?

—BEN

He is totally getting his cock pierced. Guess my job here is done!

The back of her note has information for a restaurant near the water and a designer boutique with an appointment time.

"Let's go shopping on his dime," I insist. "Then, you're so meeting that hot as fuck billionaire for dinner. Sorry, Layla-love, it's totally his dick, so no hanky-panky for you."

4

JACK

After talking with my aunt, she'll be able to subsidise some of my research and the renovations. Ben and Julian are going to find a way to fund the remainder of it, but in all honesty, their plan sounds more like a money laundering scheme than anything. Based on their projections, I'll be able to start my dig in a couple of months and I can afford to have Cam assist. The pieces are all coming together.

Packing my bag, I yell to the other room, "Cam, ten minutes."

"Shite, I thought I had twenty," he shouts back.

I huff a laugh, shaking my head. My brother may be an amazing researcher, but he has the worst sense of time. We're scheduled to deliver more findings to the British Museum later today, and I hate to be late. I wish we could've flown, but it's not in the budget until our additional funding comes in—I don't want to touch Blair's money, and my aunt's won't deposit into our account for a couple of days.

Once we have everything, I toss my bag into his truck and get on my motorbike. It's still dark, the only light on the roads being Cam's truck and my bike. A bit of fear creeps in; this is eerily similar to how Ben ended up in his accident and lost his leg. I'll need to be careful.

The wind whipping around me, my thoughts travel to my wee spitfire. Ben and Julian are in Seattle right now, but will be in New York in a month. Part of me wonders if I made the trip, stayed at the same hotel, drank whisky at the same bar, would I find her again?

I don't believe in soulmates, but what I felt in one night for a stranger has consumed my thoughts for months. I'm reminiscing for far too long when I nearly hit a highland cow in the road. I swerve to miss it and hit the brakes and swerve, my back wheel drifting for a moment before I right my bike and pull over. Cam isn't far behind me and stops in time to not hit it. I take off my helmet and approach his truck.

He rolls down his window and asks, "You alright?"

"Aye, you?"

He nods. "Sun should be up soon. Get in and we'll wait it out."

Cam knows as well as I do the dangers of driving in the dark and pulls off the road. He puts on his hazard lights and parks his truck. I slide into the front seat next to him. It should only be half an hour before the sunrise; we won't be behind schedule if we wait.

We sit and talk about his upcoming project he's doing before we continue our research. Time always passes quickly with him; he's not just my brother, he's my best friend. Few people understand and appreciate what I do, let alone get excited when I've discovered something groundbreaking. I can't wait to see what he finds on his next project.

The sun peeks over the horizon, red and orange seeping into the darkness. It's beautiful, but nothing like the one I saw months ago with my American lass.

"What's wrong?" Cam's voice pulls me from my thoughts.

"Oh, nothing."

"Fucking liar. It's that woman, isn't it? Every time you get sad like this, it's her," he laughs. "Why don't we go out tonight? Find a pretty blonde to get your mind off things."

"No, not a blonde," I growl, then clear my throat. "I mean—"

"She was blonde, got it. So, let's find you a brunette then. You can't keep pining after a woman you'll never see again. This isn't healthy. Want to come to San Francisco with me after my next project? Take your mind off things?"

"No, I need to prepare for the next castle. The layout is unlike any other we've been in. There's dozens of hidden passages, I need to make sure everything is safe before we tear up the stone. I just hope more journals are hiding in the floors, or all of this was for nothing."

He grips my shoulder. "It'll be fine. Alright, now get out of my truck and let's get the fuck out of here."

I laugh, climb out of his truck and onto my bike, taking one last look at the sunrise.

Maybe in fifty, I'll find her again.

5

AMANDA

I'm supposed to stay the night at Layla's. Since her book daddy boyfriend is getting his dick pierced, I won't need to cockblock these two. Chai in hand from the most adorable little tea shop down the street, I head to Layla's apartment, surprised to find Ben opening the door.

"Ry— Oh. Hello, Ms. Storm."

"Well, aren't you a thirsty bitch. Your fly's down, by the way." He glances down. Fuck, he's easy to mess with. "Just kidding." I push past him into the apartment. "Where's Layla?"

"In here. Just, um, grabbing something," Layla yells from her bedroom. Maybe he didn't get his cock pierced after all, these two definitely had some fun.

"Layla-love," I call, walking to her room, "home early. Didn't know you had company. If you need some..." I pause, stifling a laugh. "Alone time." She's flushed and definitely had plans for some sexytime. "Oh. Well. Have fun with the billionaire." I lower my voice. "If he's newly pierced, you're fucked in the most un-literal sense, babes."

"I know," Layla whisper-shouts. "He was all 'make a proper mess all over my face' but it's not like we could have sex. What if he got a Jacob's Ladder? That shit takes months to heal!"

"I didn't get a ladder, sunshine." I spin to find Ben leaning against her door frame. Layla groans, and I glance over my shoulder to find her hand covering her face in embarrassment. "Ms. Storm. Pick a hotel, any hotel, and I'll cover your expenses for the night. Want a penthouse apartment downtown Seattle for the night? I'll give you my key."

Don't have to tell me twice…

"Sold." I hold out my hand, awaiting his keyfob. He places it in my hand without a second thought. "Oh, shit. This might be more fun than the writing retreat at Julian's."

"Order whatever you want, my food delivery app information is on the counter by the refrigerator, but any damages to the flat will be billed to you directly."

And just like that, I have plans to order far too many whiskey sours and entirely too much food.

I'm supposed to stop these two from… I'm not entirely sure what. She's a grown ass woman, she doesn't need a keeper. I step past Ben, waving the key in the air with a skip in my step as I walk to the door. "See you in the morning, Layla-love. May you have many orgasms!"

I take a taxi to his temporary apartment and it's dull… worse than dull. It's as if a hospital designer moonlighted as an interior designer. It's so gray. I set my bag on the counter, find the delivery information Ben mentioned, and order myself lobster and two whiskey sours from the place downstairs. No reason to have them deliver it, I'll save the billionaire a few dollars and pick it up myself.

After my stomach is full and I have a nice buzz, I'm in a bit of a pickle. My laptop and all my things are at Layla's; I didn't think this one through. I wander into the office and find a few legal pads and a pen that glides on paper magnificently. Settling on the couch with a bottle of overpriced water and a pen I'm most definitely stealing, I begin writing.

Several hours later, I'm working through a plot hole I've dug myself into when there's a text from Layla. I check the time before opening her message. It's the middle of the night, why is she not asleep or fucking that hot Brit?

LAYLA

Just took either naproxen, viagra, or I'm being drugged. Just FYI.

Sounds like a good time. Just looked it up. Call a doctor if your ladyboner lasts longer than four hours. Rohypnol isn't typically a little blue pill so I think you're fine. Text me in the morning.

> Tell Ben I'll have Julian send a SWAT team or whoever he has on speed dial if you don't reply by noon tomorrow.

> And thank him for my lobster dinner and far too many whiskey sours.

For good measure, I send a quick message to Becca and Julian to let them know I've failed their little mission and continue writing until I can't keep my eyes open.

The next morning, I wake on the couch with a touch of drool sliding from the corner of my mouth. I'm staying in a billionaire's apartment and didn't even sleep in a comfortable bed. Such a fucking waste.

I put the legal pad and fancy pen in my bag. About to head out the door, I pause. I should leave him a note. Granted, it won't be sweet like I left my hot Scot. I take the pen out of my bag and scribble a note.

> **BEN'S-A-DICK,**
> **HURT LAYLA AND I'LL CASTRATE YOU.**
> **XOXO,**
> **AMANDA**
> **P.S. I'M NOT KIDDING. I WILL LITERALLY**
> **REMOVE THAT PIERCED PEEN OF YOURS AND FEED**
> **IT TO A RACCOON.**

I leave his apartment and head to Layla's. After a quick knock at the door, Ben answers. I'm actually a little proud of our book daddy, he didn't just hit it and leave.

"You're alive! No roofie!" I sing. "And… Jennifer? When did you get into town?" I head further inside and take a seat at the table next to Layla's mom. I'm sad to find her wheelchair next to her—today must be a rough day with her prosthetic leg.

"Late last night. What about you?"

"Julian flew me in a couple days ago to watch over this one," I reply, gesturing my thumb toward Layla. "Where are you staying?"

"I stayed at a hotel downtown because I didn't want to wake Layla. Seems I managed to anyway." Jennifer gives Layla a knowing look, and I can't help but laugh.

"Did you walk in on them, too? That was me yesterday. You should've called me! I stayed at Benny-boo's last night. Swanky as hell penthouse apartment; easily would've accommodated both of us." Ben gets up and brings me a glass, pouring me a mimosa. "Thank you."

Ben tops off Layla's, then offers to refill Jennifer's but she declines. She has diabetes and probably has reached her limit for sugar for the day. Ben leans in to kiss Layla's temple. "I'm going to head out so you can enjoy your company, but I'll see you tonight." He rights his posture. "It was a pleasure meeting you," he tells Jennifer, then asks me, "I take it I won't be expecting anything unusual when I return to the flat?"

"Oh, it's worse than that scene in *The Hangover*. Pretty sure there was a tiger when I woke up and everything." I keep a stoic expression as I sip my mimosa.

Ben scoffs. "Is that all? I expected more from you." He winks and adds, "Have a wonderful rest of your morning, ladies."

He retrieves his bag and phone, then his key from me—which I reluctantly give up. As soon as my front door clicks shut, I jump right in, "Start talking."

"Alright, girls, I'm going to head out for a bit. Don't get into too much trouble," Jennifer announces.

"Do you need help?" I ask.

"Of course not. You two have fun gossiping, I'll be back soon. I placed a grocery order and need to pick it up. Should only be ten or fifteen minutes." Jennifer wheels her wheelchair to the front door, grabbing her purse along the way. I fucking adore this woman's independence.

After she's gone, Layla clears the table and I wash her dishes. Once her apartment is back to its natural state of organized chaos, I lay into Layla. "You're in trouble with a capital 'T,' babes."

"You think?" Layla leans her head back on the chair and groans. "Mom already lectured me on this. *He has the worst manners of any British person I've met.* And don't forget, *who openly touches a woman in front of company?* I get it, he's socially inept, but I don't get what the big deal is. It's temporary. Why can't I just have a bit of fun?"

"I saw the way he looks at you and it's *not* casual. He looks like he's going to devour you any moment. Pretty sure if he was a caveman, he'd throw you over his shoulder and haul you off to his abode to have his way with you." *Or maybe that was just me four months ago...*

Layla raises an eyebrow. "Isn't that the definition of casual sex?"

"Oh no, I'll bet he probably has a breeding kink, knocks you up, or tries to mate with you for life. Is the caveman analogy throwing you? Ok, let's try fantasy. A 500-year-old fae shows up at your door, says you're his mate and... Wait. That's Julian's schtick. Instalove and fated mates bullshit with Becca. Ok, so I don't have a good one for this, but just know that he's super into you and it sure as fuck doesn't look casual from where I'm standing."

"I barely know him. We met two days ago."

I sigh and cross my arms. "You saw what happened with Becs. These billionaire men mean business. Think about it: how the fuck did they become billionaires? It wasn't the lottery! They saw something they wanted and took it. You think they look at women differently? Nope. You're something he can acquire, just like all of the companies he buys out. He's set his sights on you. Prepare to be wooed, wined, and dined. It's not like you're fucking for a month with that pierced cock of his."

"How did you kn—"

"Ah-ha! I knew he got it done. Cheeky bastard. I found period pads in his bathroom and you and I are synced up, so there's no way they were yours. It was a guess but thank you for confirming it." I didn't actually find period pads, but what's a little white lie?

"You're such a bitch," she laughs.

"Takes one to know one. Ok, so did you see it? Or—"

The front door opens and Jennifer struggles to wheel through with two bags of groceries on her lap. *Fuck, she's fast!* Layla and I rush over to help her.

"Here, let me grab those for you," I offer.

"Thank you. They're heavier than I thought they would be. I always forget I can get so many delicious low-carb goodies at the bakery down the street on my way back here."

"Mom, you should've let one of us go with you."

"I lost my leg, not my arms. I can wheel myself around just fine," Jennifer insists.

Layla asks what she got at the store. As Jennifer unpacks the bags, she tells us, "Meats and cheeses for a charcuterie board and everything to make tacos."

"Pretty sure Layla's taco was already eaten." My filter is shit today, but what does she expect?

Layla smacks my shoulder. "Amanda!"

"What? Deny that he didn't tongue-fuck you, and I'll take it back," I snicker.

"Girls, I really don't want to hear about my own daughter being *tongue-fucked* by the hot billionaire."

"Mom!"

"What? Amanda started it." Jennifer shrugs. "You act as if I haven't read your books or hers. I won't deny he's attractive... for an asshole."

I hug Jennifer around her shoulders. "Can you just adopt me?"

"Take the number one spot, Storm, and I'll consider it," she replies with a shrug.

Layla gasps. "Hello! I'm right here! Number four best seller for thrillers and number three for fantasy romance. Am I chopped liver?"

"Now that we're basically sisters, I say this with love: go fuck the hot billionaire," I insist. "I told Becs the same thing when she was dating Julian. Get it out of your system."

"Ok, that's enough about my daughter having sex, Amanda. Let's have lunch. I feel like my blood sugar is wonky. Don't think for one second that will get you out of telling me all about the hot Scottish man you met in New York."

"There's not much to tell." I shrug. "It was just a hot one-night stand. Would make for one hell of a book for Becs to write! Mild age gap, no names, golden retriever energy with a dirty mouth... would probably just be a novella though, since I'll never see him again. As hot as it was, I'd much rather hear about Ben's pierced dick."

"Amanda!" Layla shrieks.

Jennifer is about to respond when the intercom buzzes. We all look over and I rush over to it. "Yes?"

"Hi. I'm with Pixie Floral and have a delivery."

I let the delivery man into the building, smirking at Jennifer and Layla. Several minutes later, there's a knock at the door. Layla answers it. There are three stunning bouquets: black roses, white tulips, and one with a combination of red, yellow and orange roses.

Layla signs for them and we check the cards.

The one with black roses reads:

THOUGHT YOU WOULD APPRECIATE THE BEAUTY IN THESE. I RECEIVED YOUR NOTE AND REST ASSURED NO BEHAVIOUR OF MINE WILL WARRANT THE REACTION YOU SUGGESTED.
—BEN

Hah! He got my note!

The note for the white tulips reads:

I KNOW YOU'LL NEVER ACCEPT HELP IF I OFFER. HOWEVER, I HOPE ONE DAY YOU'LL ALLOW ME THE OPPORTUNITY.
—BEN

The final note reads:

> **YOU SAID YOU'RE MINE UNTIL I LEAVE.**
> **WHAT IF I NEVER DO, SUNSHINE?**
> **-YOURS**

"Did I call it, or did I call it?" I laugh. "The wooing has begun."

6

AMANDA

TWO MONTHS LATER

I only lasted a week in Seattle; there was no point in staying. Ben and Layla were destined to hump like rabbits and fall in love like a cliché romantic comedy. There was no point in stopping it.

I was in chai heaven about a week ago—writing my book that isn't just *inspired* by the hot Scot I hooked up with—when Ben sent me the details for his and Layla's engagement party. Mind you, they're not already engaged, he's planning on popping the question with all her friends and family there. It's a bold move, considering they've only been together for a few months, but I have a feeling the gesture will land well with my friend. As a bonus, I'm hoping that spending a few days in England will help with my book.

The entire situation is absolute madness. It was only supposed to be an interview. Layla needed to talk to a "morally gray" billionaire for her new book. Except, Ben turned out to be the furthest from morally gray.

Sure, he can be socially inept and a bit of an asshole from time to time… and, of course, there's the matter of him snatching up publishing houses left and right. But, as if he was a damned romance novel love interest, everything changed for him the moment he met Layla; he became a cinnamon roll of a man.

So, now I'm packing my laptop, my favorite mono-grammed notebook, a few smutty books—*and the sexiest dresses I own*—to fly across the world for their happily ever after. I hope Layla says yes; it'll be incredibly embarrassing for Ben to fly her mom all the way to London, only for Layla to decline.

Our friends, Becca and Julian, have already arrived in England after vacationing in France. I inwardly groan at how fucking cute they are. My jealousy has been rearing its ugly head lately while two of my friends live in seri-ous-relationship bliss.

After an internet deepdive, I learned there are only three thousand billionaires in the whole world. Light-ning striking three times, and me ending up with some hot, rich as fuck, man isn't statistically likely. While I have no need for my own billionaire—my last series took off with the horror crowd and I've made millions of my own. But who wouldn't want to feel financially secure indefinitely?

Who am I kidding? I'd live in a shack if it meant I had a man who treated me the way Ben and Julian treat my friends.

I finish packing and head to the airport. Being so close to Scotland on this trip, my heart drops into my stomach, wishing I was living in an alternate reality where I'd see my mystery man again.

The flight to London is long but otherwise pleasant. I'm sitting next to an interesting woman on her way to Scotland, with a long layover in London to meet someone for drinks. She's everything I'm not—poised, sophisticated, and incredibly stylish. I find her fascinating, and despite my initial assessment of her, we have a lot in common. She's agreed to grab coffee with me later today to discuss an upcoming suspense series I've been wanting to write. Perhaps this trip will turn out to be better than I had hoped.

After I land in Heathrow, there's a car waiting for me with a giant 'Ms. Storm' written in bold font on a small poster board. I was fine taking public transit or a taxi, but Ben insisted on sending a driver to pick me up. The driver takes my luggage—which he refuses to let me wheel myself—and we leave for Ben and Layla's home.

Ten minutes into the drive, I get a message from Layla's mom that her flight is arriving early. I ask Cliff if we should just stay at the airport, but he has strict instructions from Ben to drive me to the house first. At this rate, I'll only have about twenty or thirty minutes at Ben's place before I'll need to hop back into the car and return to the airport to retrieve Jennifer for tonight. At this rate, I might not have time to meet my new friend for a drink. I could never live this posh lifestyle regularly, I don't particularly enjoy living on the schedule of others and I'd struggle with my independence.

As if today wasn't busy enough, my old publisher, Roger Kipling, is on trial here in England. Busying myself during the drive, I read a few articles to see what the locals are saying. After a quick search, everyone in England seems to agree—Kipling got what he fucking deserved. I was part of a class action lawsuit, but Ben is testifying against him in the criminal trial later today.

People say I have really bad timing, but here we are, about to attend a proposal-turned-engagement party on the same day he's testifying. I can't help rolling my eyes at the ridiculousness that has ensued since Layla met Ben.

We arrive at the mansion in Canterbury, and I'm in awe. It could double as a backdrop to a Regency novel. As the gates open, I shake my head in shock. Ben's home feels entirely fictional, the mansion easily the size of my apartment building in New York.

Is that a fucking pond?

Mr. Darcy, feel free to emerge any moment now!

I glance at my clothes, feeling underdressed for the home sitting on acreage that could double as a small country. Taking a deep breath, I open the car door before the driver can and attempt to open the trunk.

"Miss, I can't allow that," he says as he hurriedly opens it. "Mr. Turner would be quite displeased with me."

"Mr. Turner isn't here right now, is he?" I quirk an eyebrow at him. "I won't tell, if you won't."

He sighs, worry painting his face. "Miss, please. Allow me to at least bring it inside for you."

"I'm sorry. I didn't mean to do your job for you."

Being in the service industry sucks, and my heart hurts for this guy. I'm always brought back to my college years working as a barista and how my boss would be livid if someone helped themself to a carafe of creamer. I should make his life easier, not harder.

"No apology needed, miss." He smiles and I can't help but return it.

"Can we not call me 'miss?' Please, call me Amanda."

"Miss Amanda, please head inside," he insists. "I'll ensure your bags are brought up."

I shake my head and chuckle. "We'll need to work on that. What's your name?"

"Clifford, *miss.*" He emphasizes the last word as he tilts his cap. When his eyes reach mine again, I pause. He has the most beautiful bright green eyes; they remind me of my hot Scot.

No, not my hot Scot. A hot Scot.

Perhaps my time here will be the perfect distraction if all the men somehow remind me of my one night stand from months ago. If nothing else, it could help with my book research and inspiration, like I'd hoped. Maybe I could even find a Scottish or English billionaire of my own to interview? Or, I could turn my hot Scot into a wealthy mafia heir? I'm only a millionaire, but due to the cost of living in New York City, I can't empathize with that kind of wealth.

In my internet deep dive, I discovered there are approximately one hundred and seventy-one billionaires in the UK. Only ten in Scotland. The odds of finding one of my own are not in my favor. I'm better off interviewing Ben or Julian if I need content for a book.

"It's open, miss. Mr. Turner and Ms. Thorne are waiting for you."

"Thank you, *Mr. Clifford*," I say with a wink, and he offers a sheepish grin. I rush up the steps to what can only be described as a damn palace, eager to see my friends.

Once the massive front door shuts behind me, I take stock of the entryway. The staircase to my right lacks the character I'd expect based on movies I've seen, but as I continue further into their home, I begin to see small pieces of Layla warming the otherwise sterile space—a plant here and there, a bright painting that feels otherwise out of place.

I'm about to walk into what appears to be a sitting or music room with a black baby grand piano when I hear Layla yell upstairs. I pause, trying to make out what she's saying.

"I told you, they're in bedroom four!" Layla shouts.

"Like I know which one bedroom four is! There are no numbers on them!" Ben yells back.

I giggle to myself, surprised my friend doesn't already have door numbers hung on each of them. She's used to her modest apartment in Seattle, not this monstrosity of a home anyone could easily get lost in.

"It's your house! You should know where your suits are hanging!" she replies.

"*Our* house, sunshine!"

I can't help but snicker at the back and forth between her and Ben. It doesn't sound like anyone is about to get laid, so I make my way up the stairs toward the echoing shouts to see my friends.

As I walk upstairs, they continue to bicker about bedroom placement. There's a pause and I'm met with two corridors when I reach the top of the stairs. As I'm about to turn left, Layla's voice pulls my attention to the right. "Ben! Get in here!"

"If you're not tied up and naked in our bed, I'm not coming!" he yells back.

I freeze.

Oh crap! They're totally going to fuck.

"Now is not the time! This is serious!" Layla sounds concerned and not at all in the mood for a good railing.

I'd like to see her before I leave to pick up her mom from the airport, so I make my way toward the adorable quarrel. Ben rushes from one room to another so quickly that all I glimpse is a swirl of a dark blue suit and raven black hair.

"Yes, love?" he asks as he enters the other room. *Fucking cinnamon roll.* I wait outside, just in case I got this all wrong and she's sprawled out naked on the bed, ready to be ravished.

I'm not above eavesdropping, though…

"When was I supposed to start my period?" There's a long silence, and I cover my mouth to muffle my gasp. "Ben," she warns.

I pegged Ben for having a bit of a breeding kink a while back, and I'm pretty damn proud of myself that I hit the nail on the head with that one. I know he loves her and would respect any of her wishes, but putting a baby in her would be a dream come true for that man.

I try to contain my excitement for them as he purrs, "Sunshine."

"Don't get excited," she says sternly.

He's totally excited.

"Oh, it's a little late for that," he growls back at her.

Fucking knew it.

"We have to get to the courthouse," Layla tells him, trying to contain her laughter. I should leave, but this is too fucking good.

"Unless the court you're referring to offers a marriage certificate, I'm not going. I have more important things to tend to," he growls

There's a tossing of something heavy onto a bed and a yelp. "You need to stop with the fake engagement thing. Find a new hobby," she teases.

Don't you dare propose, you impulsive twat! Wait for tonight!

They continue with a back and forth about her possibly being knocked up. I start to back away slowly; this conversation is starting to seem too serious. What's said next is muffled until I hear him clearly say, "No, love. Reach in my pocket." Intrigued, I pause.

"I swear, if it's a vibrator and remote…"

He's going to fucking propose. I pinch the bridge of my nose and groan, hoping she says no and waits for him to ask like he planned. She deserves an over-the-top, grandiose engagement, not something rushed because she's possibly preggo.

"No, love. Take it out," Ben says, full of hope. I actually wish he was talking about taking out his cock and not an engagement ring.

"Ben," she breathes.

Nope, it's absolutely an engagement ring. Fucking. Idiot.

"Take it out, sunshine, so I can ask you properly. Even if you're still in my old uni shirt and knickers. I wouldn't have it any other way."

I purse my lips and nod to myself. *Ok, that's actually kind of sweet…*

"Ben, this isn't a…"

"Sunshine, for the thousandth time, will you marry me? I was going to ask you at dinner tonight, but I don't want to wait another moment without being able to call you my fiancée, even if I'd rather call you my wife." There's a pause. "Is that a yes, darling?"

I should have popped some popcorn for this, or at least taken notes to inspire dialogue for the next main character I write with a breeding kink. This is better than any daytime soap opera. I honestly wasn't sure whether she would say yes and it would be really awkward at the engagement party.

"You really want to marry me?" Layla's voice is laced with worry. "What if I'm not—"

"Yes, I want to marry you more than anything. I don't care if you're pregnant or not, love, I want you as my wife. My intentions have always been clear. I'd rather fight with you every day about too many bedrooms, than spend a single day without you."

"And if I'm not pregnant?" she asks.

"Then, you're not," he replies confidently. "I want to marry my first and only love." While I want to throw up in my mouth a little at his declaration, it's actually kind of romantic that he couldn't wait for tonight.

"Ok," she finally replies. I let out the breath I was holding for far too long.

Ben chuckles, "That's all I get? An 'ok?'"

"Yes, *Benedict*, I'll marry you."

I'm now almost positive they're going to fuck, so I decide to make my presence known; I want to say hi before the headboard thumping begins. I knock softly on their open door and enter.

"So, did she say yes?" I ask, and they both turn wide eyed to find me in the doorway. "Can I smother you in confetti yet? I have to go pick up Jennifer from the airport in fifteen, can I use one of your fancy drivers?" I know he'll say yes, but it's a good excuse to flirt with Clifford. Maybe I should call him Cliff… or Ford. He needs a nickname.

"Amanda, what the fuck are you doing here?" Layla shrieks in delight.

"So help me, if you walk in on me and my future wife one more time, you can fuck right off and never be invited back here," Ben growls.

I raise my hands in surrender. "Fair enough, my timing is shit. Everyone will be here this evening, but Ben's A Dick decided to move up the timeline." I snicker at my immature nickname for him. Not my fault, Layla came up with it first. "Congrats on the maybe-baby, by the way."

"Did you listen to our whole conversation?" Ben asks, his British accent thicker than usual when he's growly.

I leave without answering, but hear Layla laughing as I walk down the hall.

I know I'm the queen of horrible timing, but it's not my fault these two have been fucking every waking moment since they met. They have to know that, statistically, it is inevitable that I'll walk in on them at least once—or several times, as it turns out. How was I supposed to know that they would be having a sweet intimate moment when I arrived? Ben knew I was coming, it's his own fault.

As soon as I'm downstairs, my new bestie, Clifford, is waiting with my bags. "Miss Amanda, are you hungry?"

Oh, I'm hungry all right. Too bad you're not 'Jackson.'

"We need to go pick up Layla's mom, and I need to meet someone for a quick drink. Can we pick up something on the way?"

It's a shame Scotland is hundreds of miles away. I could really go for a hot Scot for lunch.

7

JACK

I'm excited to see Ben and Layla tonight. Ben and I had a pint last night and he's nervous, since he wants to turn his engagement party into a full-on wedding, if Layla agrees to it. I'm genuinely surprised; I've never known Ben to be the least bit impulsive.

Unfortunately, before I can enjoy the possible wedding and celebrations, I have to meet with Blair to sign the investment contracts. I'd much rather celebrate Ben's happiness than spend more than a moment necessary with her. I'll be cutting it close, but I should be able to make it before the ceremony begins. I'm hoping I have enough time to change, but seeing as I'm one of the only Scots in attendance, I don't think anyone will take offence to me arriving without my kilt if I'm in a rush.

Arriving at the pub, I shrug on my brown leather jacket and retie my hair into a bun. I've been tempted to cut it all off, but maintaining a shorter hairstyle is too much work when I'm on a site. I slide onto a stool and order a whisky.

While he pours, I feel the evil aura surrounding me before Blair sits on the stool to my left. "Hello, Bartholomew," she says, her voice sickeningly sweet.

"Blair," I seeth, trying like hell to not let her sour my mood. Today is supposed to be a day of joy and levity, I won't let her take that from me.

"We'll need to make this quick, I have an appointment to be interviewed by an author I met on the plane before I head home." I stifle a groan at her words. Scotland isn't her home and hasn't been for almost a decade. "The only reason I can squeeze you in is she has to pick up someone from the airport before meeting me. So, what are your plans for the rest of the afternoon?" We've had this time scheduled for the last few weeks, and I hate her twisted truths.

"I have a wedding to attend," I admit.

Her gaze rakes my body in disgust. "In that? Whose wedding?"

"Why not?" I shrug as the bartender sets down my drink. "Or is it not good enough to impress my cousin?"

Shite. I shouldn't have said that.

A sly grin tugs at her lips. "I miss this."

"Well, I sure as fuck don't miss you."

Fuck. Fuck. Fuck. Why do I let her get under my skin?

"I need you to sign over the publishing copyright to me. I'm hoping to include it in my journal article. Also, there's the matter of where the findings will go after the project."

"Why the hell do you care about the lost belongings of the Black family?" While the findings are worth millions, I intend to have them donated to museums. They aren't simply missing heirlooms, they're stolen treasure from wars hundreds of years ago. Blair must know their value if she's attaching herself to this project—which suddenly makes much more sense why she's here in the first place. Money has always driven her more than anything.

"You know as well as I do that it's not just *'lost belongings.'*"

"It's history, Blair. I don't care about any riches we might find. I want to tell their story," I plead, downing my drink in two gulps.

Before she can reply, the bartender slides a second whisky in front of me and asks Blair, "Miss, what can I get you?"

"I'm not staying." Blair tosses down twenty quid for the bartender and slaps a stack of paperwork in front of me. "Think about it." She grabs my drink and finishes it as quickly as I did with my first one, then slips off her stool and struts out the door.

The bartender and I look at each other for a moment before he nods and pours me another drink.

I sift through the papers she left, shaking my head in annoyance when I read how she's trying to assume the credit for the entire excavation if we find anything in Skye. I'll need one of Ben's lawyers to look it over. I roll them up and stuff them inside my jacket for later. Once I'm done with my drink, I leave an additional twenty quid for his troubles—*fuck Blair for trying to pay my tab*—and head out to get a taxi.

Without traffic, it's a quick hour and a half drive to my cousin's place in Canterbury. Two, at most. Unfortunately, on an unpaved road, with a short distance to go, we manage to get a flat. I feel like a fucking damsel in distress on the side of the road with a carriage. There's no cell reception, and I inwardly curse at my predicament. The driver's spare also has a flat, so we're stuck in the middle of fucking nowhere until someone happens to pass by.

We wait for two long hours. I shake my head; this whole thing feels like a comedy of errors.

I take out the tie in my hair and ruffle it a wee bit. As soon as this project is over, I'm getting a haircut—*even if the American lass loved it long.* I'm tying it back up when there's a rumbling of a car passing us. My driver yells at them to stop. They don't but the driver of the other car looks remarkably similar to a man who works for Ben, and he's transporting two women in the same direction —one of them is blonde and looks a lot like…

Spitfire?

No. There's no fucking way. It can't be her, but there's only one way to find out. I plead with my driver, who has fought me for hours, "My cousin's home is only three miles away. I don't think anyone else is coming."

He sighs in defeat. "You're right. I can't reach my mate to come help me with the car. I think we might need to walk?"

You mean what I've been suggesting for two hours?

Fuck, it can't be her… can it?

"Good plan," I reply, trying to not offend him. He's easily twenty years my senior and has been avoiding travelling by foot this entire time. "Are you sure you don't want me to go ahead and call for a ride for you?" I offer for what feels like the hundredth time.

"Oh, nonsense. I'll come with you."

I sling my leather duffle over my shoulder, and we spend the next hour walking what would've taken me half the time. Unfortunately, when we arrive at my cousin's home, I'm a bit of a sweaty mess. I click the intercom at the gate entrance.

"Turner residence," a woman's voice says.

"Yes, hello, it's Jack. Here for…" Unsure of whether or not I should be divulging that this is a wedding or engagement in front of the driver, I go with the latter, "The engagement party. But my ride seems to have gotten a flat down the road. I'm wondering if you can help with that?"

"Of course, Dr. Jackson."

We're buzzed in without another word. Ben's driver, Clifford, approaches as we walk up the steps of Ben's home, his eyes widening when he spots me. "I'm incredibly sorry, sir. I had strict instructions to get the women I was transporting home. They protested that I should stop, but, well, you know Mr. Turner."

I huff a laugh. "No offence taken. Can you help my friend here?"

"Absolutely. The ceremony has begun but, forgive me, might I suggest you freshen up first?"

This time, I let out a full laugh and pat him on the back. "That's a braw idea." *Especially if my spitfire is here.*

We say our goodbyes. I walk inside and up the staircase to shower and change. When I arrive in the room I normally stay in when I visit, there's a black, hardshell suitcase on the bed. I glance around, wondering if I'm in the wrong room. It's been a while since I've stayed here, and with seven spare bedrooms, there's a chance he may have given this room to someone else. Surely, they won't mind if I take a quick shower; I don't want to miss any more of the ceremony than I already have.

There's a familiar perfume lingering in the air, and I pause to breathe it in—a mix of thistle and something sweet like honey, reminding me of my wee spitfire.

Was she here? Is this her room?

No, that's impossible.

I toss my duffle onto the bed and take out my kilt and a fresh shirt. I'm missing part, if not all, of the ceremony, so I move quickly to undress, shower, and change. As soon as I'm ready, I make my way back downstairs, taking them two at a time in hopes of seeing her.

There's a swirl of caterers and staff rushing up and down the hallways the moment my feet touch the final step of the staircase. Between my meeting with Blair, the car, and now this circus of a house, I'm drained. Unsure where this is all taking place, I stop one of them, "Excuse me, where's the wedding?"

The man looks down at my kilt and smiles. "Ah, you must be Jack. I believe they are in the library." He then yells down the hall, "Sage, the cousin's arrived."

A tall, blonde woman with a cane approaches. "Dr. Jackson?" I nod. "Follow me."

The woman leads me into the library and gestures to the happy couple. Layla, her mum, and a blonde woman are talking with Ben. She has a similar figure to my American lass; I can't help but get my hopes up.

I approach, but grab Ben's attention, clamping my hand on his shoulder. "Shite, I'm late." I'm here for him, first and foremost, feeling like a bit of an arsehole.

He turns, brings me in for a tight hug, and claps me on the back twice before releasing me. None of this is typical for him—he's not an affectionate man—and only adds to the odd events of the day.

"Yes," he laughs. "You missed the wedding, but you made it in time for the reception. Where are my manners? Jack, this is Layla's friend, Amanda. Amanda, my cousin, Jack."

Finally, I get a good look at the woman.

Fuck. Me. It's her. I found her.

The hotel bar, the bakery, the bookstore, the outdoor pub where I danced with her under the stars. All the memories from that night come flooding back, and it takes every ounce of restraint to not haul the blonde goddess over my shoulder to make love to her all night.

Instead, with all the restraint in me, I take her hand in mine, kissing her knuckles. "My wee spitfire, what are you doing here?"

8

AMANDA

Time stops.

No. No no no…

A zing courses through my body.

What is happening?

The air crackles between us.

Wait, did he say Jack?

My breath hitches and I feel the blood drain from my face. I knew there was something familiar about Ben when I met him. While Ben's eyes are blue and Jack's are green, they have the same shape. Also, when Ben and Jack smile, the same dimples appear. Now that they're standing side by side, there's no doubt they're related and part of me is kicking myself that I didn't notice it sooner.

Fuck Becca and Julian for putting soulmate shit in my head.

He's here. How is he here?

"I'm sorry, do you know each other?" Ben asks.

I open my mouth to reply but no words come out. Layla gasps, then leans in and whispers, "It's him, isn't it?" I manage a nod, unable to take my eyes off my hot Scot.

Not yours! Just a hot guy you fucked once… and then fantasized about for months.

I shake off whatever spell he has me under, close my gaping mouth, and clear my throat. As I take a breath, I manage, "Yes. Well, sort of. We met in New York."

"Small world," Ben laughs, thankfully not catching on to the war of emotions I'm feeling.

"The smallest," Jack agrees, his gaze still burning into me.

"I should go check on, um…" I have nothing to check on and dart away before anyone can stop me.

I only make it five or six steps before a hand envelops mine, stopping me in my tracks. A shiver cascades across every inch of my body at his touch, even as I try to fight off the attraction—which hasn't faded in the slightest.

"Not here," I tell him, closing my eyes briefly and refusing to face him.

Sensing my discomfort, he whispers, "Fair enough, spitfire."

Has he known who I am this whole time?

He leads me away from the library and down a hall. Out of earshot of guests and staff, he asks, "What are you doing here?"

"Me?" I cross my arms over my chest. *The audacity of this man...* "My friend is getting married. How was I supposed to know you'd be related to the groom?"

Fuck. On top of everything else, I have to rethink my entire character for my book—I can't write about 'Jackson'... *Shit. I'm in hell.* I'll have to change his name and the title of the book, too.

Jack closes the distance, so I take a step backward, then another, until my back hits the wall. He props himself up with his hand above my head and leans in. "I shouldn't have left for my meeting that morning," he says softly, pain etched in his eyes.

"It was only supposed to be one night." My voice comes out shakier than I'd like, but I can't help it. The one man who ruined me for all others is standing in front of me, and every inch of me is begging to be touched by him again. I have the urge to run, but my feet are glued to the floor.

He snakes his free hand to the small of my back and pulls me flush against him. "We were never supposed to be one night."

My breath heavy, I retort, "Yes, it was. *It is.* We—"

My words are swallowed as his mouth crashes into mine. A whimper escapes me as I quickly lose all resolve to keep my distance from this beautiful man. I take his face in my hands, kissing him back harder, aching to get closer to him.

His beard is scruffier than I remember, and his hair a little longer, but he has the same whiskey lingering on his lips. It transports me back to six months ago and I'm lost in a highlight reel in my head, longing to recreate it.

I found him.

A throat clears loudly behind Jack, but he doesn't stop kissing me. They clear it a second time and a growl erupts from him as we finally break apart. His lust-filled emerald eyes remain on me as he responds to the man behind him. "Whatever it is, it can wait."

"Your cousin has requested you both join them for dinner."

"We'll be right there," I reply, unable to tear myself away from Jack's intense eyefucking.

The man walks away and I'm about to follow, but Jack doesn't release me. "Not so fast, spitfire."

"We can't make out in a dark hallway all night at your cousin's wedding," I joke, since that's exactly what will happen if I stay with him a moment longer.

His eyes darken. "You know I'm capable of so much more."

What am I doing? I can't do this, not with him. I need to get out of here.

Panic setting in. This man ruined me once, he'll do it again. I manage, "Head to dinner, I'll be there in a few. I need to freshen up first." I attempt to remove a smudge of my lipstick from his bottom lip with my thumb, but as I wipe it away, he grips my wrist and kisses my palm.

"I thought I'd never see you again." He shakes his head. "Can we talk after?"

"Of course." I nod but the lie weighs heavier on me than I thought it would.

Jack releases me and squeezes my hand one last time before letting go and walking in the direction of the library. My stomach is in knots as I mentally catalog my options:

Go to dinner, flirt with the hot Scot.

Go to dinner, avoid the hot Scot.

Go to dinner, fuck the hot Scot.

Run. Run back to New York and pretend today never happened.

Door #4 it is…

The one man who ruined me is here. If I consider staying, I'll end up spending another incredible night with him. He's the kind of guy you settle down and make babies with. That's not on my mood board, and even it was, how would that even work? I live in New York, he lives… Where *does* he live? I'm not going to stick around to find out.

I rush down the hall and up the staircase to the bedroom I'm supposed to stay in tonight. Sitting next to my suitcase and dress bag is a brown leather duffle with the monogram BWJ on it. I giggle to myself that this poor guy's initials are BJ, but Clifford must've had someone send a bag up to the wrong room. I set the duffle at the foot of the bed and quickly strip out of my dress and strapless bra.

In search of my most comfortable clothes, I dig through my overstuffed suitcase, settling on a pair of jeans and an oversized NYU hoodie. Fuck putting on a bra, no one will see my nips through the thick fabric. Packing the cute dresses was a fucking waste.

Or was it? I got to see my hot Scot again…

Fuck. He's related to Ben.

I zip up my bags and haul ass downstairs in search of Cliffy. When I reach the front door, guilt creeps in; I'm leaving on Layla's wedding day—the happiest day of my best friend's life. *I'm such an asshole.* I take out my phone to text Layla and Becca.

> Sorry, have to run. Emergency.

BECCA
> Bullshit.

LAYLA
> It's Jack, isn't it?

> Jack being here is absolutely an emergency.

BECCA

> Jack? The archaeologist? Fuck, he's hot.
> Don't tell Julian I said so.

I don't reply as text bubbles dance at the bottom of the screen, but a familiar voice pulls me from my phone. "Where are you headed?" Ben asks playfully.

"Oh, uh, sorry. Emergency. I was just texting Layla." I wave my phone as if that's proof that what I'm doing isn't fucked up. "Congrats, by the way."

"It's my cousin, isn't it?" *Fuck, is it written on my forehead?* "I can ask him to leave if he makes you uncomfortable."

I shake my head. "No, I'm not uncomfortable. He's just…" My shoulders fall as I sigh, unable to admit to Ben's face that I've been fantasizing about his cousin for half a year. That night wasn't just sex for me, which is why I need to go. Right fucking now.

"He's been talking about you for months, but I didn't know it was you. Come back and celebrate with us. I'll make sure he's on his best behavior." Ben offers a beaming smile, one that meets his eyes. Eyes that, if they were green…

"No, sorry. I need to go. Love you guys." I give Ben a quick hug and rush out the door, pleased to find a car out front with Clifford at the wheel. He spots me approaching and rushes out of the car to help me with my bags.

"I wasn't aware you were flying back so soon." Cliffy opens the back door for me, but I open the front one instead. He places the bags in the trunk and joins me. "You know, Mr. Turner—"

"Please just drive?" I shut my eyes tight, swallowing my emotions and burying them deep—where I'll hopefully never find them again.

9

JACK

"What do you mean she's gone?" I growl at Ben.

"I don't know what the fuck you said to Amanda, but she was one foot out the door when I ran into her." I don't appreciate his accusatory tone.

The woman who has consumed my thoughts for months appears out of nowhere, only for me to lose her? No. Absolutely not. "Where is she going?"

"A hotel? The airport? I don't fucking know. She had her luggage with her and couldn't get away fast enough. I didn't ask, but I'm sure she told Becca or Layla." I storm past Ben, only to make it a few feet before he catches me by my elbow. "Don't you dare drag my wife into this," he seethes.

"I'm not going to let her slip through my fingers. You'd do the same if this was Layla. Julian would if it was Becca. You can't expect me to let her go." I shrug out of his hold and continue walking away from the library where everyone's enjoying dinner.

Ben follows, sighing in defeat. "You're right. If Layla left, I'd chase after her. But Amanda isn't like Layla, or even Becca. She threatened to serve my cock to a raccoon if I messed things up with Layla. She's also stubborn as hell." He blows out a long breath. "And, fuck, if that woman doesn't have the worst possible timing in the bloody world, but she's one of my wife's most loyal friends. I'm not going to let you fuck this up and upset Layla on the happiest day of my life. Taming a wild stallion takes patience. If you chase after Amanda, she'll never come back to you."

My jaw tics and I swallow hard. "There's something about her—"

"Let her go. We'll find another way to get her back. She's visiting in a couple months for Layla's book sign-ing. We'll come up with something. Who knew a quick shag in New York would have you all twisted up like this?" He laughs, shaking his head. "Come have a drink or two and celebrate with me."

My heart is stuck in my throat. He's right—if I go after her, I'll lose my chance with her. She's no longer a mystery woman from one of the best nights of my life. I know her name, she knows my family, we have mutual friends. I reluctantly take Ben's advice and return to the celebration, even if my wee spitfire remains on my mind the entire evening.

At dinner, Becca offers to personally ensure Amanda attends Ben and Julian's upcoming charity gala. While she refuses to give me her address, she does, however, allow me to include a note on the back of the invitation prior to getting it to Amanda.

I need to find out more about my mystery lass. The day we met, Amanda recited a line from Becca's book. I'm not sure how much information I'll get out of Becca, but since Becca and Layla are authors, there's a chance Amanda isn't just a reader; she could be an author. If she is, the moment I get home, I'll be purchasing every-thing written by her.

I carefully ask Becca, "What's Amanda's last name?"

"Storm, why?"

"Storm?" I choke on my own air.

"Have you read any of her books?" she excitedly asks, taking out her phone.

As she's typing Amanda's info into the browser, I keep from telling Becca that I've read *Maybe in Fifty* a dozen times, hoping I'd find a clue as to who my spitfire is. Never once did I consider the answer was on the front cover.

Sure enough, Amanda's picture appears with the search of her name, along with a list of books she'd written.

Fuck. This whole time...

Ben's right. If I bide my time, I might have a shot with her, even if the next few months are going to be fucking torture.

I found her.

10

AMANDA

TWO MONTHS LATER

After a quick trip to the gym—*ok, so I just used the sauna and hot tub*—I check the mail and head up to my apartment. Once inside, I toss down my keys and sift through bills and junk mail. There's a burnt orange envelope that appears to be an invitation. I check the back for a return address and can't help my smile; it's Ben and Julian's new charity providing accessibility options for various disabilities. I fucking hate dressing up, but I'll do it for their gala.

Layla's morally gray-ish hero took a sharp turn onto Good Guy Avenue, and I couldn't be happier to see it.

My book is coming along, even if I haven't changed Jack's name or the title yet. It's morphed into the typical romantic suspense book I'm known for, and I've added in several unexpected twists and turns, thanks to the advice from my seatmate a few months ago. The minute I returned home, I put horror movies on in the background as I wrote, so my male main character would lose his golden retriever vibes.

She's a fucking saint. Every time I have a question, she hops on the phone with me and helps me workshop the scene. My female protagonist is a hitwoman and she's helped me really dive into the character's motives. Meeting her on the plane was nothing short of a blessing.

I plop down on my sofa with my laptop, about to transcribe a scene I wrote in my notebook, when her name comes up on my caller ID.

"Hey," I answer excitedly, "I just finished writing the clean-up scene. You're going to love it."

"I can't wait to read it! When is the release date again? My colleague was asking when I told her about your book and I wasn't sure."

"Probably in a few months. I still have to run it through a round of beta readers and send it to my editor." My shoulders sag. I miss the old days of indie publishing, when I wasn't beholden to deadlines of a publisher. "I almost forgot to tell you, my friend is doing her book signing in London in two weeks. Are you still going to be in the UK? Or is that the week of your conference in Germany? I'd love to meet for a drink or dinner while I'm there."

"Yes, the project I'm working on won't begin for at least another month here in Scotland. I can probably meet you in London, or if you'd like to sightsee, you're welcome to come visit me here."

My stomach drops. I'd love to visit Scotland, but knowing Jack is there somewhere, I don't know if I can do it.

What am I thinking? Of course I can! It's a huge fucking country, it's not like I'll run into him.

"That sounds amazing! A castle tour, maybe see those cute cow-sheep. Definitely drink entirely too much whiskey."

"They're highland cows," she laughs, "and they are indeed adorable. I know of a few amazing distilleries. We could get into a bit of trouble."

I could really use a wing woman to find me a hot Scot to get my mind off Jack, even if the thought currently makes me sick to my stomach. After Layla's wedding, I did a quick internet search for 'Jack Turner' that came up empty and I've resisted the urge to call Layla or Becca to find out more about him. It's better this way. But, I'm not getting any younger; at some point, I need to get back out there and date. I should find myself a boring accountant, settle down, have 2.5 kids and a dog. Not a golden retriever.

"I know you're hoping to rekindle things with your ex-husband, but are you up for a night on the town while I'm there? I could use a growly Scottish man who is up for throwing me around for a night," I tease.

She nearly chokes while laughing. "I'm still working on him, but maybe I can convince him to come out to dinner or drinks, and invite his brother. Actually, he mentioned he'll be in London around the same time you are. I'll arrange it and make the trip to see you."

"Let's do it! I'll send you my flight info as soon as I have it."

We hang up and a pang of guilt hits me. I haven't told her about Jack yet. Part of me feels that, if I mention him, he becomes more real. The past couple of months, I've enjoyed living the lie where he's only a hot guy I met at a bar, never to be seen or heard from again.

From what little she's told me about her ex, he's a little like Jack—sweet on the outside and spicy on the inside. We don't talk much about our personal lives, and I don't want to pry, but she's such an amazing person that I hope they have a second chance romance in the end.

11

JACK

Layla's book signing is tonight, and I'm a nervous wreck. I've been stuck in Scotland the past two months making arrangements for my upcoming dig and haven't seen Ben or Layla since their wedding. I'm looking forward to visiting with them, but knowing Amanda might be here has me on edge.

In a rush packing, I forgot my contacts, forcing me to wear my glasses for the next few days. I haven't worn them in years and the prescription is slightly outdated. I did, however, remember to bring my brown jacket. While it's not quite cool enough for a jacket, I'm hoping it'll spark nostalgia for my spitfire.

I arrive at the pub and grab a whisky at the bar. It's a bit unorthodox to have a reading at a pub, but Layla insisted that she wanted an experience like she had back home in Seattle, where she enjoyed doing readings at bars and distilleries.

Amanda is nowhere to be found; she must be running late. Ben and Layla walk in the door a few minutes after I do, and seeing them so happy lifts the grey cloud that's been hovering over me these past few months.

Ben helps Layla get ready for her live reading and comes over when he spots me at the bar, bringing me in for a tight hug. For someone who has hugged me no more than four times in our entire lives, two of them have happened since meeting Layla. My cousin, who was once deemed the coldest of the family, is now one of the warmest.

"How is married life treating you?" I ask, sipping my whisky and adjusting my glasses.

"How's Amanda?" he counters.

I cough on my drink. I should've expected his question but it still takes me by surprise. "I don't know what you mean. I haven't seen her since the wedding."

It's not entirely a lie. I haven't seen Amanda in person but I now follow all her social media accounts under a fake one. She's writing a new book that she refuses to share spoilers about. While her readers are enjoying the mystery, I'm not. I've read her entire backlist since learning who she is, and am genuinely curious what she's writing now. She's an incredible storyteller and it translates beautifully on page.

Fuck, I feel like a stalker.

"Right. Well, I think I've solved your funding situation for the additional research you wanted to do. Can we chat after the gala?" Ben asks.

"Of course, I'll give you a ring."

He claps me on the back and I find a seat in the back rows.

Layla steps up to the podium and Ben sits in the front row. She talks for a few minutes about how her project began as a story about a morally grey billionaire, but she found writing one about a villain who becomes a hero to get the girl was far more interesting.

After her quick reading, she receives a standing ovation from the crowd. Ben joins her at the podium, takes her in his arms, and leans in to whisper something to her. My heart swells at seeing them together. I can't help but hope that one day I'll be attending one of Amanda's book signings, sitting in the front row, stealing glances as she tells one of her stories.

My American lass isn't here tonight, hopefully I'll have better luck tomorrow at the gala. I make my way to the front to congratulate Layla, then leave the bar.

The gala is at one of my favourite libraries in London. I confirmed earlier today with Julian that Amanda RSVP'd to the event, but I'm running late so there's a chance she's already here. I jog up the steps when a woman in front of me trips. I catch her by the waist before she falls.

"Are you ok, lass?" The familiar scent of honey and this-tles gives me pause. *Amanda*. I resist holding on to her a moment longer than necessary, no matter how much I desperately want to.

"Oh, yes, thank you. I'm fine." Amanda rights herself and dusts off her dress. She turns, and her beautiful blue eyes darken the moment she recognizes me. "Hi, Jack."

"You got my invitation, I see." I can't wipe the smile from my face. She's a vision and there's no way in hell I'm taking my eyes off her all night.

"Your invitation?" she asks, quirking her eyebrow. "Ben and Julian invited me."

"You didn't get my note?"

"What note?"

"On the back of the invitation?"

She frowns, then sifts through her bag and takes it out, finding my handwritten note on the back.

> **IT MAY HAVE ONLY BEEN ONE NIGHT, BUT I CAN'T STOP THINKING ABOUT YOU.**
> **—JACK**

A beautiful crimson creeps from her neck and chest, up to her cheeks, as she fidgets with her necklace. "Sorry, I didn't see this before. We should head inside."

"May I escort you?" I offer her my arm.

She reluctantly settles her hand in the crook of my elbow. "Sure."

I lead us up the rest of the steps, attempting to steal glances. My spitfire doesn't give in until we reach the door. We hand the attendant our invitations and she insists, "Well, thank you for the escort. I can take it from here."

My face falls. Without another word, she rushes through the crowd to our table. Though, the disappointment is short lived as I chuckle to myself. Little does she know, she won't be getting away that easily tonight. I walk to the bar and watch as she checks the name plates, likely relieved she's not sitting with me. When you're the third generation of Bartholomew Jacksons, your family gets creative; I've been Jack since I was a child. She probably thinks she's sitting next to some rich arsehole tonight and will be in for a surprise.

Her drink arrives, so I make my way to the table and take a seat next to her.

"Sorry, I think that seat's taken." She gestures to the nametag reading '*Bartholomew Jackson, III.*'

"Aye, by me."

"Bartholomew?" She stutters over the realisation. "So, what, is Jack a nickname? Or a pseudonym?"

"Nickname. Would you rather call me Bart?" I ask, wiggling my eyebrows.

She laughs. "Absolutely not."

Layla takes a seat to her right and sighs, "Fuck, I'm tired." She's pregnant with twins, and Ben couldn't be happier about it.

"How are my favourite little friends doing in there?" Amanda asks Layla, rubbing her belly. I didn't peg her for someone to fawn over children and babies. There's so little I know about her and it's a welcome surprise.

"They're being little assholes, I still have at least six months before they decide to show their faces. Whoever said pregnancy is amazing is a fucking liar." I have to laugh at the contrast between Layla and my cousin. While he's typically void of all emotion, she lights up a room.

Ben sits next to Layla and a small smirk tugs at his lips as he sees Amanda next to me. "Jack. Amanda, how was your trip?"

"Oh, it was fine," she sheepishly replies, finishing her drink in three quick gulps and getting the attention of a server to order another.

Amanda keeps quiet whilst Ben takes the pass and recaps the thrashing the Rangers received in the Champions league last week. I'm distracted, but notice that Amanda's now on her third drink and has bid on several excursions in a short amount of time—including a castle tour in Scotland and a whisky tasting in Ireland.

Is she planning on staying a while?

No matter how much I try to get Amanda's attention tonight, she brushes me off. After some time, I remember that I'm going about this all wrong. When we first met, I pretended to ignore her and she practically ran into my arms. I should've heeded Ben's warning to not chase her.

She signals the waiter in an attempt to order a fourth whisky sour, but I stop her. I rest my arm behind her chair and pull her raised hand into her lap, covering it with mine. "Easy there, sprite, I think you've had enough. If you drink any more, you'll be leaving here broke with all that you've bid on."

For the first time tonight, she's looking at me, and her eyes are full of hunger. The same hunger that drew me in the moment we met. Every part of me is fighting to not touch her, kiss her, grab her hand and run like hell out of here.

"You're right, I'm actually quite drunk," she giggles, biting her lip and looking up at me through her lashes. I love that she's flirting with me, but I hate that it took whisky for it to happen.

"Why don't I get you a ride back to your hotel?" I offer.

Amanda shakes her head, looks around to ensure no one is watching, then leans in and whispers, "Only if you come back with me." She nips at my ear as she pulls away, and I can't help the groan that escapes me.

She's quite pleased with herself, her mischievous grin giving her away. "No, my wee spitfire. I'll ensure you get back safely, but I won't be staying the night."

We're halfway out of our seats when Julian stops us. "Before you go, we have a proposition for you both."

Frowning, we both sit. "What kind of proposition?" Amanda asks.

12

AMANDA

I wake up hungover, not remembering much from last night, other than I bought some outlandish activities to do while I'm here. I'll never drink a whiskey sour again... or at least for the next week. I turn over and find Jack laying on top of the duvet, wearing an undershirt and boxer briefs.

"Jack," I shriek. "What are you doing in my bed?"

His eyes flutter open. "Mornin'."

"Don't you *mornin'* me, mister. What are you doing here?"

"You asked me to stay and do... other things." He wiggles his eyebrows. "But I'm a gentleman. Besides, I could never take advantage of the woman who is my new investor."

"I'm sorry, your what?" My voice comes out shrill but I have no clue what's happening.

"Go check the paperwork on the desk. I was honestly surprised you agreed to it."

I throw back the duvet and rush to the desk, not caring that I'm only in my underwear. It's nothing he hasn't seen before. I sift through them and find verbiage that states Ben will give me $2.5 billion if I invest $1 billion in Jack's research. This feels like a bad spam email or pyramid scheme. The only stipulation, other than monetary, is that I'm on site for the six month dig. The area he's researching will yield millions of dollars worth of lost artifacts and is critical to his research, but I now vaguely remember them mentioning that there's another investor they want me to keep an eye on there.

"So, I fund your quest for fortune and glory, and in six months, I'll be a billionaire?" I just need to hang out with a sexy man who is digging up old pottery shards. It can't be that bad, right?

Jack props himself up on his elbows. "That's it. You can review it with your lawyers, but I was in as much shock as you when Ben presented it last night."

"And what of the note?"

"Ah, yes, well… that does complicate things, doesn't it? But what do you say, my wee spitfire, are you up for an adventure?"

"Yeah," I answer honestly, scanning the pages. I look up from them and swallow hard, my voice coming out meeker than I'd like. "Are you sure about this? Six months is a long time."

Can I do this? Six months with a man who can make my heart stop with just one look?

Jack laughs and slides off the bed, stalking toward me. "If you need, you can pretend New York didn't happen, shove down all the emotions painted on your face, and join me in Scotland for half a year. You'll walk away a billionaire and my research will be funded."

"Or?" I stupidly ask.

He grins, the smile meeting his eyes; my favorite little wrinkles appear at the edges. My ass is pressed against the desk, there's nowhere for me to go. He cages me in and leans forward, speaking softly beside my ear, "Or you can let me get to know you when my face isn't buried between your legs." He pauses and presses chaste kisses on my neck before continuing, "Making you come over and over until you're begging for my cock is an ungodly experience, but I want more than your delicious cunt."

My breath is heavy, synced with his. He trails soft kisses up my neck to my jaw. I shouldn't let him continue. I should end his seduction, but my body and my head are at war with each other.

"How are you supposed to get to know me if you can't keep your hands off me?"

He chuckles against my skin and nips in the same spot he marked me with a dark hickey that night. A whimper escapes me, remembering how it lingered for well over a week.

"My hands aren't on you, sprite, but I know you want them to be."

"Yes," I breathe. A rumble vibrates against my bare shoulder as he peppers soft kisses across it.

Fuck it.

"Touch me," I beg.

There's no way we could fuck on the desk, given how tall he is, but damn if I don't want to try. He grips my ass, pulling me to the edge, and I wrap my legs around him.

No words pass between us when our eyes meet. His burn into me as if he can see straight to my soul.

Jack tucks my hair behind my ear, then cups my neck, his thumb brushing my jaw. "Fuck, you're beautiful," he whispers.

I huff a laugh and look down at my tits as I joke, "They really are, aren't they?"

He tilts my chin to look at him. "Don't." His words are more firm than I anticipated and his fingers graze my neck, leaving goosebumps in their wake, until he rests his palm on my chest above my heart. "*You* are beautiful, Amanda. While I have every intention of worshiping your body, I want more. It scares you and it's why you ran when I found you."

I suck in a breath. I love and hate that he knows why I can't do this. "You were supposed to be a hookup," I say quietly, mostly to myself.

"You weren't supposed to claim me for yourself and never let go. Well, my wee spitfire, it's my turn. But I'm not going to fuck you, not when I know it'll push you away."

"You're going to say no to a topless woman, wet and ready for you on a desk?" I jest to hide my disappointment. He's right, of course, but that doesn't mean I don't want him desperately.

"I'll say yes when I can guarantee you'll be mine after."

Before I can respond, there's a knock at the door. "Amanda? Are you up? You're not answering your phone and Becca wants to get tacos. *Ow!* Ok, fine, I want to get tacos," Layla shouts through the door.

"This is my karma, isn't it?" I mutter to myself.

"Tell them ten minutes," he growls and I feel it everywhere.

Jack pulls out the chair from the desk and takes a seat, lifting my legs onto his shoulders. Tugging my panties to the side, he wastes no time as he licks up my slit and swirls his tongue around my clit.

"Ten minutes," I breathlessly yell back to my friends, then tell Jack, "I thought you said you weren't going to —" He nips at my clit, cutting me off and forcing a scream from me. "*Fuck me,*" I finish, but it comes out as a command.

My friends' footsteps retreat in the hall. I know ten minutes isn't enough, but I want him too fucking much that I'll take whatever he gives me. My head lulls back as Jack continues licking and sucking, teasing the fuck out of me. He slides two fingers into my soaked pussy and I can hardly hold myself up as he curls them, hitting right where I need him.

Part of me is afraid he'll edge me like he did that night in the bookstore. "*You come on my face or my cock… or not at all.*" His words from that night while he refused to let me come on his fingers echo in my ears.

He continues the delicious torture as I wind tighter and tighter, my orgasm almost within reach. My breath quickens, and I'm ready to let go… until he abruptly stops. "Jack!" I cry out in frustration, popping my head up to figure out why the hell he would do this to me.

Jack looks up through his lashes as he kisses the inside of my thigh, his beard tickling me. "Yes?"

"What the fuck?" I groan.

"Tell me you won't run, and I'll let you come."

My fear is coming to fruition—this asshole is really not going to let me come.

Two can play that game…

I grip his wrist and pull his fingers out of me, then bring them to my mouth to suck them clean. His eyes darken as I remove them from my lips with a pop.

"Don't give me an ultimatum, Jack," I spit. "I can make myself come." I slip my ring and middle fingers inside myself, ready to finish the job. "I don't mind fucking myself. I've been doing it for months while I remembered how your thick cock felt inside me."

Jack's nostrils flair and his jaw tics; it's too much for him. His molten eyes don't leave mine as I drive my fingers faster and harder and allow myself to gasp and moan, loving that it's making him feral. He stands, grips my throat, and brutally kisses me. I might not trust him with my heart right now, but I will absolutely let him own this piece of me. With his free hand, he fists his shirt at the nape of his neck, breaking our kiss for a fraction of a second to tug it over his head and toss it who the fuck knows where. I reach for his hard cock through his boxer briefs, but he swats my hand away. He takes it out himself and begins long, slow strokes up and down his shaft.

With each swipe of his tongue over mine, I give in to this man. I want him to take from me until I have nothing left. I need him to lose control, throw me on the bed, and fuck me for the next twelve hours.

Is he losing control, or am I?

He removes my hand from my pussy and grinds his length against my clit, "I told you I wasn't going to fuck you, and I'm a man of my word. But you're still going to come all over my cock."

I whimper against his lips and pull him closer, increasing the friction. I was already so close, it only takes a minute of him rubbing his cock against my clit and I come undone. My orgasm tears through me hard and fast. "I'm... *oh fuck!*" Lifting enough to bite down on his shoulder, I sink my teeth into his flesh like a fucking vampire, claiming him as mine.

Jack growls and continues grinding against me, prolonging my orgasm as he chases his own. He pulls back a couple inches as he comes, aiming right for my pussy like a damn shotgun. I'm painted, marked by him. He then palms my clit, making me cry out. With three fingers, he pushes his cum inside my pussy.

A smirk tugs at his lips. "You branded me, spitfire. Only fair I returned the favor." He slowly removes his fingers, and replaces my soaked panties. "Open for me." His fingers trace my lips and I open my mouth more than willingly. He drags his coated fingers across my tongue, then surprises me by sucking his fingers clean before kissing me. I tangle my hands in his hair as I kiss him back harder, tasting both of us.

True to his word, he didn't fuck me. He did something far worse: he made me his.

13

JACK

I rest my forehead against hers.

What is she doing to me?

When Amanda challenged me, I snapped. My inexplic-able need to claim her, own her, was significantly stronger than my desire to keep her. I slipped up. There's a good chance she'll have lunch with her friends, then pack her bags and be on the first flight to New York.

"I should—"

"No," I growl, sinking my fingers into her thighs. I can't help it. After months of thinking I'd never see her again, now that I've found her, there's no way I'll be able to let her go—at least not like this.

"Sign the contracts," Amanda finishes softly.

I pull back. "What did you just say?"

"I should sign the contracts," she repeats. "It's six months. Your work needs to be funded. I'll have a lawyer review them and I'll sign this afternoon."

"What about this?"

"What *about* this? You probably shouldn't come all over my cunt as a morning wake up call, but I don't see why I can't spend six months in Scotland. The only thing that doesn't make sense is why they'd want me on-site. It says something about keeping an eye on an investor but I'm an author, not an archaeologist."

I chuckle. "You're a buffer. My ex-wife is a major donor and will be there. Ben and Julian suggested having someone else there to ensure my work isn't stolen. Don't you remember from last night?"

"Too many whisky sours," she laughs but her face falls quickly after. "Your ex? Is she also an archaeologist?"

"I'd rather not talk about my ex-wife while I'm still hard," I tease.

She looks between us. When her gaze returns to mine, it's filled with a swirl of emotion. "I promised them ten minutes. Let's take a quick shower and talk more about this later?"

I press a soft kiss to her lips and help her off the desk. Without another word, I lead her to the shower. I refuse to let her out of my sight, especially after this morning. I'd invite myself to lunch with her and her friends but it'd likely backfire.

Turning on the water, I ensure it's extra hot—just like months ago, even if it would nearly sear the flesh off my bones. I strip her out of her ruined underwear and toss them in the bin.

"Hey," she protests, though it's lacklustre compared to the fire I expected.

"Get in." I gesture to the shower, steam rolling out the open door.

"Aren't you going to join me?"

I shake my head. "And risk accidentally fucking you? Not a chance, spitfire."

"How do you *accidentally* fuck someone?" she laughs.

"Simple." I guide her backward a few steps until her back hits the wall beside the shower. "Like this." Gripping her thigh, I hike her leg above my hip, and slip the tip of my cock into her warm, wet cunt. Her gasp quickly turns into a moan, and it takes everything in me to not continue. I pull out and release her leg. "See? Accident."

Amanda's eyes narrow, and I bite my lip to stifle a laugh. "How the hell do you expect me to spend six months with you when you pull a little stunt like that?"

"I thought I was clear." I rest my hand above her head on the wall and lean in. "Or were you too hung up on the thought of me tasting you until you're craving my cock inside you?"

She straightens her posture and lifts her chin, as if it would make any difference. We both know where this is headed, no matter how much she tries to fight it. I lean in further and nip at her ear, eliciting another delicious moan from her.

"You're right," she whispers, sliding her hands up my stomach to my chest. "Showering together is a terrible idea."

"Think you can tempt me, sprite? You have tacos to get to, I already had mine. But don't worry, I'll be having seconds later when you return."

"*If* I return," she corrects.

"You will," I reply confidently, swallowing my fear of her not coming back. "Get cleaned up, have lunch with your friends, then you and I have plans."

"I already have plans. I'm supposed to meet a friend for drinks tonight."

"I have plans later as well. I have to meet my brother for a pint," I say carefully, omitting that Blair will be there. I'm not about to drag Amanda into the situation with my ex-wife. My ex asked that my brother join us to discuss logistics, since he's agreed to be on-site for me for the project. Thankfully, Cam's in London to deliver items from the last dig to a museum, otherwise I wouldn't bother him with yet another ridiculous request of Blair's.

As a fellow archaeologist, Cam's the best choice to join me on the dig, and I'm excited to work with him on this project. Though he doesn't chase missing diaries, he's currently researching mediaeval bridges and castles. It'll come in handy when we begin cataloguing our findings. He's taken an interest in other projects, and I recently helped him recover a fascinating collection of Kildalton Cross jewellery, which he donated to a museum in California.

Amanda smothers a smile and teases, "How do you expect to squeeze in a sex marathon with your busy schedule?"

"The next time I'm inside you, you'll be mine after. Until you're ready for that, my cock is off-limits." I tilt her chin and bring her lips within a breath of mine, lowering my voice. "After your lunch with the girls, we have plans before you head out for drinks."

She takes a deep breath, then concedes. "Alright, you win. Are you going to share what these plans are?"

"You know, on second thought." I turn off the shower. "I quite enjoy the idea of you going out with nothing under your dress, feeling a little of both of us dripping down your legs." She reaches behind us to turn the water back on but I grip her wrist and bring it to my lips.

There's a pounding at the door. "It's been more than ten minutes," Becca shouts.

Amanda's eyes haven't left mine. Neither of us move, despite her friend's relentless knocking. She cups my cheek and kisses me, unlike any kiss I've experienced before from her. It's both gentle and raw, full of unspoken promises. We hardly know one another but she's already relinquishing control to me, trusting me with more than just her body. I don't take it lightly.

When we break apart, she whispers, "Stay here. I'll be back in an hour."

I half expect her to turn on the shower. Instead, she leaves the bathroom, shouting to her friend, "Getting dressed. I'll meet you downstairs."

14

AMANDA

This whole thing is a mess. I know nothing about archaeology. Zero. Zilch. Nada. What if he's a fraud? Do Ben and Julian know?

You know he's not a fraud, you stupid cunt. You're just trying to come up with a reason to not be in the same room with him.

An idea strikes me as I rush down the hall to the elevators to meet Becca and Layla for tacos. At our friend Harriet's bachelorette party a few months ago, I met Harriet's younger sister, Lizzy, who works at a museum. Lizzy's a black cat in a human body, if nothing else, she would be the perfect person to make sure I'm not fucking a hot archaeologist for six months.

Jack didn't confirm whether or not his ex is an archaeologist. *What if she is? Will they get to live their happily ever after, leaving me pining for a man I know virtually nothing about?*

I get into the elevator and check my contacts, thankful that, even after a fun night of celebrating her sister, I have Lizzy's number.

> Hey, it's Amanda.

Fuck, it's the middle of the night in California.

> Hope you don't mind me texting you at this weird hour, but I vaguely remember you saying that you work for a museum?

LIZZY

Hi! It's only 4am here, so it's not that weird.

Yes, I work for a natural history museum.

> 4am? Fuck, I'm old if you think that's not weird.

> Do you have any experience with Scottish shit?

Define shit ;)

> Old paintings, jewelry, etc.

I'm listening...

> Ok, so I got roped into this project in Scotland and the archaeologist is that hot AF guy I told everyone about at your sister's bachelorette party.

What the fuck?

Exactly. So, I need someone here who knows what they are doing as a buffer between me and my hot Scot.

You know, distract him with boring facts about broken pots and shit.

Sure, count me in. Send me the details!

You're amazing! Thank you!

The faster I'm away from this Jackson guy, the better.

Wait, are you talking about Cameron Jackson?

I pause for a moment and shoot her a quick reply as the elevator doors open and I spot my friends.

No.

Who is Cameron Jackson?

I stuff my phone in my purse and join them in the lobby.

"How was sex with your hot Scot?" Layla asks, wiggling her eyebrows.

"We didn't have sex."

"Such a fucking liar," Becca laughs. "Your post-orgasm glow says otherwise; you totally got laid."

"I didn't," I insist, then add, "but I definitely came."

"You're such a bitch," Layla jests, playfully smacking my arm with the back of her hand. "He strikes me as a man who likes to eat, glad you got to be his breakfast. So, is this a thing now, or what?"

"No, definitely not a thing." We begin walking out to the street to hail a cab and my stomach grumbles. "Fuck, I'm starving."

"So, he got to eat, but you didn't? Selfish bastard," Becca says with a smirk.

I roll my eyes. "Why do I tell you guys anything? I actually had to enlist Harriet's sister, Lizzy, to come to Scotland with me. Since she works at a museum, she can bore Jack with archaeology talk."

"I mean, if he's not tongue fucking you, he needs to keep his mouth busy somehow. Good plan." Layla winks at me, then gestures to the black town car that's approaching.

"I thought we were taking a cab?"

Becca and Layla laugh as Becca replies, "Have you met our husbands? If we tried, they would both get growly as fuck. Especially Ben. With this one knocked up, he's a little overprotective." She then asks Layla, "When do you need to be back for Sir Grumpypants?"

"Whenever. Ben's busy with Cam," Layla replies. "There was some huge find recently with old crosses, or something. I don't know, I wasn't following. It has something to do with Jack and Cameron's research."

"Did you say Cameron?" I ask them.

We all slide into the car and Layla answers, "Yeah, Ben's cousin, Jack's younger brother."

I dig out my phone before getting in the car. The driver closes the door behind me and I open Lizzy's messages.

LIZZY

> I just put away a collection of jewelry that was donated to the museum. It was a bunch of old Kildalton Crosses from Scotland.

> I just figured it was the same guy.

> If your hot Scot isn't him, who is he? I'd like to do my research before I come.

Fuck. For all the research I did on Ben when Layla started dating him, I know nothing about Jack or this Cameron guy.

I leave her message for later, it's time for some recon. I exit out of the messages and open the browser app.

I type *Bartholomew Jackson, III.*

Clicking on the first link, I scroll to find his accolades and published works. He seems to be the real deal. There's an article co-written by Cameron Jackson and I click on it.

...the Black family took extreme measures to ensure their stolen fortune wouldn't be found. While the excavation yielded more questions than answers, it led us to Swarthmore Castle, which was previously occupied by the family.

Ewen Black's recovered diaries will be donated to the British Museum in London.

While I continue to read and fidget with my grandmother's necklace, Becca's voice startles me. "Earth to Amanda?"

"Sorry. You said Cameron will be on-site in Scotland?"

Layla answers, "Yep. You'll be with *two* hot Scots."

Fuck my life.

"I'm glad Lizzy agreed to come. The last thing I need is any more alone time with Jack. Take that, forced proximity! You can go fuck yourself."

We all laugh. While it's one of my favorite tropes in books, I don't want to live it. While I like him, if his ex is another investor and on site with us, I need to keep my distance. If I don't want to live a forced proximity trope, I certainly don't want to be involved in a love triangle.

I send Lizzy the article and text her that Jack is the hot one night stand. She doesn't reply, but it's also 4am for her, so she's probably asleep.

Becca, Layla, and I have a leisurely lunch that turns into one too many rounds of margaritas—virgin for my super preggo friend. After talking things through with them and sending a quick message to my accountant and lawyer, I electronically sign the document Julian sent me to invest in the project. It's a fairly simple contract, and I trust my friend's husband to not fuck me over.

When I get back to the hotel, I check into a different room. I need a chance to clear my head before returning to Jack. The hotel bar was too loud, and the nearest cafe was bustling. I need a quiet room, a hot shower, and probably a nap. There's also the fact that we'll be spending six months together, we can't be fucking every chance we get.

I get to the room—which is an identical set up as the one I slept in last night—and toss my bag onto the small table by the entryway. I glance at the desk, and shake away the flashes of what we did earlier.

For a brief moment, I consider going back to my old room to see if he's waiting for me. No good would come of it if I did.

Six months. I can handle six months. Then, I'll walk away a billionaire and never see Jack again.

Except, I want him…

Fuck it. You only live once.

I text Layla, asking for Jack's number. In seconds, she sends me his contact information.

> Hey, it's Amanda. Busy until tonight. Up for a nightcap?

I'll still get to see him once I figure this all out and after drinks with my friend.

The time at the top of my phone can't be accurate. I glance at my watch and realize it never synced properly with the time zone.

"Fuck! I'm late!" I shriek and rush to the bathroom to fix my hair and makeup. Blair needs a wing woman, I can't show up looking like I've been tongue-fucked all afternoon or like I survive off a diet of margaritas and tacos—even if both those things are true.

15

JACK

Amanda never returned to the room after she left for lunch with her friends. I don't have her number but feel like an arsehole asking my cousin for it. Ben texted me that Amanda electronically signed the contracts and that Cam would bring me a physical copy when we meet with Blair later. At least this means she'll be coming to Scotland; she's not running.

The pub Blair chose is walking distance from the hotel. I need the time to get my shit together and not obsess over Amanda for the next hour. There's too much at stake where my ex is concerned; I need to stay focused. As I'm walking, I get a message from Cam.

CAM

Blair's friend appears to be late or a no-show. Care if I bail early?

Why? Don't tell me, Blair is already boring the fuck out of you.

I'm two minutes out. Grab me a pint?

Cunt.

A few minutes later, I arrive at the pub and spot Cam at the bar getting drinks, looking particularly irked. I join him and he gestures to the table where Blair sits alone. He slides a beer over to me and grumbles, "Can we get this over with?"

About to reply, my phone vibrates in my pocket. In case it's Ben or Julian, I check it, but It's a message from an unknown American number

UNKNOWN

Hey, it's Amanda. Busy until tonight. Up for a nightcap?

I can't help my smile and tell Cameron, "Looks like I have plans later. So, yes, let's make this as short as possible."

"Plans?" He frowns.

"Remember the fiery American lass I told you about?"

"I thought she went home after Ben's wedding."

I shake my head. "She's back."

His eyes widen and he replies with a gasp, "No fucking way."

"Aye. Saw her at the gala, and this morning. She just sent me this." I show him the message.

"Attaboy." Cam claps me on the back. "It's been ages since I've seen that smile. Let's rush through this meeting so you can meet up with your dream girl."

Amanda is everything I've ever wanted in a woman. That night we spent together in New York meant more to me than the last couple decades combined. She's full of fire and the polar opposite of Blair. I glance at the table where she's sitting, busying herself on her phone.

This meeting needs to be fucking quick, I want to get back to my girl. She's not mine yet, technically, but if I have any say, she will be soon.

Thankfully, my meeting with Cam and Blair is brief, coming to an end before I've even finished half my whisky. Blair requests accommodations for the duration of the dig, and Cam and I agree she can pay her own way. She suggested staying with me but I told her my room is already full. I don't share my hope that Amanda will stay with me, and I don't so much as hint about Ben and Julian's investment through Amanda either.

I'll fill Cam in on any missing information later.

After I've devoured every inch of my wee spitfire that I've craved for months.

Back at the hotel, I make my way up to Amanda's floor, brace myself on the doorframe, and knock on her door three times. I swear I can still taste her on my lips and am desperate for another round with her.

There's no answer for a minute. I knock again.

No answer.

I press my ear to the door, hearing nothing, and take out my phone to message her.

> Ready when you are.

There's no reply for a couple minutes. At risk of looking like a desperate arsehole, I walk downstairs to the bar, grabbing a quick whisky to pass the time and figure out my next move. I slide onto a stool, staring at the message for far too long.

The bartender refills the drink I finished a little too quickly. As I'm about to take a sip, a familiar scent of sweet thistles pulls my attention. I look to my left, then my right, finding my wee spitfire on the seat next to me. I can't help my smile.

"What's a pretty lass like yourself doing in a place like this?"

16

AMANDA

I rush to the bar, pub—whatever they call it here—to meet Blair. I don't want to bother my friends with their fancy chauffeurs. Besides, it's only a few blocks from the hotel. I power-walk to my destination.

New York prepared me for this.

I enter the bar that looks like a typical English pub back home, though this is significantly more welcoming. I only make it two steps before I spot Blair in the thick of a heated argument with two men with matching physical builds. I pause when I see one of their profiles.

What is Jack doing here?

She's hung up on an ex... bringing his brother...

Jack's meeting his brother.

No. No, no, no. Fuck.

Either Jack or his brother are Blair's ex-husband, and I'm not about to find out which. I pivot quickly and leave the bar, hoping no one saw me.

I type out a quick message to Blair.

> Sorry, something came up. See you soon!

See you soon? Nope. Not after tonight.

How did I not put this together earlier?

This has to be some sort of cosmic way of punishing me for something I did in a past life.

I rush back to the hotel and check with the front desk staff that all my things were brought from my original room while I was out. I wouldn't normally have splurged on a second night here and checked into a cheaper hotel, but if I'm about to be a billionaire, why the fuck not?

Since Jack said he had plans, I strategically waited to ask the staff to move everything until I knew he couldn't possibly be still lurking in my room. With everything settled, maybe the universe isn't against me after all.

No, his bag is in my room, too. *Fuck my life.*

I sift through my luggage for new clothes and take a long hot shower, washing away the reminisce of what Jack and I did earlier today. I fucked my friends' ex, or my friends' ex's brother. Either way, I'm not about to be center stage in a soap opera plot. What next? Someone gets amnesia?

The suds wash away and I crumple to the shower floor, tucking my legs to my chest. How could this happen? I feel more for Jack than I have for any other man I've dated, and we never even went on a real date. I've lost someone who isn't even mine—it ended before it began.

I shut my eyes tight, letting the hot water wash away the pain I refuse to let myself experience. We hardly know one another. We've spent less than forty-eight hours together total. How can I feel so much for him? A stray tear leaves my eye, but I shake away the hurt I don't deserve to feel. Best case scenario, he's the brother.

Yes. He's the brother…

No. His ex is a major donor. Blair is his ex; it's the only logical explanation, and there are too many coincidences for her not to be. She's been wanting to get back together with her ex—with Jack. I was going to be her wing woman.

Fuck. She's the one I'm supposed to keep an eye on?

I'm craving the touch of a stranger, who I'm now financially tied to… and is also my friend's ex-husband. Nothing about this is ok; my therapist is going to have a field day when I get home.

I shut off the water, bracing myself against the wall, and take a moment to process everything. I'm torn between wanting to pursue something with Jack and walking away completely.

The contract. Fuck! Why did I sign it?

As I get out and dry off, I continue piecing it all together. Blair's going to be in Scotland, on-site with me, Jack, Lizzy, and probably Jack's brother.

I need to get out, clear my head, and fill my social cup. The hotel bar should be a safe bet, since Jack is preoccupied with Blair. I'm not worried about going home with anyone tonight, so I keep my makeup minimal and slip on a pair of dark skinny jeans and a black tee. A drink at the bar and a little chit chat with a stranger should fix everything. If nothing else, a fun story might inspire a scene for a book. With one last check in the mirror, I grab my purse and head out.

Once downstairs, I locate the hotel bar on the other side of the lobby. I pause at the entrance the moment I see him.

Jack.

I check my phone for the first time since I sent him the text and find a reply.

JACK

Ready when you are.

My heart stops.

He doesn't know I'm friends with Blair.

He doesn't know I want nothing more than for him to take me in his arms and whisper sweet praises as he kisses me.

He doesn't know I've never truly been in love and don't know what the hell I'm doing.

He doesn't know it wasn't just sex for me, and I'm his.

He doesn't know that, for the first time in my life, I'm ready to fall.

But… can we do this?

With Blair in the mix, I should run far away from him, but can't bring myself to do it. I can't fight this anymore. After the whirlwind of today, only one thing is certain: I want him. Even for a night.

I swallow hard and face my fears, walking in and sitting next to him. He exhales a contented sigh, a smile lifting at the corner of his mouth before he turns to face me.

"What's a pretty lass like yourself doing in a place like this?"

17

JACK

"Can we talk?" Amanda asks, chewing nervously on her bottom lip. Despite her ominous words, all I want to do is take her lip between my teeth and kiss her until sunrise.

"Aye, but we know that nothing good ever comes from those three little words." I intend my reply to lighten the mood. Instead, her beautiful eyes fill with worry. Tucking her hair behind her ear, I cup my fingers behind her neck, keeping my thumb in place on her cheek. "What's wrong?"

Her hand covers mine and she leans into my touch. This is a softer side of her, one I haven't seen yet. Granted, we haven't spent much time together, but this isn't the same woman who's been fighting me at every turn. Something's wrong.

"I'm sorry," she whispers.

Fuck. Is she going to run again? I close the distance and brush a ghost of a kiss to her cheek. "There's nothing to apologise for," I insist.

She unconsciously toys with her pendant necklace. "She's my friend. Your ex-wife is my friend."

My brows furrow. "I'm not following."

Amanda sighs, and I don't like the sound of it one bit. "Earlier..." She kisses my palm and sets it on her lap. Still holding my hand, she continues, "I was supposed to meet Blair, her ex-husband, and his brother for drinks. I walked in and saw the three of you. She's your ex-wife, isn't she? Not Cameron's."

Oh fuck.

"Yes, but—"

"She's been wanting to get back together with you. I was supposed to help her win you back," she explains softly.

I grip my glass tightly. "Hell will freeze over before that happens." She nods in understanding, but remains otherwise quiet, so I ask, "What else is bothering you? I can see the wheels turning."

Amanda blows out a long breath. "Do you remember what I said to you at the bar in New York?"

"We said a lot of things that night," I chuckle.

"Well, you wanted to take me out, but I said I might start liking you."

"Aye." Hope fills my chest; there's the smallest chance the woman I need more than oxygen might feel the same for me. "Did I succeed?"

"A little too much," she admits.

The conflict is written all over her face. She wants this as much as I do, but doesn't want to hurt Blair. I don't know how they met, and frankly, I don't give a fuck. For months, I craved this woman in front of me. I'm not giving her up—no matter who she's friends with.

"Come out with me tonight?"

She frowns. "Where?"

"I wanted to take you to see some of my favourite spots around London, but you never came back to the hotel."

"Oh, right. I checked into a different room. I, um… lunch ran late and I wanted time to process everything without my friends' commentary. I needed some space. So, I switched rooms and—"

"You could've just said something," I laugh, cutting off her rambling. "You didn't have to reserve a whole other room."

"I'm not used to, well, the green flags. It's throwing me a bit."

"When was the last time you let someone in?"

A swirl of emotions fill her eyes—an equal combination of fear and lust. Amanda takes a deep breath and replies, "You think you're going to be that guy? I like you, Jack, but what you're asking is..." She shakes her head and backpedals. "It's just sex."

"You know this is more than that." I drag my hand over my face. "I don't just want that perfect round arse of yours, or that cunt I crave to taste again. Is it so hard to believe that I want you to be mine? I'm not saying we should run off into the sunset like one of your books, but don't we deserve a chance?"

"You just like the chase," she teases with a light laugh.

"No, my wee spitfire, but I'd happily chase you to the ends of this earth, if you admitted I have a real chance with you. Why are you fighting this? I've been yours since the moment you walked into that hotel bar in New York. I think it's only fair you let me know where I stand and not make a numpty of me."

"I'm not the girl to settle down with—not the girl anyone settles down with. Blair is ready and waiting for you." She pulls back. "I shouldn't be here. All of this was a mistake."

I bark out a laugh and keep her close. "Are you serious? Fuck. I don't want her; I haven't for years. I want *you*. Don't worry about my ex, or any other made up obstacle you've come up with. I know you feel this, too."

"It'll hurt her."

"Aye, but it'll hurt me more to know I lost the perfect woman."

"I'm not perfect," she scoffs.

"You're perfect *for me*."

Amanda shakes her head, closing her eyes. "Setting aside that cheesy as fuck line, please don't make this harder than it needs to be." When they open, she says the one thing I refuse to consider, "Let's just get through the next six months and—"

I know what I want and won't dance around this. "Do you want to be with me?"

She swallows hard and her eyes pin me with hunger, though she's still fighting a war inside that beautiful mind of hers. "It doesn't matter," she whispers.

"It absolutely does. Do you want to be with me?" I repeat. When she doesn't reply, I admit, "For months, not a day passed when I didn't think about you, wishing I had stayed in New York. Thinking I'd never see you again but hearing your laugh ringing in my ears when someone told a joke. Not being able to smell honey or thistles back home without remembering how your scent lingered on my skin for days after you were gone. Watching the sunrise but its beauty paled in comparison to the one we experienced. Wondering if, in some twisted world, we might find each other again."

Fuck. I'm falling in love with her.

"I'm all in, spitfire. Give me one chance to prove that this—you and me—isn't fiction. Give me one shot at having something real with you."

In a quick movement, Amanda hops off her stool, stands between my legs, wraps her arms around me, and kisses me. It's cautious, not full of her usual fire, but I'll fucking take it. As we break apart, she nuzzles her face into the crook of my neck. I hold her closer and don't let go.

With a heavy sigh, and a shaky breath, she says softly, "I don't do relationships, or love, or feelings. But, *fuck*, I'm tired of fighting this. I want to trust you, but so help me, if you break my heart—"

"You'll break mine first."

"Can you give me six months? I don't feel right being with you since..." Her words trail off but I know she means Blair. After being haunted by the memory of a single night, I'm not giving her up that easily. It's completely irrational, but I'd trade this project for her to be mine.

I kiss her neck, my lips lingering on her soft skin. "Starting tomorrow."

Amanda pulls back to look at me, but I keep her close as she asks, "What's tomorrow?"

"I want to spend the night with you."

She bites her lip to hide her smile. "Sleeping together is a terrible idea."

"Aye, but who said anything about sleeping?"

_____

18

AMANDA

I don't know much about Jack, other than I am entirely too into him and he's a sexy as fuck archaeologist—*and basically, every woman's dream man.*

Maybe fucking him will get whatever this is out of our systems and we can walk away from this like it never happened…

Who am I kidding? I'm going to fall in love with him if I'm not careful.

"I came back for you that morning," he hesitantly admits.

"After your meeting?" I ask and Jack replies with a small nod. "I went back that night…" *Fuck, I shouldn't be telling him this.* "I didn't have a key card, so I couldn't access the elevators. I went to the hotel bar, hoping you might be there." *For a week.*

"Oh, my wee spitfire." He closes his eyes and shakes his head before returning his gaze to me. "I asked the front desk to extend my check out for you, in case you wanted to sleep. I was hoping to find you when I returned, but you were gone. I flew home that night."

Taking out a small paper from his wallet, he unfolds it and hands it to me—it's the hotel stationary I wrote on. My hand flies to my mouth as I gasp. He kept it this whole time.

**MAYBE IN FIFTY, WE'LL FIND EACH OTHER AGAIN.
XO, YOUR WEE SPITFIRE**

"Do I have to wait fifty?" he asks, his voice strained.

I quickly retrieve my wallet from my purse, finding the note he wrote me.

**MY WEE SPITFIRE, THANK YOU FOR THE BEST
NIGHT OF MY LIFE.
-J**

"Was it really the best?"

His smile soft, he replies, "It was… Until now."

I wrap my arms around his neck and kiss him. I can't run from this, it would hurt too much if I did. "Six months," I say into his mouth. "We can wait six months."

Jack pulls back an inch. "I'm not waiting six months to touch you again." I laugh, shaking my head. "What? I'm not going to lie to you." His thumb briefly grazes my bottom lip, and I have to resist taking it in my mouth. "I refuse to keep my hands to myself tonight. If I have to spend six months without touching you, I want to memorize how you clench around me as I drive deeper into your tight cunt, how you taste like both of us after you've had my cock down your throat, and the sound of you screaming my name after begging me to let you come."

My voice trembling despite myself, I admit, "The last time you fucked me, you ruined me."

"I never fucked you. That night? That wasn't fucking. You stole a part of me I never got back." He rests his forehead on mine. "I meant what I said, I want all of you. If you want to wait six months, then that's what we'll do."

I lean in closer and whisper, "If we only get one night, what if I'm not me and you're not you?"

He finishes his drink, the glass clinking loudly as he sets it back down on the bar. Without a word, he flags down the bartender, who retrieves his check. I grab it before he can and include my room number to charge it, but Jack snatches the pen from me, scratching the numbers out. He places cash on top of the bill, grabs my hand and swiftly walks us out of the hotel bar and toward the elevators. When we reach them, he growls, "Room key."

The low rumble of his voice makes my stomach dip and my whole body feels like it's on fire. The mild adrenaline from his command has me fishing the key from my purse in record time. I place it in his expectant hand, and he swipes it on the sensor.

The doors open, and once inside, I press my floor number. The moment the doors click shut and we begin ascending, I back Jack up against the elevator wall and crash my mouth against his. He chuckles against my lips but kisses me back harder. For months, I wanted a ghost of a man, a stranger I thought I could never have again. A man who, in one night, made me fall for him.

And now he's here. I have him, if I want him.

We reach the second floor and reluctantly break apart. The ache between my legs is unbearable, I'm desperate for him to touch me again. His words from that night ring in my ears, *"You said you wanted me to touch you, never said that you wanted to come."*

I silently remind myself to be careful what I ask for.

"234," I manage through labored breaths. "The room. 234."

Jack presses a final kiss to my lips and leads us out of the elevator and to my room. His hand poised to scan the card, he pauses and looks at me. "If you're mine, spit-fire, it's not just in there."

I consider it for a moment and swallow hard. He's right.

I'm his.

19

JACK

I scan Amanda's hotel key and hold the door open for her as she walks in. The instant it clicks behind us, I reach for her. Not touching her feels wrong. I grip her thighs and wrap her legs around my waist, carrying her further into the room. I take a seat on the edge of the bed, keeping her close. No words pass between us, I don't kiss her, but I can't tear my gaze from hers.

Brushing her hair off her shoulder, I kiss her neck and break the silence first. "Have you eaten yet? We should go out. If we stay here, I'll have my cock buried inside you for the rest of the night."

"I had plans to…"

I know I'll regret asking, knowing damn well it has to do with Blair, but I can't help myself. "What were your plans?"

"I was supposed to be on a double date with your broth-er," she laughs.

I chuckle against her neck and nip at her jaw. "Plan on upgrading to a younger version of me, spitfire?"

"Not a chance." Amanda's pupils dilate and, upon seeing the fire in her eyes, it takes everything in me to not strip her bare right now. "But you should probably tone down the growly possessive bit if I'm supposed to spend six months with you," she adds with a laugh.

"Are you serious?" I toss her onto the bed and lean over her, bracing myself on the mattress. "You're the one who growled '*mine*' while I was inside you."

She narrows her eyes. "I didn't growl."

"You absolutely did, and it was fucking adorable." As much as I want to spend the night between her legs, I need to get her out of here before I push for too much, too soon. I press a single kiss to her forehead and lift off the bed. "Come on, let's go. Grab your bag."

Propping herself on her elbows, she asks, "Where are we going?"

I do my best to hide my smile as I take my phone out of my back pocket and text my brother.

> Want to meet my spitfire? I need a ride to the airport.

CAM

> Can't. I'm already at the airport.

Shite. I was hoping to catch him before he left. He has to be in San Francisco in the morning to drop off two of the crosses the museum didn't have space for here.

Also, why are you texting me and not fucking the woman you've been obsessed with for months?

I look up in a silent prayer that my cock will forgive me. A chuckle escapes me and I glance at Amanda, but she's no longer on the bed. Her purse is slung over her shoulder and she's leaning against the hotel door. As she plays with her necklace, she openly drinks me in, looking at me like she could pounce on me at any moment. I don't address Cam's question, instead wish him a safe trip and stuff my phone back in my pocket.

"I was going to see if my brother could drive us to the airport, but it looks like we'll need to get a taxi."

"Airport?"

"Aye. Where's your luggage?"

"You told me to grab my bag." She gestures to her purse. "You didn't say I needed my suitcase."

I spot it next to the bed and shake my head with a light laugh. It's the same luggage I found on the bed in the spare room at Ben's house at the wedding. I could've had her months ago. I look back at her, a puzzled look still painting her face. All at once, I'm flooded with the memories of the one night we had together.

The unsexiest food she could find.

The sweet couple who let us sit with them.

Her taking my hand in the cab.

The bookstore where I kissed her for the first time.

Dancing with her at the bar.

Making my wee spitfire come over and over…

"I'm taking you home." I wheel her luggage behind me and open the door for her.

"What?" She pauses, not walking through.

I close the door and playfully reply, "I know my accent is thick, but you heard me just fine. I'm taking you home."

"I'm supposed to fly home in a couple days. And what about the room?"

"I'll cover your room. Swap your ticket for Edinburgh if you want to, but you're coming home with me tonight."

"Edinburgh? I can maybe come for a few days, but—"

I close the distance, her hitched breath cutting off her rebuttal. We stand there in a silent standoff for a moment, until I cave first. "Stay, spitfire," I tell her softly. "The project doesn't start for a few weeks. Until then, stay here… with me."

Amanda shakes her head. "I didn't plan for any of this. It was sprung on me after too much whisky. I need to get back to New York, tie up loose ends and whatnot. Fuck, all I have with me is that suitcase and my dress bag in the closet. I need to go home before you start digging up old pots and shit."

I stifle a laugh at her last remark. While I understand where she's coming from, I went months without her. Now that she's here, I'm afraid she might slip through my fingers, just like she did last time... and the time before. I couldn't bear to lose her again.

"What if you stayed for a few weeks?" I shouldn't have let her go when I saw her at my cousin's wedding.

Amanda cups my cheek and I cover her hand with mine as she sighs, "I'm not Becca or Layla. I don't do the whole 'whisked off to a foreign country' thing. Don't get me wrong, it's sweet, but I don't need any sort of grand gesture. I don't need St. Tropez's beaches, or a house that could fit a family of fifty in Canterbury. Nothing about that kind of wealth impresses me, I'd much rather spend time with you like we did in New York. At some point, I'll see your home, where you work... all of it. But I can't just drop everything in my life like we're living in some kind of fucking romance novel. This is real life, Jack."

I keep her close. Despite her words, I feel her pulling away from this. "I know. I just want—"

"No more declarations. Please. I like you... more than I should." She presses her forehead to my chest, fisting my shirt, and takes a deep breath. "I just need time to process this." Her gaze lifts to mine and I swallow hard, finding hope in her eyes. "I'm on deadline to get a chunk of my book to my editor and I'll need time to write. If you can promise me time to do that, I'll come to Scotland... for a week."

A small smirk tugs at my lips as I ask, "What if you fall madly in love with me in a week?" *I fell in a fucking night.* "Would you stay longer?"

"No." My shoulders sag at her simple reply, until she wraps her arms around my neck and brings her lips within an inch of mine. "But you know I'll come back to you. I found you. After months of not being able to stop thinking about you, you're here, right in front of me. That means something to me. I'm not dismissing it, but one of us needs to be the practical one."

"It's normally me," I admit with a small laugh.

"Well, then let's go have an adventure, my hot Scot." She smiles and it's one that meets her twinkling blue eyes. "One week where I'm not me and you're not you. One week where we're just two people who found each other again. And when the week's over, I'll go home to New York to make sure everything is in order before the dig begins. I'll come back to you, and we'll go find this missing treasure of yours."

I brush my nose to hers, then close the distance and kiss her softly. Speaking against her lips, I tell her, "You know, you ruined me, spitfire."

She kisses me harder, and when we finally break apart, she laughs, then clears her throat before speaking as if she was narrating a story, "Little did he know, he unexpectedly ruined the wee spitfire."

20

AMANDA

We arrive at the airport, and as we approach the line for the ticket counter, I take out my phone to check my bank account. A last minute plane ticket swap could cost me a pretty penny. While I'm not broke by any stretch of the imagination and Jack offered to cover my room, most of my money is tied up in stocks and other investments.

I type in my username and password in my banking app, chewing on my lip. The page refreshes and...

Available Balance: $2,500,034,098.22

I zoom in to double check, nearly dropping my phone in shock. Fuck, Julian and Ben work fast. My eyes wide, I turn to Jack to explain, but the words are stuck in my throat.

"You ok, spitfire?"

"I, uh…" I show him my screen and my breathing becomes more rapid.

He chuckles and wraps me in his arms, kissing the top of my head. Not removing his lips, he speaks against me, "Deep breaths, it's just money."

"Just money?" I whisper-shout. "Just money is losing fifty bucks to a slot machine. And this isn't losing money, this is obscene. Two and a half billion dollars!"

Jack strokes my back, keeping me grounded. I close my eyes as I try to catch my breath. "You can return the money and we can rip up the contract, if that's what you want."

Fuck, he smells good… and those bright green eyes are fucking gorgeous… especially with those hot as fuck glasses… No, bitch, focus.

I pull back enough to look at him, resting my chin on his chest, and take a deep breath. "No, I want to help fund the project. But I'll talk to Ben and Julian about the extra money. It's too much wealth for one person."

"It's yours to do whatever you want with. You could donate it to charity? But save a wee bit for yourself, for a rainy day."

"A wee bit? What, save half a billion dollars under my mattress? I…" My eyes wide, an idea striking me. I should keep it for now. I've never written about a woman billionaire before and this could be my chance to see what it's like to have entirely too much money before I donate the rest to charity. "First class is on me."

I wriggle from his hold and glance around for the first class line that bypasses the rest of the travelers. When I spot it, I take Jack's hand and drag him to the counter. He says something in protest, but I'm a woman on a mission.

"Two first class tickets on your next flight to Edinburgh, please," I say with a confidence that I absolutely don't have today.

The attendant doesn't search her computer, instead simply replies. "Unfortunately, none of our flights to Edinburgh have a first class option. We do, however, have business class, which offers wider seats than economy."

My shoulders sag. I've flown business countless times, but never first class. "Can we rent a plane, or something?"

"There are a few private airports that can charter a flight for you, but as an international airport, we do not offer that service." Damn, this woman is stuffy and a killjoy.

"Alright, well, two business class tickets, please," I sigh.

She types for a moment, then says, "I have two seats, but not together. Each seat is £297.53, shall I book them for you?"

I do a quick calculation, and it's less than $400 each. *So much for treating myself to an overpriced flight.*

While I'm distracted by my disappointment, Jack snakes his arm around me from behind, splaying his hand on my stomach. He leans in, his breath tickling my neck as he whispers, "I got this, spitfire," and hands her his credit card. His hand doesn't leave my belly; instead, a single knuckle of his forefinger slips into the top of my jeans.

"We won't be sitting together," I whisper.

The attendant swipes his card and asks for his ID and my passport. While she's processing everything, Jack kisses my neck and whispers back, "It's an hour and a half. Think you can go that long without me touching you?"

"I know you can't," I playfully reply.

Jack tugs me closer until every inch of me is flush with him. He's about to say something when the woman hands him back his card and ID, while I put my passport in my purse. With a nod to her, he stuffs them in his back pocket, not letting go of me. She hands us our tickets and checks our bags.

Jack takes my hand and we make our way to security. His grip is tighter than usual. I can't help but ask, "Is everything ok?"

He offers a small smile. "Can I be honest?"

"Of course."

"I hate that you ran." He glances away briefly, but then his beautiful green eyes find mine again, worry etched in every inch of his face. "I'm afraid in a week you'll do it again."

I squeeze his hand tighter. "I'm not running anymore. But let's just take this one day at a time. You know, like normal people."

Before entering the security line, Jack stops abruptly. Brows pinched, he insists, "You, my wee spitfire, are the furthest thing from normal. That one night I spent with you fucking ruined me for months. There's nothing normal about obsessing over a nameless woman." He tilts my chin and kisses me softly.

"Come on, we're going to miss our flight," I say against his lips.

He groans. "It's going to be the longest flight of my life."

Jack keeps my hand firmly in his while we wait in the security line. My phone buzzes in my bag. I take it out to find a voicemail from a New York number. "Mind if I…?" I give my phone a shake.

"Of course not." He pulls me close and kisses just above my temple. "You never need to ask."

Jack grabs a tray for his things as I click play and the message begins, "*Good morning, Ms. Bl—*"

"Spitfire, one bin or two?" Jack calls, gesturing to the stack. I hold up one finger and he sets it next to his.

"...*transferred to your account within the next few hours,*" the woman continues. "*Mr. Evans would like you to meet with him in New York within ten business days to transfer the funds to the Swarthmore Castle project. Please give us a call at your earliest convenience.*"

I save the voicemail for later, along with a mental note to call Julian or Ben tomorrow.

21
___

JACK

As predicted, it's the longest flight of my life. Amanda's sitting in the row behind me, writing in a journal. Every so often, I hear her chuckle to herself, the sound immediately bringing a smile to my face.

All those months ago, all it took was one night for me to fall for this stranger. Waking up next to her this morning, I fell all over again. I teased Ben and Julian relentlessly for marrying their wives after knowing them for less than a year. Here I am now, suddenly thinking it wasn't so impulsive of them after all. I want to keep Amanda for myself, and I have every intention of doing so when my project's complete.

We land in Scotland and I wait for the cabin doors to open before standing. Two hands slide down my chest from behind me, briefly startling me. I take Amanda's hands, holding them in place as I look up to find her bright blue eyes above me. I'm half tempted to pull her around the seat and onto my lap.

"How far is your place?" she asks through a yawn.

"Just down the road."

I release her so we can disembark, but the moment we're off the plane, I pull her to my side, not letting her move an inch away from me. Having her home with me makes a lightness settle in my chest that hasn't been there in years.

We pass the baggage claim and nearly leave without our bags. "Shite! We almost forgot the luggage."

Amanda shakes her head with a small chuckle. "Was someone a *wee bit* distracted?" she asks, in the worst possible Scottish accent I've ever heard. Yet, hearing her adorable laugh keeps me from cringing.

After we find our flight number, we linger at baggage claim since the luggage hasn't begun unloading. I pull her close to me and kiss her. She sighs against me but doesn't part her lips for me to taste her. Her laugh gives her away. *Fucking tease.* I groan but playfully nip at her bottom lip.

"You know, rumour has it there are first class lounges where you can rent a room to... *work.*" Amanda's gaze hasn't left my lips since I stopped kissing her. I try to keep from laughing, knowing full well she's referring to Ben shagging her friend in an airport earlier this year.

I keep my voice low, and lean in to whisper, "You want me to touch you in the airport, spitfire?"

Amanda slides her hands inside my jacket and around my back. "No, I remember your rule. You won't let me come. I'll be a good girl and wait to be properly serviced by that mouth of yours, instead." She lifts onto her toes and kisses me, though only a peck, before stepping back.

Once we have our luggage, we walk to where I parked my motorbike before leaving for the book signing and gala. When I reach the sliding doors to the airport parking, I stop abruptly and guide her back into the airport.

"Whoa, wait, where are we going?" Amanda glances behind us into the garage.

"I'll call you a taxi. I have my motorbike, you'll have to meet me at my flat."

"What are you talking about? I'll ride with you."

"No chance in hell," I growl, squeezing her hand tighter.

Amanda stops me before we can go any further. "Why not?"

I swallow hard. "That's how Ben was injured. You want to ride with me? We'll go home and fetch an extra helmet and I'll wrap you in fourteen layers of leather. Only then will I let you ride with me."

"I get the whole needing a helmet thing, but if it's so dangerous, maybe you shouldn't be riding either?" She quirks her eyebrow.

"Well, you have luggage," I counter, desperate to ensure she's safe. There's absolutely no way I'll let her ride with me.

"Fine," she replies, rolling her eyes. "Leave the bike here, we'll figure it out in the morning. Let's get a cab and grab a bite to eat, I'm starving."

So am I, spitfire.

I stifle a groan at the thought of tasting her again and take her hand, needing to touch her in some small way. This morning, I claimed her as mine, and I intend to do it over and over again for the next week. I gave up rationalising what I feel for her months ago. I fell in love with my wee spitfire that night in New York, and now that she's home with me, I'm not letting her go.

The next morning, I wake to the sound of a car horn blaring outside my apartment, followed by shouts from my neighbour. I really need to move, but with my upcoming dig, there's no point; I'm never here.

I'm met with the sweet smell of honey and thistles, but not the fresh ones I ensured were on my bedside table all these months. This is the real thing, what I've truly been craving. *Amanda.* I reach for her, only to find the other side of my mattress warm but empty. I sit up and glance around the room, finding her luggage in the corner. I breathe a sigh of relief. *She's still here.* I fall back onto the bed, hardly able to keep my eyes open after the day we had yesterday.

"Spitfire, get your arse back in my bed. It's too early," I call, arm covering my eyes.

There's a patter of footsteps and I look to the door once they stop. She's leaning against the door frame, arms crossed, stark naked except for a scrap of fabric barely covering her cunt. Her beautiful dark blonde hair cascades over her shoulder and faux pout dances on her lips… it's too much.

"Fuck, you little siren, get over here."

She pushes off the doorframe, rolling her eyes. "They're boobs, Jack. Nothing you haven't seen before."

"Why didn't I wake up to them in my mouth or hand then?" I retort.

"You need an emotional support tit?" She takes a few steps closer, remaining just out of my reach. "Or would you prefer I just deprive you of oxygen with my pussy on your face?"

"Don't tempt me. I'm starving after that bunny food you forced me to eat for dinner last night." I prop myself up on an elbow and turn my body to face her. "Get over here." I lift off the bed enough to reach for her wrist, and pull her onto me. She laughs as she falls on top of me, leaving only a duvet and our underwear between us.

Amanda's hands fold on top of one another on my chest. She rests her chin on them and playfully asks,

"What are we doing today?" Her tongue lightly licks her top lip, raising an eyebrow at me in challenge. I don't reply. Instead, I flip her onto her back, pinning her on the bed as I hold both her hands above her head with one of my own. "I approve of your plan."

I settle between her legs, though there's entirely too much fabric between us. "Admit you're mine and I'll fill you right fucking now."

My feisty spitfire doesn't try to tug out of my hold, she fucking leans into it. "I thought I told you to stop with the declarations." Her voice softens when she adds, "I need you, Jack."

Fuck. Me. Hearing my name from her lips is indescribable.

I kiss her hard, needing her more than the air in my lungs. Gripping her arse with my free hand, I slide it down her thigh to pull one of her legs up over my hip before returning it to its rightful place and toying with her thong. She might run again, but right now she's here in Scotland with me and I need to know she feels this as deeply as I do. I risk the only card I'm holding. "You're mine, spitfire. You can lie to both of us if it makes you feel better, but we both know you became mine the night we danced under the stars."

"I need what you did to me that night," she admits, and I trail kisses from her neck to her lips. When I reach her mouth, she speaks against me, "I'm yours. Ruin me again."

It's a lot of pressure to put on a man, but the most beautiful woman I've ever known has demanded I take from her until she has nothing left to give. Who am I to deny her?

22

AMANDA

I shouldn't give Jack this much control, but I've craved him for so damn long, I can give up a little… *right?* I've fucked myself countless times to the thought of his mouth and hands on me, and no other man has ever compared to him. I'd be a fucking idiot if I stopped him. He wants to be the alpha today? Go for it, my hot Scot.

Jack kisses me harder and a deep moan escapes me. I try to free my hands, needing to touch him, but he doesn't release me. I tug a second time and he growls, "Tell me to stop and I will. But you know damn well what the consequences are."

"Are you going to let me come?"

His dark chuckle is all the confirmation I need to know he intends to edge me again, just as he did the night we spent together and yesterday morning. My breath is shaky and my heart is racing, but a part of me loves his torture.

Jack releases my wrists as he slides down my body. He tears away the duvet and rips my thong on one side. He moves further down my body and kisses the inside of my hip before taking the fabric between his teeth and dragging it down my leg, discarding it on the floor.

In an instant, my legs are over his shoulders as his tongue licks up and down my pussy. While it feels incredible, we both know I need more. He doesn't make me wait, and I feel two fingers press inside me as his tongue swirls around my clit. How he knows exactly what I need from just one night in New York—and devouring my pussy in London—is a fucking mystery, but regardless of how he's managed to memorize my body so quickly, I glide my fingers in his hair and selfishly grind against his face.

His muffled groan against me spurs me on as he continues licking, sucking, and touching me. He flattens his tongue and applies extra pressure as he drags his fingers out of me. I whimper at the emptiness.

As he continues his torture, I focus on my impending orgasm—afraid he'll stop at any moment. He dips his tongue into my pussy, adding the friction I've been missing. I can't hold on any longer. As if he can sense it, he licks back up to my clit and drives his fingers deeper, holding them in place and expertly curling them. It only takes mere moments before I'm seeing stars and my thighs are shaking. I come hard, harder than I have in months—with exception of the hotel room yesterday. My whole body is both on fire and shivering, and Jack's rhythm on my clit matches my pussy pulsing around his fingers

"Your turn," I pant, unable to catch my breath.

He slows his pace and kisses my inner thigh before slowly peppering kisses up my body. "I don't have condoms… but don't even think about me fucking that pretty mouth of yours. The next time I come will be inside you. I have a lifetime to come down your throat, so for now, I'll wait."

A lifetime?

Despite my better judgement, my words tumble from me, "Come inside me."

I've never had unprotected sex, except the one time he fucked me in the shower that magical night of ours. Even then, he finished in my mouth.

Maybe he doesn't want to? Fuck, am I an asshole for pressuring him?

"Or don't?" I timidly correct, but my words are stolen with a searing kiss. "It's ok, no breeding kink, got it," I tease between kisses, tasting myself on him. In a small way, I feel like I've claimed him as mine and it makes me want so much more.

I don't have time to process it before his cock is inside me to the hilt in one quick thrust, making me cry out. Jack doesn't move, neither do I, but he continues kissing me. I tilt my hips to take him deeper, unable to get close enough, making him groan.

I'm falling for a man who is essentially a stranger. I want more than just sex with him, but the idea of it not working out between us after his project hurts more than I'd care to admit.

Oh, fuck. I'm not falling. Right?

I try to shake the thought away but it lingers. He's right, I can lie to myself and say all I want is a good lay, but the truth is... I want Jack. All of him—the whole fucking package. I want what Layla and Becca promise in their books. Hell, I want what Layla and Becca have with Ben and Julian. I want my happily ever after, no matter how much the idea of an actual relationship makes me nauseous.

Jack slowly pulls out, thrusting back in harder than before. I wrap my legs around him, needing more. We both do. It's not enough, because with him, it never is. His kisses become urgent, desperate. My grip on his back tightens, making him groan.

"Shite." He settles inside me, but doesn't come. At least, it doesn't feel like he did.

"What's wrong?"

Kissing me softly, he replies, "You feel too good, I was going to come."

"Then fucking do it." I clench my pussy around his cock, making him hiss.

He kisses my neck, murmuring against my skin with a soft chuckle, "What do you think you're doing, sprite?"

"Nothing." I clench again. "No idea what you're talking about."

In a quick movement, he pulls out of me and flips me onto my stomach, making me giggle. He grips my hips and yanks them up to meet his. I eagerly wait for him to fuck me again as he slides his hand up my back and grabs a fistful of my hair and carefully tugs. I gasp, but the prickling on my scalp has me so fucking wet for him, I silently beg him to do it again.

"Just for that, spitfire…" Jack's voice is dark and lust-filled. He slams into me, using my hair as leverage to get deeper. "You'll come when I let you." His thrusts become faster, harder, making me wind tighter and tighter. I fist the sheets and push back into him. We find a rhythm that has his breath ragged and mine broken. I tighten my pussy around him, and he practically roars as he comes, emptying every last drop inside me.

I feel like I won. Though, I'm not sure what, seeing as I didn't come. His cock twitches as I purposefully clench impossibly tighter around him, making him growl. He palms my ass and I anticipate a strike of his hand that never comes. I'm desperate for my own release and continue pushing back into him. Unfortunately, my plan to steal my orgasm backfires when he releases my hair to grip my throat and pulls me to him until my back is flush with his chest.

"Please, Jack."

"Oh, did you want to come?" His voice is playful, but there's the same darkness to it that makes me so fucking wet and has my hand travelling between my legs to relieve the ache he's caused. He swats it away, then releases his other hand from my neck, tracing with a feather-light touch over my breast. My chest heaves as he rolls one of my nipples between his fingers before pinching hard. I yelp at the sting, but it's cut short, quickly turning into a whimpered moan. He settles a hand between my legs and circles my clit at a pace that will quickly have me undone if he continues.

"Do it again?" I pant.

Jack moves to my other breast and tweaks my nipple, keeping his pace on my clit. His beard tickles my shoulder as he kisses my neck and I can't help but sigh into his touch. Unlike how he was fucking me moments ago, this is slow, sensual. He draws a mouthful of my flesh between his teeth and sucks hard, bruising the side of my neck.

I let him. I let him claim me, mark me, willingly. *Fuck, what's wrong with me?*

He wraps his arm around my middle as he continues teasing my clit. His touch is intoxicating. As he slowly pulls me back onto his cock, I feel him get hard again inside me, rubbing against my g-spot.

"I know you're close, but you're going to be a good lass and let me play with this pretty cunt of yours a little longer."

My pussy tightens at his words and I can't hold on any longer. My hot Scot can play another day. As if he can sense it, he thrusts into me and increases the pressure against my clit. It's enough to send me over the edge. He doesn't stop touching me as wave after wave of my orgasm hits me.

As I finally catch my breath, I whisper, "Fucking. Ruined."

"Ruined? We've only just begun."

23

JACK

I've fallen for her. My heart aches when she's not with me, and it's like I can't fucking breathe. I've never experienced this kind of attraction with someone and my only hope is that it's not just because my cock is still inside her. I need to find a way to keep her when my project's over.

Amanda's breath is still laboured after making her come another three times, and I can't help wanting her close. With her on top, I keep my hands firmly on her hips. She traces the small spot on my shoulder where she marked me with her teeth yesterday morning as she came. "How are we going to stay away from each other for six months?" she asks earnestly.

"Can we worry about that tomo— *Fuck*, can you not clamp down on my cock while I'm answering you?"

She chuckles softly. "How can I not worry about it? There's billions being funnelled into your treasure hunt... but I also can't imagine another six months without being touched by you." Her hand traces up my neck and tucks a stray tendril of hair behind my ear. "I'm yours, Jack. It's stupid, irrational, and absolutely ludicrous, but here we are. How am I supposed to be on site with you when every part of me aches to be..." She swallows hard but doesn't continue.

"We were never supposed to be one night." I kiss her neck. "I don't know what this is, but I'm yours, too, spit-fire. I got a message while we were on the plane that Julian want us in New York in a week. So, let's have this week, just the two of us. We can deal with the rest later."

"Yeah, I got a voicemail about meeting them." I expect her to push back. Instead, she kisses me. It's soft but desperate, as speaks against my lips, "I can't be with you for six months, or until your project is over."

My beautiful spitfire isn't going to get away from me that easily. I hold her tighter and thrust up into her, my cock twitching and ready for her again. "You're mine, Amanda. I don't care if I have to wait a month, six, or twenty-four. You stole a piece of my soul that night. I don't want it back, I want yours in return."

"Six months without you was torture."

"It was closer to eight," I reply, making her chuckle.

"I'm doing the one thing I swore I never would after watching Becca and Layla," she grumbles.

"What's that?" *Stop fighting me, spitfire.*

Amanda kisses my cheek as she says softly, "Fall for a stranger."

I breathe a sigh of relief that she's not running. "You want to know more about me? I'm an open book. Where should I start? I like the quiet before a thunderstorm with a good book. I fucking hate dancing. I can never give you the home or security you deserve. I—"

"Whoa, whoa, whoa... what do you mean home or security I deserve?"

"I'm no billionaire, I'm project to project. Sometimes, I have tight months. For fuck's sake, we're staying in this tiny apartment tonight and—"

"In what world did I ever indicate to you that I want fame, fortune, or glory?" She pauses. "Other than as a joke. I'm serious about this, though. I have millions of my own. I don't care about the $2.5 billion, or lavish vacations, or a home that requires a staff for upkeep. I want a man who wants me for... me."

"Oh, my wee spitfire," I sigh. "I want you more than I've wanted anything in my life. I'd happily live here, if that's what you wanted. I just don't want to disappoint you."

Amanda takes my face in her hands and kisses me roughly, enough that I've nearly forgotten anything I've said to her these past few minutes. "You, my hot Scot, could never disappoint me." She grinds further onto my cock, then teases, "But if you dare question that I want anything or anyone more than I want you right now, you won't be coming again today."

"A castle?" she squeals. We haven't left the bed most of the day but I'm finally telling her about my project.

"Aye, but not just any castle. This one has dozens of underground passages." I grab my phone from the bedside table and pull up a few of the photos I took in my initial survey. "I spent a few weeks checking stability and mapping it out. Nearly got lost a few times."

Amanda takes my phone and scrolls through the photos. "I read the article you wrote with Cameron. There was something about journals. I've joked about it, but it sounded an awful lot like an actual treasure hunt."

"I suppose it is a treasure hunt of sorts," I laugh. "There were millions of pounds worth of lost artefacts—art, jewellery, even first edition books. They were hidden, but moved after wars. Each generation of the Black family left a journal for the next one with clues to where they hid it. The last journal we found was Ewen's but he's left us a couple. I'm worried the next generation didn't carry it on."

"It's fucking cool that you're finding them, I'm sure their family is so thankful."

"From what we've seen, there might not be any living relatives. We've worked with historians, and a few ancestry websites have been helpful in tracing back several generations, but the last Black passed away about five years ago. We don't know if she had any children."

Amanda hands me back my phone. "That's so sad. I've never done one of those DNA tests. I probably should, though. My grandmother told me I had a great-great-great—probably eighteen greats—uncle who was supposedly some sort of aristocrat in England. I had to do a genealogy project in high school, but there wasn't a lot of information on him. The internet wasn't that great back then. Now, the name is so common, I'd probably never find anything on it."

"What about your mum?"

Amanda stills in my arms. "Oh, um. She died during childbirth. I was raised by my grandmother."

"Fuck." I hold her tighter and kiss the top of her head, then whisper into her hair, "I'm sorry."

She snuggles closer to me, fidgeting with her necklace. "Thanks but you don't need to apologise. I didn't know her. My grandmother was amazing though. I miss her."

I trace her necklace, landing on the key pendant. "Is this from her?"

"Yeah, it's all I have left of her. She told me it's hundreds of years old, passed down for generations, but I'm pretty sure she just bought it at a jewellery store," she laughs.

I pull back to take a closer look. "I noticed it the night we met, it's not something you would buy in a store. Do you know what that is in the handle?" I ask, tracing the Kildalton Cross.

"No." She tilts her chin to look down at it. "A cross? She wasn't religious, I just always thought it was pretty."

"It's beautiful. Cam researched Kildalton Crosses for years and could tell you more about it."

"Kildalton?"

I type it into my phone and pull up one of his research papers and pass it to her. "See." As she scrolls his article, I add, "Your nan could've been Scottish."

"Maybe," she chuckles and hands me back my phone. "If that's the case, then I am too." She laughs, then sits up abruptly and slides off the bed.

"Where do you think you're going, sprite?"

Slipping on her bra and clasping it in the back, she replies, "I didn't fly all the way to Scotland to lay in bed with you all day. I'm hungry and I want to sightsee. Who knows, maybe even bump into a long lost relative. We only have a week before I have to fly back to New York, we should make the most of it. When I come back, you're off limits. You say you want more than just sex, so let's go out and not have sex." She puts on her shirt, but then climbs back onto the bed, straddling me. My hands slide up her thighs to her waist but I resist grinding her against me. Leaning in until her breath is

tickling my ear, she whispers, "But I expect to be properly fucked when we get back." An involuntary growl
comes from my chest, making her laugh. She pulls back
and presses a single kiss to my cheek. "Come on, my hot
Scot, let's have an adventure."

24

AMANDA

Edinburgh is absolutely beautiful. Jack's apartment is close to the water in the little neighborhood of Leith. He's shown me a couple of his favorite places, and it was adorable to see him light up as he shared facts about some sort of royal yacht. I didn't follow most of it, but apparently it's fairly popular.

I can see why he'd want to live here—the port has an old, cozy feel to it. Walking along the waterline with the cold sea air filling my lungs, I'm inspired, wanting to capture the essence of this place on page.

"Mind if we sit for a bit?" I ask, gesturing with our joined hands toward what appears to be a small shopping complex with restaurants and small stores.

Jack kisses the back of my hand and replies softly, "Of course not."

Every time he kisses me, touches me, or insists on taking my hand, my heart leaps into my throat. We've already managed a level of comfortability I've never had with anyone else. Our amazing night together was nothing short of magical, but being here with him feels like I've known him all my life.

In search of a smaller and less busy cafe, we walk past a bookstore. I can't wipe the stupid grin off my face as I peer through the large windows. Jack pauses in front of it. "Shall we?"

"I won't get any writing done if we do."

He leans in, his hot breath fanning my ear as he whispers, "And I wouldn't be able to keep my hands to myself." I close my eyes, my thighs clenching at his words as a soft whimper escapes me. "Since you need to write, give me five minutes to pick up a book, something to fill the time while you work."

As he pulls back, his smile meets his eyes, making my favorite little crinkles appear at the corners. I can't help smiling back. "Fine, five minutes, but I'm waiting out here."

"Not a chance." Keeping my hand firmly in his, he guides me into the bookstore and directly to the romance section. "Pick one." He gestures down one of the aisles.

The thought has been in the back of my mind for months. I have to ask. "Did you... did you read my book?"

"Dozens of times. I'd hoped there was a clue you left for me about who you were, or where I could find you. After Ben's wedding, I read the rest of them."

My eyes wide, I squeak, "All of them?"

"Aye."

"Even my book that came out the day we met?" *Fuck, please say no.*

"Read that one twice."

I shake my head in disbelief, my stomach in knots. "Why?" I wince.

Jack closes the distance and slides his hand into my hair, bringing our lips a breath apart. "I may not know how you take your coffee, or your mum's name, or your goals and dreams... but in time, I will. Your books were the closest thing I had to knowing you after you ran."

I lift onto my toes and kiss him. This man read my entire backlist to get to know me. All at once, my heart breaks, knowing that, for half a year, I won't be able to be with this sweet man. We'll be in the same place, in the same rooms even, but I won't be able to touch or have him. What we have right now will be... gone. Or at least on hold, I guess. It isn't just Blair, it's the money. It's all so complicated. If it wouldn't ruin his upcoming dig, I'd return the money so I could be with him.

I don't want to give him up. I can't.

"I prefer extra spicy chai lattes over coffee, my mother's name was Isla, and I have too many goals and dreams to count," I whisper against Jack's lips. He pulls back and kisses my forehead, wrapping me in his arms. "Three minutes, mister. I still need to find a book for you."

"That you do," he chuckles, but doesn't release me. He lets out a defeated sigh.

"Have you read all of Becca and Layla's books?"

"I haven't read Layla's recent one because I heard it's loosely based on my cousin."

"Oh, yeah, that could be a bit awkward," I laugh, but it's cut short as I realize I've done the same thing with him. "Shit," I mutter.

Jack pulls back enough to look at me but it's as if he refuses to let me out of his arms. "What?"

"I'm writing about you. Well, sort of. It's a romantic suspense, but the main character is Scottish, sexy, and seductive, and—"

"You think I'm sexy?" he laughs.

I playfully smack his chest. "Now isn't the time to feed your ego. I'm serious! I wrote a character because... I missed you. So, I have to change it."

"Don't. Keep it in. I don't mind."

I look between his earnest eyes while silence passes between us and the world around me falls away. While I appreciate his blessing, I don't want to write about him,

I want to keep our story to my journal. I don't want to share him with anyone.

"If we stay here any longer, we'll have a repeat of New York," I tease.

I feel a rumble in his chest, making me smile. He leans in beside my ear to whisper, "Don't tempt me. I'd risk getting barred from the shop to hear your stifled moans as I get you close."

I swallow hard and whimper, "Please?"

"Later, my wee spitfire," Jack chuckles darkly. "I have all night to touch you. You need to write."

"Damn it. Why do you have to be a voice of reason?" I playfully whine. Jack pulls me impossibly closer, making me gasp. "Ok, fine, I'll pick a book."

Finally releasing me, Jack takes my hand and lets me lead the way to the erotica section. His eyes widen as we pass cover after cover of half naked men. I scan the shelves, looking for the one book I've written that I know he hasn't read.

"G, G-r, G-r-a... Aha! They have it." I remove the book from the shelf and hand it to him triumphantly.

"Delicate Danger by Amanda Gray?" he asks, quirking his brow.

"Pen name, baby. I wrote it years ago but since my romantic suspense series was taking off, I wanted to keep it separate." I take the book back, flip it to the copyright page, and hand it back to him, pointing to the date and my LLC, Pitch Black Publishing, I used when I published independently. "See."

"So, what's this one about?"

I bite my bottom lip to hide my smile. "You'll have to read it to find out. Just know that we are definitely trying chapter seven at some point."

A grin dances across his lips. "Alright, sprite, I'll read it. But only because I need to know what's in chapter seven."

Jack tucks the book under his arm and takes my hand as we walk toward the registers. The woman ringing us up looks at me, then to Jack. "Is this a gift?"

"Oh, it's the gift that keeps on giving," I laugh. "No, just for this one," I correct and gesture with my thumb to Jack. He coughs and I can't wipe the goofy grin off my face. She's about to place it in a bag when I ask, "Do you have a pen?"

She passes one to me, and when she hands me the bag, I take out the book and sign it.

TO MY HOT SCOT,
WHIPPED CREAM IS MESSY. BUT IT'S STILL FUN
TO EAT OFF OF A PUSSY.
XO, AMANDA GRAY

"You're the author?" she asks excitedly. My cheeks heat knowing she read what I wrote to him.

"Aye, she is," Jack replies, wrapping his arm around me proudly. "Best porn I've ever read."

"I don't know about the best," I nervously laugh. "But yes, I wrote this one and others under another name."

"I don't have any more of this title in stock. What's your other pen name? If I have it, would you be willing to sign them?" she asks.

"Of course." I do it back home for smaller bookstores often, but it would be fun to post on social media to say I have autographed copies in Scotland. "It's under Amanda Storm."

Her eyes widen even further. "Amanda Storm? I... I have dozens of copies to be signed. I couldn't trouble you with that."

"No trouble at all. I have to get writing done, but maybe we can come back later today? I'd be happy to do it." I look at Jack, finding his emerald green eyes already on me. "Is that alright?"

He frowns. "Why wouldn't it be?"

I shrug and look back to our cashier, checking her name tag. "We'll be back later, Olivia." I put the book back into the bag and hand it to Jack. "Here's your porn, babe."

Jack lets out a hearty laugh. "Come on." He keeps his arm around me and guides us out of the store.

We continue toward a few of the restaurants and cafes, finding one that doesn't look too busy. It's casual, too similar to the coffee chains I'm used to back home. I want something unique, I won't feel inspired here. We keep walking until I spot an adorable coffee shop that has more of an artsy vibe.

Perfect.

Jack opens the door for me, and as I walk inside, I'm met with the smell of freshly ground coffee and buttery pastries. We approach the counter and I scan the menu board. As I'm searching the tea options, looking for my beloved favorite, Jack asks the barista, "Do you serve chai?"

"No, sir," he replies. My shoulders sag with disappointment.

"What do you normally order?" I ask Jack.

"I don't normally drink tea, but when I do, I like an English breakfast tea with milk."

Gross. "And for coffee?" I wince.

He chuckles and tells the barista, "Two black coffees, please."

"Oh no! Sorry, no," I quickly correct. "That's even worse. Just one black coffee. I'll take a black tea, but without milk, please."

Jack's deep laugh has both the barista and I joining in. As Jack takes out his wallet to pay, I retrieve mine from my bag faster than him. "My treat," I insist.

His laughter immediately ceases and his eyes narrow and darken, a low growl rumbling in his throat. He leans in and whispers, "You may be a billionaire, but under no circumstances are you to pay for us. Let me dote on you." As he pulls back, he presses a chaste kiss to my neck, sending shivers down my spine. I nod and he pays for our drinks.

I notice there's no tip jar, so I ask Jack, "Did you remember to tip him?"

"The only time you tip here is at a restaurant, and even then it's ten, maybe fifteen percent of the bill. If I'm at a bar, I'll usually buy the bartender a drink. Americans pay their staff shite, sometimes below minimum wage. It's not like that here."

I hum with a small nod of understanding. Still, it's so strange to me. I think back to my favorite coffee shop in New York and wish my barista friend, Jackson, was paid better. I can see why Layla would want to move to the UK to be with Ben, and if things continue the way they have been with Jack, I wouldn't hesitate to move here. Hell, I could even get a job at a coffee shop to fill my time when I'm not writing.

Fuck, why am I thinking about moving?

I'm pulled from my thoughts when our drinks are ready and Jack finds us a table. He takes out the paperback as

I remove my monogrammed notebook from my bag. Before I dive into writing, I take a sip of the tea and wince. "I'll be right back, I need to add sugar."

I take my tea to the handoff counter and ask the barista for sugar. He points me in the direction of a small table with sugar and napkins, hiding his amusement. I shrug with a laugh. Once added, I return to the table, finding Jack frowning.

"What's wrong?" I ask.

His face relaxes, but only a little. "Your notebook?"

Now, I'm frowning. "Yes?" He points to the monogram with my initials AMB, the B larger and in the center. "My initials..." I say, confused.

"Shouldn't it be S?"

It takes me a moment, but then I laugh, "You know 'Storm' is a pen name."

"No, I didn't."

"What are you talking about? You know my last name is Black."

25

JACK

"Black?" No, I would definitely remember that. I've been researching a family with the same last name for years. "When were you going to tell me?"

"Excuse me? You knew!" Amanda insists.

"Your nameplate at the gala said 'Storm.'"

"Yeah, there were dozens of book people there. Ben is a book publisher, for fuck's sake. Why would I put my real name?" She sits back in her chair, crossing her arms.

I rub my hand over my face. "I didn't know your last name until now."

"It's literally all over the contract," she deadpans.

"I didn't read your contract; it's between you, Ben, and Julian. Sorry, this is…"

The reality hits me. I've been inside her bare and didn't even know her real last name. I've been so wrapped up in the fantasy of her that I've lost my damn mind. We don't know each other, finding this out makes me feel like I've rushed things far too much. I haven't had a chance to properly date her.

"I never hid anything from you," she says softly. When I don't respond, she gets up, moves her chair next to me, and sits again, taking my hand in hers. I bring our joined hands to my lips, kissing her knuckles, then place them back on the table. "I'm sorry, I assumed you knew."

"No," I reply, shaking my head. "I'm sorry."

Fear seeps into her eyes and worry paints her face. "Are we ok?"

I tuck her hair behind her ear, tracing her jaw as I retreat, but take her chin between my fingers and thumb to bring her lips to mine. She sighs against me, a soft moan escaping her as we break apart. "Yes, of course, we are. I'm obsessed with you, my wee spitfire. That's why I'm sorry. I'm cross with myself that I haven't spent enough time with you to really get to know each other… and that's not fair to either of us. I feel like an arsehole for not knowing your last name."

"We'll have months for that. But please know that I'll never keep anything from you—at least not intentional-ly." Amanda cups the back of my neck and kisses me. "For the record, I'm obsessed with you, too." She takes a sip of her tea and adds, "I need to write, so… enjoy reading my porn."

I chuckle and kiss her one last time, then settle back into my chair, my smile returning. She attempts to move hers to the space across from me, but I grip the chair to hold it in place. I shake my head at her, and she rolls her eyes with a laugh as she sinks back into her seat. Sliding my hand onto her thigh, I keep her close. Reading one-handed will prove to be an issue, just as it was in New York. She takes out a pen with 'Turner' etched into it. I chuckle and she looks up at me, then follows my gaze to the pen. "Oh, yeah, I totally stole this from Ben."

"Anything else stolen that I should know about?"

"Nope," she replies, popping the 'p.' "I may be a Black, but I'm not one of those pillaging ones you've been researching for years." She laughs to herself and begins writing.

A minute later, I'm about to lift my hand from her leg to turn the page when she reaches over to turn it for me, offering me a soft smile; the gesture takes me back to that night we shared. Her gaze lingers on me for a moment and I can't help stealing a kiss from her. How can I not want things to move fast with her? She's fucking perfect.

———

Amanda wrote for an hour while I read her book. I didn't make it to chapter seven, but I intend to later tonight. The weather here is cooler than she packed for, seeing as I sprung this trip on her, so we stopped into a couple shops to pick up a few things. Despite her insistence that she needed lingerie, there's no point. I'd rather her sleep naked with me.

I get out of the shower, towel wrapped around my waist. Walking into the room, I find her on my bed with her laptop, wearing pyjamas that cover her from neck to ankles, her hair braided over one shoulder. "What are you wearing?"

"A onesie," she replies, not looking up from her computer. "Look, it has pockets!" She briefly stuffs a hand into one as proof. "I'm on deadline and need to be comfy. Also, it's harder to fuck me in this. Win-win."

"You think a glorified bathrobe can stop me, spitfire?" I laugh.

"No, it's to stop me." She looks up, her eyes roaming my body. "Fuck, you can't walk in here looking like some sort of sex god and expect me to be able to write."

Amanda sets the laptop onto the bedside table and slides off the bed. Prowling toward me, her gaze is heated, making my cock twitch. The movement catches her attention, her eyes dropping to my towel. She lightly licks her lips and practically shoves me onto the mattress. As I fall back onto it, the towel loosens.

"What are you up to?" I chuckle.

"I'm writing a spicy scene and need inspiration." She drops to her knees, looking up at me through her lashes.

"Then why aren't you naked?"

"Power move," she replies with a smirk, taking the base of my cock in her hand and licking up my length. "Research."

"Fuck," I groan. Sitting up, I cup her neck and brush her cheek with my thumb as she wraps her mouth around my cock. It hits the back of her throat, making her gag; the vibration makes me desperate for more already. "Tap my leg if it's too much." She hums in agreement and I'm about to thrust into her, but before I can, she takes me deeper—all of me. Her eyes water, but she doesn't tap out.

Shite, *I'm* going to tap out; it feels too fucking good. She continues sucking and massaging her tongue along my shaft as she brings me closer to the brink. It's too much, I need to be inside her. I grip her braid to pull her lips off me. "Naked, right now," I growl, releasing her hair.

Amanda keeps her hand firmly on my cock, swirling her tongue around the head as beads of precum leak from it. "You never said who had to be naked," she teases, throwing my words from yesterday back at me.

Fuck, this woman is going to be the death of me. She continues her torture, fisting my cock as she licks around the head. It's simultaneously too much and not enough. She slides back onto my cock, her warm, wet mouth making my balls tighten. Moving up and down my length, she picks up her pace, bringing me close again.

As I'm about to come, she chuckles, but it's dark, sinister. In an instant, she pulls off my cock and sits back on her heels. "Thanks, that's all I needed."

"Are you sure about that, sprite?" I keep my voice playful, but I need to fucking come. She's toying with me, and I intend to win this game of hers. I grip my cock and slowly stroke from base to tip.

Her lips part, her gaze fixated on my hand movements. "Yep, that's all," she breathes.

"Eyes on me." Her eyes dart to mine. *Attagirl.* "Now, tell me again how you don't want me to touch you."

"I…" She clears her throat. "I never said that."

"Then, you won't mind if I come without you, will you?"

Even through her thick pyjamas, I can see her chest rise and fall with her heavy breaths. "Don't mind at all." She bites her lip but quickly schools her expression.

I've got her.

"You have enough inspiration for your scene, spitfire?"

"I suppose I could use a *wee* bit more," she replies, a playful smirk escaping her otherwise neutral expression.

"Take it off," I command, my gaze falling to her pyjamas. "I want to see you."

"I should be writing," she says, contradicting the unzipping. She shrugs the onesie off her shoulders and shimmies out of it until it drops to the floor with a thud. Stepping out of it, she climbs on top of me. I line my cock up with her entrance, waiting for her to sit. She does, but only an inch. As much as her mouth feels amazing, it doesn't compare to her perfect cunt. I stifle a groan as she lowers herself one more inch.

I resist pulling her onto me. "I never said you could fuck me, sprite."

"Never said I couldn't." She takes another inch and holds. "Should I stop?"

Don't you fucking dare. "Tell me about the scene you're writing," I whisper.

Amanda slides down the rest of my cock until I'm fully seated inside her. "There was no scene."

I bark out a laugh. "What? You're fucking joking."

"Nope." She kisses me, rocking back and forth, using me to make herself come. Between moans, and manages, "Fuck, that feels good."

"Aren't you supposed to be writing?" I tease, gripping her hips and matching her pace as I thrust into her. I'm close and, so help me, if she tries to edge me again…

I kiss her neck and suck hard enough to mark her. "I will, as soon as I—*oh fuck.*"

"As soon as you what?" I ask, nipping at her ear.

"*Jack,*" she breathes, her cunt tightening around me as she continues to chase her orgasm.

"Let go. Come with me, love," I growl into the crook of her neck. She cries out, and the moment she clenches around my cock, I let go and come with her. I wrap my arms around her, and even with our bodies flush, I still need her closer. Our breaths synced and ragged, I empty myself inside her.

"I guess you'll need another shower," she chuckles.

"There's no point. As soon as you're done writing, you'll be riding my face, then I'm taking this beautiful arse of yours." I squeeze it once before playfully smacking one of the cheeks.

She yelps, then says, "We can't, we have to go back to the bookstore for me to sign the copies."

"Bookshops aren't open late like in New York. It'll be closed in half an hour."

"Shit!" Amanda attempts to scramble off me but I keep her close. "Hey, we need to go."

"We can call the shop and let her know you'll pop by in the mornin'."

"You just want and excuse to fuck me again," she says with a playful grin.

"Aye, but you need to write. I'll call the shop for you, and as soon as you're done writing, you're mine, spitfire."

She slides her hands into my hair and kisses me roughly, muttering against my lips, "Deal."

I know there will be surprises the more I get to know her, but one thing's for certain, if she's still kissing me like this in six months, her last name won't be Black for long.

26

JACK

The last week has been incredible, but bittersweet. I haven't spent a moment apart from Amanda—the only exception being my short trip to pick up my motorbike from the airport. There's no way in hell I'll survive this project without being able to touch her, or even have her in my arms. Mostly, I'll miss having her here with me. We'll have two weeks when she's in New York making sure her affairs are in order, while I'm here preparing for the castle excavation. It's going to be the longest, and the worst, two weeks of my life.

Cameron should be back from San Francisco today. With Amanda and I leaving for New York to meet with Julian, we'll be ships passing in the night. Cam stayed an extra two days—something about meeting with a museum staff member who needed his help. I'm close enough with my brother to know when he's lying; something else kept him there, but I'll address it when I'm back in Scotland in a couple days.

Ben and Julian insisted that we not fly commercial, but Amanda's a stubborn sprite and bought two first class tickets for us on a major airline. She's always wanted to fly first class, so I wasn't about to deny her the experience. A first for both of us; I've never flown first class either.

While in New York, we'll have to iron out Amanda's travel arrangements—she can't be in Scotland for the entirety of the project. She can stay in Scotland for up to six months without a visa, but it'll be cutting it close. We've been advised for her to return to the states for a week or two in the middle. Even then, the rest of her trip will be under the guise that she's a tourist here.

We board our flight and take our seats, and I'm grateful this flight won't be like the one from London to Edinburgh. This time, I'm sitting next to my wee spitfire. We're both exhausted from late nights, her chapter seven reenactment, and daily excursions we went on. The flight attendant takes our drink order and offers us blankets. I'm confident that this will be the first and last time I fly first class; I don't need the extras. Though, the seats are significantly more comfortable.

Amanda drinks her whisky sour and I sip my whisky neat. Comfortable silence passes between us but it's as if we're both afraid to say what we're thinking. My mind can't stop circling three:

I already miss you, even though you're still here.

I can't imagine a day without you, much less two weeks.

Stay with me when my project's over.

I know it's irrational to fall in love with someone I've only spent a week with, but there's no other explanation for what I feel for her. I knew she was special when we met, and there's no use denying that I'm hers, and have been since that night. She's everything I've ever wanted in a woman and so much more. I have no idea how I'll convince her to stay with me when I have nothing to offer her.

Once we finish our drinks as everyone boards the plane, Amanda settles next to me with her head on my shoulder, keeping my hand in hers. Her breathing slows as I brush my thumb along hers. I rest my head back on the seat and close my eyes in hopes that sleep will find me.

We take off, and the cabin isn't quiet enough for me to fall asleep completely. Amanda stirs and whispers something unintelligible. I'd ask her to repeat herself but I don't want to wake her. I kiss the top of her head and tell her quietly, "I've fallen for you, spitfire."

For a little while, I allow myself to live in a fantasy where she feels the same.

Hours later, we land in New York, more exhausted than when we took off. Amanda's eyes are heavy and I can hardly keep mine open. We disembark and make our way to baggage claim to retrieve our luggage and to meet the driver Julian insisted on sending for us. A man with a sign reading "Ms. Storm and Dr. Jackson" waits for us as we get our bags.

"Mr. Evans is running behind and asked that he meet both of you later. Would you like me to drop you at your apartment, Ms. Storm?" he asks.

"Yes, please." Amanda replies through a yawn. "We could use a couple hours of sleep before meeting with Julian."

He nods and leads the way to his parked car. I know Ben and Julian are used to personal drivers, but I'm more than happy to take transit or a taxi. With Amanda now a billionaire, I'm beginning to wonder if she'll change and want chauffeurs, a personal chef, or even a damn butler, like my cousin. I hope money doesn't change my wee spitfire.

We slide into the back seat and Amanda returns to the same position she was in on the plane, resting her head on my shoulder with a long sigh. Thankfully, it's a short drive to her apartment and I'll be able to take a quick shower before a nap.

I've never seen her flat before, but it's exactly as I imagined it. It's around the same size as mine, yet so full of life. It's open-concept with fake plants scattered throughout, coordinated furniture that has mismatched pillows, a bright red kettle on the stove that matches mine, and it smells like her—sweet like honey mixed with thistles. Stacks of books and notebooks cover most surfaces, which doesn't surprise me—my place looks the same.

"The bathroom's down the hall on the left, if you want to shower first," she says sleepily.

I take her in my arms and she wraps hers around me. "No, you're tired. Go first and I'll make tea."

"Are you sure? It might be one of those long showers where I wash my hair, apply a face mask, shave everything but my head, and then contemplate my life choices for twenty minutes."

"What?" I laugh.

"You know, a 'girl shower.'"

I shake my head. "Take your time. I'd join you, but we both know I won't be able to resist touching you. You need to rest. Go take your girly shower, your tea will be ready when you get out."

She lifts onto her toes and kisses me. "Alright, you win."

27

AMANDA

I wasn't kidding when I said I was going to contemplate my life choices in the shower. There has to be a way out of this. I adore Blair, but because of her presence on the excavation, I can't be with the man I want more than I should. I gave Layla and Becca so much shit for falling hard and fast for their husbands, and here I am doing the same damn thing. I don't want to go another half a year without him. It'll be worse this round because I'll see him every day. He'll be there, but I won't wake up in his arms, I won't have sunrises looking out on the water, I won't have endless orgasms...

Damn, I'm a selfish bitch.

Blair can't find out about Jack and I—it'd crush her. I need to come up with a way to be with him without hurting her.

Hair washed, body shaved, and hardly able to keep my eyes open, I shut off the water. I step out and wrap myself in one of my fluffiest towels that I warmed on my heating rack. Once dried off, I wipe away the steam on the mirror, and for a moment, I almost expect to find a man standing behind me. I've been deep in edits with my book and my main character is a bit of a stalker, it's getting the best of me. I quickly blowdry my hair and slip into my robe. I'd prance around my apartment naked, but since I didn't have the heat running while I was away, it's practically an icebox in here.

I open the bathroom door and find Jack scrolling his phone and leaning with his back against the counter. I take a moment to drink him in and appreciate how attractive he is. He's wearing his contacts today, which is a shame—he looks so damn hot in his glasses. My stomach grumbles. He hears it and his gaze quickly snaps up.

"How was your shower?" he asks, stuffing his phone in his back pocket. He pushes off the counter and stalks toward me, taking me in his arms.

"Good." I hold him tighter and breathe a contented sigh.

"Loads of contemplation?"

"Yep," I laugh.

He chuckles and kisses the top of my head, then releases me to pour tea. "Give it five minutes to steep. I'll take a quick shower and join you in a few. But you need to eat something."

I cup my mug with both hands and breathe in the fragrant scent of chamomile and lavender. "I'll be ok. We can grab something to eat before meeting with Julian," I insist.

"Alright. Let me know if you need me to pop into a shop and pick up something before then." He kisses my temple, but then smacks my ass as he leaves to the bathroom, making me laugh.

I give the tea time to steep, but unlike my chai, I prefer chamomile weaker. I pull the bag after three minutes and throw it away. Padding to the bedroom, I hear the shower running and pause at the bathroom door. As tired as I am, I'm tempted to join him. I resist, sipping my tea, and continue to my bedroom.

Jack fits in a little too perfectly here. When his project is done, I can't help but wonder if he'll want to come back to New York with me.

I take a few more drinks and set the mug on my bedside table, then rummage through my drawers to find comfortable pajamas. I settle into bed, close my eyes and doze off.

Unsure of how much time has passed, I stir when there's a dip in the mattress that would wake even the deepest sleeper. I keep my eyes shut as Jack tucks in behind me and slides his hand under my shirt. He splays his hand across my stomach and pulls me to him. His sweet, subtle touches light me up more than when his hand is between my legs.

Content in his arms, I begin to fall back asleep when Jack kisses my shoulder and whispers, "I love you, my wee spitfire."

While my breath hitches, the four little words feel honest, and surprisingly don't scare me.

I turn to face him. "Is that so?"

"Fuck, I thought you were asleep!"

I laugh and toy with his beard, unable to meet his gaze. He tilts my chin to look at him, anyway. My laughter ceases as his green eyes pierce me with an intensity I've never felt before. "Do you?" I ask, my voice caught in my throat.

"If I say yes, will you run?"

"No," I reply earnestly, shaking my head.

Jack presses a gentle kiss to my lips. "Then, yes, I love you."

"What if I said I was going to run?"

"I'd find you," he chuckles. "I fell in love with you. I didn't mean to, it just happened. I didn't want to tell you, because I can't lose you. I can't imagine not having you in my life."

"You're not going to lose me. But I don't think I know how to love. I told you I don't do relationships, but I want to try. I know we haven't talked about it but do I dare ask what this is?"

"I'm yours, Amanda. That's all. I don't care if you want to call me your boyfriend, your lover, or whatever label you want to put on this. This week"—he sighs—"fuck, this week changed everything. I'll never be able to walk away from you, not unless you walk away first." Jack brushes my hair away from my face and kisses my forehead. "I know this brilliant mind of yours doesn't want to fall, because you know when you do, you'll give me all of you. You're the most extraordinary woman I've ever known, I'll spend a lifetime waiting for you, if that's how long it takes for you to fall in love with me."

"Did you read that in one of my friend's books?" I tease, hoping to lighten the weight of what he's suggesting.

"No," he laughs. Our legs tangle together and he holds me tighter. "Get some sleep. You can profess your undying love for me another day."

I snuggle closer and allow myself to selfishly absorb every ounce of love from this man, even if I'm not ready to return it.

28

JACK

"Ok, so I have an idea," Amanda says, chewing her lip. Meeting with Julian and a room full of lawyers is intimating, but it doesn't rattle my spitfire. "What if I invest everything? Will it cover what Blair has thrown into the pot?" Her lawyer whispers something to her but she shakes her head.

"Have the contracts been signed by you, Dr. Jackson?" one of them asks.

Fuck. I hate when people speak to me so formally. I feel like I'm preparing for my dissertation review all over again. "No. I haven't signed it. She wants full credit for the excavation, which I refuse to do. Cameron and I have worked too hard on this to put someone else's name on it."

Amanda squeezes my hand tight and whispers, "She wanted credit? Why didn't you tell me?"

I'm about to reply when another man's voice pulls our attention to him. "If the contracts aren't signed, and you wish to invest the remaining funds required for the renovation project, then we can draft the paperwork this afternoon. You'll only need to cover half a million dollars."

"Yes," she says without an ounce of hesitation. She then whispers to me, "Can Lizzy still come? Can we afford it?"

"Whatever you want," I whisper back, pressing a chaste kiss to her cheek that I'm sure someone at the table noticed, but I couldn't care less. I'm going to have the woman I love all to myself without having to worry about Blair. I raise my voice to tell everyone else, "We'd like to add…" I look to Amanda, not remembering her friend's name.

"Elizabeth Alexander," Amanda offers.

"Right. I'd like to add Elizabeth Alexander as a junior researcher. Feel free to deduct from my stipend so she can join us."

Julian eyes me curiously. "Are you sure about that?"

"I understand the hesitation, seeing as she's Emma's daughter, but I assure you, she's qualified," Amanda insists. Emma is the President of a publishing house in San Francisco that Julian and Ben invested in a few months ago. Julian has every right to be concerned. "There's no favouritism here. She works at a natural history museum that has received several of the Jackson brothers' finds—she's familiar with their work."

"How do you know that?" I ask her quietly.

"Shh, we'll talk about it later, but trust me, you'll want her help."

Amanda whispers something to her lawyer and he chimes in, "We can make sure that Ms. Alexander has an appropriate stipend that won't affect Dr. Jackson's. If that's settled, the only thing we need to discuss is Ms. Black's travel arrangements, which can be done privately."

"Are you sure about all of this?" I ask her, squeezing her hands.

She looks over at me in the corner of her eye and nods once, but fidgets with her necklace. I've found she only does it when she's nervous, so I squeeze her hand tighter and bring our joined hands to my lips before setting them back in her lap. The corner of her lip tilts up as she tries to keep her expression neutral. I know I'm being unprofessional, but I don't like the idea of her not being one hundred percent confident with her plan.

Julian narrows his eyes at me, but he has no room to talk, especially with how he acts with his Becca. He'd do the same thing in my shoes. I know having Amanda invest in my project isn't the brightest idea, but it'll keep my ex-wife far away from me and my research. It also means if she comes to Scotland for my project, she'll be doing it because wants to and not because of her contract.

We wrap up the meeting and will have to return in the morning to sign everything before I fly back home. The idea of leaving Amanda here makes my stomach churn. As we walk hand in hand to the elevators, Julian stops us, "Hey, what are you two up to tonight?" His tone is a stark contrast to minutes ago.

"We have plans," Amanda says brightly, then looks at me with a mischievous smile, biting her lip.

"Oh, well, what time is your flight tomorrow?" he asks me.

"Late mornin'," I reply, unable to tear my gaze away from my spitfire.

"Shit. I was hoping we could've grabbed a bite to eat or a drink while you were here."

Amanda finally looks to Julian. "We can grab a drink later. I know just the place. I'll text Becca the address. See you later?"

"Sure, have fun you two," Julian chuckles, a wide smile appearing that I haven't seen in a while. I don't know if it's the mention of his wife, or seeing me with Amanda. I told him all about her when we met the morning after the night that changed my life.

Amanda drags us to the elevators, calling over her shoulder, "Oh, we will."

"What are you up to, spitfire?"

The elevator doors open, filled with men in suits and briefcases. I'd hoped for an empty one; the need to kiss her is becoming overwhelming. My heart aches even when she's here with me. I'm not sure how I'll survive the next few weeks without her.

While Amanda may be putting up someone else's money, it's because of her my project won't be at risk. I won't be forced to pretend I'm not in love with the most incredible woman I've ever known. I don't deserve her but I will do everything in my power to keep her.

29

AMANDA

"Two onion bagels with schmear and lox, please," I tell the cashier.

Standing behind me, Jack whispers beside my ear, "Unsexiest in the city." Though, his hot breath on my neck and low timbre of his voice is anything but unsexy.

The booth we sat in with the adorable older couple the night we met is available. We take a seat while we wait for our order to be made. I slide in, expecting Jack to sit across from me. Instead, he takes a seat next to me. It's the first time I've eaten here since that night. I'd pass by it often, but my heart would leap into my throat if I considered walking in.

"What do you say we come back here in fifty years?" he asks, his smile reaching his eyes. There's teasing in his voice, but I know he's serious.

"We're not college sweethearts. You'll be ninety!" I laugh. "I'll have to wheel you in here. I'll probably have to take out dentures to eat my bagel." His face falls. Shit. "What? What's wrong?"

"Nothing," he insists, though it's anything but.

"No, what's wrong?" I repeat.

"It's just, fuck, I don't want to talk about it. I don't want to ruin today."

I take his hand in mine. "Tell me."

"I—"

Our order is called out. He kisses the back of my hand and slides out of the booth to retrieve it. When he returns, he sets one in front of me. He picks up one of the bagel halves to take a bite, most likely to avoid the conversation. Before he can, I place my hand on his wrist and stop him. "Not so fast. Tell me first."

Jack huffs a laugh and sets down the bagel. "Blair. We were university sweethearts. We met at Cambridge. She was finishing her masters in psychology, I was starting my doctorate."

"Oh," I sigh.

"I don't want to talk about her." He shakes his head and picks up his bagel, taking a bite. I feel like I've ruined everything by pressing, and wish I hadn't asked in the first place.

I take a bite of mine, and when I finish chewing, I glance over at Jack to find his eyes on me. "What?" I wipe the corner of my mouth.

He slides his hand into my hair, keeping his thumb on my cheek. "We can talk about Blair, or anyone you dated before me, but not today. We only have tonight before I have to fly home without you. I want tonight to be about you and me, even if we're meeting Julian and Becca for a drink later."

"It's been you and me all week," I tease.

"And it'll be you and me for the rest of my life, if I have any say about it."

My eyes wide, I shriek, "What?"

"What?" He echos, casually taking another bite of his bagel as if he didn't just insinuate that I'm spending forever with him.

"What did you just say?"

"Nothing," he replies with a mouthful, but a small smirk still tugs at his lip.

What am I going to do with this man?

"You're just as bad as your cousin," I laugh, taking a bite of mine. Unlike him, I wait until I'm done chewing to add, "Any other declarations I should be worried about?"

Jack wipes his mouth with his napkin. "Fresh out. What else is on the agenda?"

"Oh, you know, a little bookstore edging, reading a boring as fuck castle book, having a whiskey or two..."

He barks out a laugh. "I'll have you know, that book is far from boring. You just missed where one of my projects was mentioned."

"Oh, I didn't skip over it," I lie, unable to keep from smiling. He gives me a knowing look. "Ok, fine, I did."

"Exactly. But what of the edging, spitfire? It's not the middle of the night. I can't have my hand in your trousers without getting arrested."

"We can't have that, can we? I don't think orange would look very good on you," I tease, tugging at his chocolate brown leather jacket.

His voice a deep whisper, he leans in and says, "But it would be worth it. I love that you get feisty when I don't let you come."

My lips part as my breath catches, then clear my throat. "No, I don't."

Jack kisses my neck, nipping at me. "Yes, you do. But, truthfully, nothing beats you sinking your teeth into me and growling that I'm yours when you come."

"That happened *one* time," I breathe.

His beard tickles my jaw as he pulls back. "Aye, but it won't be the last."

After bagels and skipping the bookstore to avoid one of us getting arrested, I text Becca to meet us at the same bar Jack and I celebrated his birthday at. We get into the cab and I'm actually grateful I'm not being chauffeured around the city by Julian's driver. I may be a billionaire, but I would rather spend my money on something more meaningful. Keeping Jack's hand firmly in mine, we arrive at the bar and order our usual drinks. I tip the bartender entirely too much, making Jack chuckle.

We find an empty porch swing and I jokingly sit on the opposite end, as I did the night we first met. The cover band is set up, tuning their guitars and testing their microphones. They begin playing a song I don't know, but it doesn't stop me from setting down my whiskey sour on the table, standing, and offering my hand.

"Dance with me?" I ask, biting back a smile.

"You know I hate dancing," he replies, but his grin couldn't get any wider.

"Shut up and dance with me."

Jack stands, puts down his drink, and pulls me flush with him by the small of my back. I wrap my hands around his neck, letting myself get lost in his emerald eyes.

After all this time, we found each other again.

Swaying off-beat to the music, just as we did that night, I bring his lips to mine. These next few weeks, I'll miss kissing him whenever I damn well please, I need to get my fix while I can. He nips at my bottom lip, teasing and demanding entry—which I give more than willingly. A soft moan escapes me as his tongue sweeps across mine. I'd normally fight to keep an upper hand, but I relinquish control, and give myself to him. A growl rumbles in his chest, making me chuckle against his lips. He'd happily haul me off to have his way with me; being in public is his only obstacle.

An obnoxious throat clearing behind me has me letting out a full laugh. "Hi, Becca," I say without breaking away from my hot Scot. Unfortunately, he pulls back, but keeps me close, eyes fixed on me.

"Julian was right," Becca teases, "you can't keep your hands to yourselves."

I turn in Jack's arms and counter, "You're one to talk, *my Becca.*"

Julian approaches with two Manhattans, handing one to her and kissing her temple. "What did I miss?"

Jack picks up our drinks and gestures to a table, "Don't think you're up for cuddling on a swing."

Becca wraps her arm around my shoulder and jokes, "Are you kidding? I'd love to."

Becca and I both laugh, link arms, and walk to the square table. We all take a seat and once the boys are chatting about castle shit, Becca leans in and whispers, "You're in so much trouble. That man is *obsessed.*"

"He, uh… he told me loves me," I whisper back.

"What?" Her voice raises enough that Jack and Julian look at us. "I mean, that's so exciting, your book is almost done," she lies.

Once they return to their conversation, I deadpan quietly, "Good save, Becs," but Jack's eyes haven't left me.

"Do you...?" Her eyes discretely gesture toward Jack.

"I don't know," I answer honestly. "But I'll never give you or Layla shit ever again."

Becca chuckles. "He's a good man. I'm so happy for you. I heard you're covering the funding so he doesn't have to work with his ex."

I fill her in on Blair helping me with my book, and while she raises concerns, I'm not worried. I don't know that I could be close friends with Blair since I'm falling for her ex-husband, but I hope we can still be friendly when this is all over.

We spend a little over an hour catching up. I'm in the middle of hearing about Becca's work in progress and don't notice Jack getting up. He startles me when I feel his beard brushing my neck as he kisses just below my ear. "Ready, spitfire?"

Becca chuckles. "Oh, she's ready."

"Becs!"

"Oh, come on, you two were sucking face when we arrived," Julian says with a wink as he pulls out Becca's chair. "Maybe keep to opposite sides of the table tomorrow when you sign the agreements?" He's right, Jack shouldn't have been as affectionate as he was in the meeting today. But I would be lying if I said I didn't love it.

Jack pulls out my chair, then Becca and I share a long hug goodbye. She whispers, "Don't be afraid of falling in love," as we break apart.

Once they've left, Jack and I take our empty glasses to the bartender. I slide my hand into his and he brings our joined hands to his lips—just one more thing I'll miss when he's back in Scotland.

"Where are we headed next, my wee spitfire?"

"Let's go home," I sigh. Even though I'll spend tonight in his arms, tomorrow he'll be gone, and two weeks of torture will begin.

30

JACK

TWO WEEKS LATER

Longest two weeks of my life. The time difference has made things difficult for us—I have to call early in the morning, or late at night if I want to talk to Amanda. Even then, it cuts into her writing time and our conversations are briefer than either of us would like. She doesn't contractually need to be here with me, but she's promised six months to see where things go with us.

She's choosing us, choosing me.

I'm stuck at Swarthmore Castle, so Cameron offered to pick up Amanda and Elizabeth at the airport in Edinburgh for me; I can't spare the ten hours roundtrip it would take. I found a couple passageways this week that I hadn't previously mapped out. Safety is important to me, and with Amanda here, I want to ensure there's no chance we can get stuck or lost.

They'll be here any minute, and I'm rushing to finish one of my outlines due to a publication next week. I'm hunched over my desk when two hands slide down my chest from behind.

My wee spitfire.

I take her hands in mine. About to kiss the back of hers, I notice her nails are longer and sharper, impractical for a writer. I glance down and quickly swivel in my seat to find the last person I want to set eyes on. "What the fuck are you doing?"

"I thought we could have time to talk, just the two of us, before Cam arrives." Blair's voice is sultry and makes bile rise in my throat. She reaches for me again but I wrench back.

"Don't fucking touch me." I look around my room, making sure no one saw whatever the fuck that was. No one but me is at the castle, but the last thing I need is Amanda walking in at the wrong time, thinking something is happening that's not. "What are you doing in my room? Fuck, what are you doing *here?*"

She pulls out a stack of papers and tosses them onto my desk with a smile. "You forgot to sign."

"I don't need your money, I'm not signing," I say through gritted teeth.

"I suppose that's better. It's a brilliant plan, removing me from the project; no conflict of interest." There's no teasing, she honestly believes I want to be with her after everything.

"You and I will never be together, Blair. I'm in love with someone else. Even if I wasn't, I'd never consider being with you again. We've been divorced for years. What would make you think I'd want you? It's not as if I was ever good enough for you when we were married," I spit.

"Fuck, Ben's wrong." Amanda's voice fills the room and I turn to watch her push off the doorframe. "I have the best possible timing." My heart swells seeing her, even if she's wrong, and her timing is shite.

"Amanda? What are you doing here?" Blair seethes.

Amanda glances between Blair and I. Eyes wide, her mouth opens and closes a couple of times, at a loss for words. I answer for her, "She's mine."

Conflict painting her face, Amanda melts at my words as fear creeps into her gaze. "I'm sorry, Blair. I didn't know he was your ex-husband."

"But you did at some point, didn't you?" Blair narrows her eyes at Amanda. "You know how I feel about Jack, how dare you patronise me. How long have you known?"

"Since London," Amanda replies softly in defeat. "When I was supposed to meet you. I saw you at the pub and—"

"You fucking tart. You knew this whole time?" Blair whirls toward me. "And you? Fucking around with my friend?"

"That's enough," I growl. "Don't you dare bring Amanda into this delusion of yours. You and I have been over for years."

"You've known each other, what, a few weeks? You'd throw away years together for some slut?" Blair scoffs.

"I said that's enough!" I tower over Blair. "Get off my dig site, and stay the fuck away from me, and don't think about coming within a hundred miles of Amanda." My anger softens as Amanda places her hand on my shoulder. "Go home, Blair."

"Jack, she has every right to be mad." Amanda then tells Blair, "I'm sorry. I didn't want to hurt you. I—"

"Fuck you. Fuck you both." Blair storms past us out of the room.

This wasn't the welcome I wanted for Amanda. I envisioned her running into my arms, not into my ex. "Are you ok, sprite?"

Amanda offers me a small smirk. "I've been better." She wraps her arms around my middle and I envelop her in mine as she rests her cheek on my chest and lets out a long, heavy sigh. I missed her so fucking much, having her here almost doesn't feel real. I can breathe for the first time since returning to Scotland.

I kiss the top of her head, refusing to let go. "Welcome home," I whisper into her hair.

"Home?" She looks up at me with a furrowed brow.

"This is our home until the project's over."

She looks around at our small room. "I'm staying with you?"

The question gives me pause. "You don't want to?"

"I never said that. We just never talked about it."

"So, you'll stay with me?" I ask hopefully.

Amanda's hands slide up my chest and around my neck, pulling me in to kiss her. Her lips are soft and warm, tasting like cinnamon and cloves—my spitfire must've had a chai on her way here. Her sweet kiss, but still full of fire, is enough for me.

I bend to grip her thighs and wrap her legs around me. I press her against the wall, wishing I had her naked right now. "Where's my brother and your friend?" I manage between kisses, not wanting a moment when my lips aren't on hers.

"Kitchen, probably fucking," she laughs.

I still and reluctantly pull back. "What?"

"I just spent five hours in your brother's truck with those two. They are definitely fucking right now... or have at least fucked before... or are about to fuck in a little bit. Either way, your brother is getting laid."

"You're full of shite." I release her legs, and she slides down the wall a few inches until her feet hit the floor.

"I'm not. But what do you say you give me a quick tour of this castle of yours before you fuck me so hard I can't walk for a few days?" she asks, biting her lip. I love that Blair being here didn't rattle her and she's still my fiery sprite.

I kiss her neck and nip at her ear. "Fuck, I missed you. Don't worry, if I make you that sore, I'll kiss it and make it better."

31

AMANDA

"This place is fucking huge," I say in awe. Jack's shown me no less than forty rooms but this one is by far the largest. "Who the hell needed this much space?"

"The last family to live here was over a hundred years ago. They had seven children," Jack says, huffing a laugh.

"Seven? I mean, by today's standards that's a lot... *Seven?* Talk about stretching a woman out." I blow out an exaggerated breath.

I take in the music room, where furniture is covered in dust cloths. Beneath them, I can make out there are several seating options and two pianos.

Who the fuck needs two pianos?

I peek under one of them. "May I?

"It'll probably be out of tune, but, sure," Jack says as he pulls the dust cloth up enough to reveal the covered keys.

I lift the hard protective cover over them and slide it back, taking a seat on the bench. I crack my knuckles and silently double check with him that this is ok. I attempt to play the one song that I remember by heart: Mozart's Piano Sonata No. 16 in C-Major. Within the first measure, it's obvious he's right, the piano is severely flat. I press on, missing the feel of keys under my fingertips. I haven't played in years and am honestly impressed at my muscle memory.

Jack takes a seat on the bench and I stop playing. "Fuck, spitfire. That's incredible."

I shrug. "You're right. The piano needs a good tuning."

He angles my chin to look at him. "Don't do that. It was beautiful. How often do you play?"

"I haven't touched keys in probably ten or fifteen years. My last lesson was in high school. My grandmother taught me that one, though, which is why I remember it."

His eyes wide, he shakes his head. "And you remember how to play after all this time?"

"It's not a big deal." I cover his hand with mine and pull it onto one of my thighs.

"It's a big deal to me. Will you play it again?" When I don't answer, he adds, "Please?"

I roll my eyes and concede, "Sure."

Jack keeps his hand on my thigh, and my foot returns to the petals. I pick up a few bars before the spot I left off and continue playing. When the song ends, he kisses my neck and whispers, "Thank you."

I'm about to pull the cover toward me, but the knob snaps off before I touch it. "Fuck!"

He looks down at the spot the knob should be, then we glance at each other. I expected a threaded screw, or it to be flush from snapping. Instead, it's a thick pin with the initials 'EWB' etched on it.

"EWB?" I ask, frowning.

"Those are Ewen's initials," Jack mutters.

I instinctively reach for it but he takes my hand. "No, it came off by itself. It could be one of his clues. Where did you say Cam was?"

"The kitchen."

Jack jumps up from the bench, holding his hands out in front of him in a cautious gesture. "Stay here. I don't want you to get lost. But, don't touch it. I need to find Cam."

"Sure, yeah," I reply, attempting to sound excited, but I'm a little annoyed that he's treating me like a child.

He rushes out of the room, leaving me tempted to do the one thing he asked me not to.

I'm a grown ass woman, I can touch something if I want to.

No, what if it's important and I fuck it up?

What could I possibly fuck up? It's just a couple of initials. It came off all on its own, anyway.

Curiosity gets the best of me. I run my fingers over the initials and the pin sucks into the piano. "Shit, shit, shit!" I grasp at the small, empty hole where the pin was. "No, no, no! Fuck, I should've listened to him," I mutter.

I look around and under, wondering where the hell the pin could've gone. I lift the cover that can't be more than a quarter inch. There's no way it could just disappear.

"Where the fuck did it go?" There's a creak to my right, the last white key is lifted. "Shit! How did this get worse?" I scramble to push it back down. In an instant, the pin on the cover appears. "What the fuck?" A moment later, Jack, Cameron, and Lizzy rush into the music room. Jack's nostrils flair and a small growl comes from him.

Oops.

"Amanda," he warns. "What did you touch?"

"Nothing," I lie, my fingers still on the white key at the end. I quickly pull my hand away and into my lap. Cameron slides up next to me. It's scary how much he looks like Jack, except he's closer to my age and his beard and hair are shorter.

Cameron whispers. "I get it, I would've done it too."

I try my best to not laugh, but a small chuckle escapes me. I glance up at Jack, who is most definitely not amused. "Ok, fine, you caught me. I touched the pin like this and…" I graze it as I did the first time. It sucks back into the piano and the last white key pops up again. "Sorry," I wince.

Cameron lights up and lifts the key half an inch. "You brilliant, curious lass." He pulls out a small piece of parchment with a set of tweezers and places it in a small bag. "Come on, let's get it to my work station."

Cam rushes out of the room as quickly as he came in and Lizzy follows, looking back at me once. Jack offers his hand and I hesitantly take it. He helps me from the bench and pulls me to him, taking my chin between his thumb and forefinger and kissing me softly.

"I take it back," he chuckles. "You can touch whatever the fuck you want, spitfire."

"Anything?" I ask teasingly, playfully wiggling my eyebrows.

"Anything."

Amanda and I join Cam and Lizzy in our work room, where Cam is carefully unfolding the parchment. Thankfully, it's in great condition but we press it in glass to preserve it.

It reads:

SONATA FACILE IS ONLY THE BEGINNING.
CARSE IS A FARSE.

"Mozart," Amanda breathes.

"What?" I ask her.

She takes a moment to process my question, blinks away whatever she was thinking, then replies, "Sorry. Sonata Facile is the name of the song I played. It's Mozart. Who's Carse? If they're a pianist, I don't know them."

"Quick search says a carse is land by a river." Lizzy's declaration catches our attention. "What would a river-bank have to do with Mozart?"

"Maybe it's a song?" Cam asks. Lizzy types in her phone for a moment, shaking her head. "Or maybe a musician?"

Lizzy shakes her head again. "No, only thing that could be remotely close to it would be Alexander Carse." Lizzy continues typing and scrolling. "Scottish painter." She glances up. "Could that be it?"

"That doesn't make sense. Why would he be a farce?" I ask.

Lizzy shrugs. "I don't know, maybe he used a different name? Or he was accused of something?"

The four of us pull out our phones and look up every possible reason that a riverbank or a painter could be deemed fake. Nothing seems to fit. While I'm scrolling through articles and photos, I find a sketch of Leith that looks familiar, but it could be that I've been staring at art for too long, or I've seen the scene in person.

We continue looking but Amanda's stomach starts rumbling. I laugh to myself; my girl is always hungry and I love that she has no issue eating whatever she wants in front of me. She covers it with her hand to stifle the growls that give the impression of her stomach eating her backbone. "You hungry, spitfire?" I don't give her a moment to protest before I stand. "I'll make us some-thing." I kiss her cheek and leave before she can stop me.

As I make my way down the hall, I ponder, something isn't sitting right with me. Cam and Lizzy are insistent that it has to be something to do with a hidden river and are researching old maps. Yet, there's something about the artist that keeps pulling my attention back to it.

The kitchen is fully stocked, so I make quick work to prepare tea and sandwiches. The kettle is whistling, but before I can remove it from the stove, Amanda beats me to it. "What are you doing in here, sprite?"

"Thought you could use a hand," she replies with a small shrug, pouring the water into the four mugs I prepped. "Where would I find milk and sugar?"

I gesture with my butterknife to the fridge. "You'll find fresh milk in there, and there's sugar in the larder."

She pauses. "The what?"

"Pantry," I chuckle and gesture behind me. "But you don't have—"

Amanda wraps her arms around me from behind. "You can't always take care of everyone. It's just tea. Let me help." She kisses my back and releases me, finding the milk and sugar and setting them on the counter. "I'll bring all of it to the work room. I don't know how they take theirs. Do you have a tray?"

"There should be one under the counter here." I find it quickly and set it on the counter. She begins placing everything on the tray. "Come here." I glide my hand into her hair and kiss her softly. I bite back the three little words I desperately want to tell her, and opt for the safe option, "Thank you for being here."

"I just hope you find what you're looking for."

My wee spitfire, I already did…

We fill two trays to bring into the work room. When we enter, Cameron's behind Lizzy pointing out something at the desk, his lips dangerously close to her neck. He hasn't heard us come in. I take in the sight of his body practically flush with hers and have to admit that Amanda's right: there was or is something going on between the two of them. I clear my throat to announce our presence. Cam glances back, eyes wide, and steps away from Lizzy.

"We may have found something," he offers, rubbing the back of his neck. I'm genuinely surprised he's taken an interest in Lizzy; he's more than a decade older than her, but the project is more important than his love life.

"What's that?" I ask, giving him a knowing look.

"There's a painting in the modern art museum in Edinburgh. We think there's a clue."

I keep my voice low so only he can hear. "Does that clue include sleeping with junior researchers?"

He lets out a deep, full laugh. "Such a hypocrite, Barty. If we want to examine it, we'll have to go to Edinburgh." I fucking hate when he calls me that; he knows it pisses me off.

"Fuck," I mutter, dreading heading back home.

"Aye, it's all shite."

"Who's the painting by?" Amanda asks Cam.

"Alexander Carse. We've ruled out the possibility that it's an embankment," he replies.

Amanda chews on her lip. "What if it is a riverbed like you previously thought? Maybe it just looks like the one in the painting. I doubt this guy leaving clues would make you travel all over Scotland on a wild goose chase. Why not pull up a map of rivers from the time the art was made, and cross reference it with ones that are here in Skye?"

"That's... fuck, that's actually a good idea," Cam admits. "I'm fucking starving." He glances at Lizzy. "Let's eat, then take a look at it after." He takes a large bite of his sandwich, not caring that the girl he's trying to impress is right in front of him. He's taking 'unsexy food' to a whole new level. Lizzy stifles a laugh, so perhaps I'm wrong, and my brother knows exactly what he's doing after all.

We finish eating and Amanda is doing her best to hold back her yawns; the time difference must be tough on her. I take her empty plate and place it on the tray, then kiss her cheek and whisper, "Let's get you to bed, spitfire."

"Are you going to tuck me in and tell me a bedtime story? Or maybe dive back into chapter seven again?" she teases sleepily.

"As much as I'd love to have my face between your legs until you're screaming, you need to rest. Come on, let's get you to bed."

I lead her into our bedroom and help her unpack a few things. Amanda takes a quick shower and when she returns to the room, she's not wearing a towel. Her hair is sopping wet and water drips down her beautiful, naked body. Sitting on the edge of the bed, I gesture with the crook of my finger for her to come to me. She prowls, chin lifted, and climbs on top of my lap. I don't care that she's getting my shirt and trousers soaked.

"What are you up to?" I ask, unable to help myself as I glide my hands up her thighs and tug her closer.

"Nothing. Just going to bed."

"I have a wee bit of work to do. If you're still awake when I'm done, I'll play with that pretty, tight cunt of yours."

She kisses my neck and whispers, "You have a deal."

Amanda climbs off me and I pull back the sheets for her. Even if we don't have sex, I want the feeling of her soft body against mine tonight. "Get some rest."

She nods and closes her eyes. I leave her to rest and return to Cam and Lizzy. I'm almost afraid I'll walk in on them doing something inappropriate, as Amanda predicted. I knock twice as I enter, just in case. I glance around, not finding Lizzy. Before I can ask, Cam offers, "She was tired, too. Went to bed."

"Does she have her own room?" I ask with a raised eyebrow.

He chuckles. "Aye, why wouldn't she?"

"Keep your cock in your trousers, Cam. At least for her first night?"

"If you insist," he replies with a smirk, rolling his eyes.

We wrap up some preliminary research on the art and go to bed. Amanda may be onto something, and there's a chance that the painting may unlock another clue. Amanda and Lizzy will likely be up early—they're still adjusting to the time difference—so Cam and I decide to go to bed in anticipation of an early start as well.

I climb into bed with my spitfire. She turns to face me, resting her cheek on my shoulder and slinging an arm and leg over me. I slowly caress her thigh, savouring the feel of her skin under my fingertips. I kiss her forehead and whisper against her skin, "Goodnight, my love."

"Night," Amanda whispers back, snuggling closer to me. She murmurs something else, but I can't make it out. I'm nearly asleep when I hear her say into the darkness, "Mine."

I hold her closer. "Yours."

33

AMANDA

Being here for the last week has been all but inspiring for my writing. I finished my book, but I don't love the ending. I changed Jackson's name and the title of my book, removed all traces of Jack, and now it's a mediocre duplicate of every other romantic suspense I've ever written.

I fucking hate it.

Despite my book not going as well as I'd hoped, I love spending time with Lizzy when she's not fucking Cam— which I know she's doing, even if she denies it. Cameron is also hilarious and tells some of the best stories I've ever heard. Jack is everything I could ever want in a man and, despite being scared shitless, I've fallen in love with him. This project, though, has been dead end after dead end. It doesn't deter Jack, but leaves me defeated on his behalf.

I'm walking through one of the halls lined with art when I find one that looks familiar. Unlike the other oil paintings, this one was done with pen and watercolor. I've been looking at art all week, but for some reason, this one calls to me; it feels out of place among the rest. I step closer to see if I can make out the signature. Unfortunately, it's just a scribble.

I take a picture on my phone and upload it to my search engine as a reverse image search. I gasp, my hand flying to my mouth as the name Alexander Carse comes up.

"Jack!" I yell down the corridor. He must be down in the basement, dungeon, or whatever it's called in a castle. "Lizzy? Cam?"

No one comes.

I move closer, looking for something like the pin on the piano. Nothing stands out. As I'm about to give up, I spot a small 'EWB' engraved in the right corner of the frame. I look left and right, then hesitantly reach to brush the initials like I did with the piano.

Nothing. This whole thing is in my head. But what if…

I carefully lift the thick frame a few inches off the wall to peek behind it. Still, nothing. Carse is a farce? Maybe it means the painting is real? No, that's fucking stupid. This Black family and their clues are worse than the first draft or one of my romantic suspense novels.

I could do so much better.

"If you were my book, you'd have another clue," I laugh to myself. "Classic example of the book is better. One star. Poorly written, Black."

"Reading your reviews again, spitfire?" Jack's low, playful question from behind startles me. His hand slides to my stomach, pulling me against him.

"Shit! You can't be sneaking up on people. This castle is haunted, you know," I tease back, resting the back of my head on his chest.

"What did you find?" He pauses but a moment later lets go of me and steps closer to the art. "What is this doing here?" he says to himself.

"Which one of these is not like the other?" I sing.

He looks at the other paintings on the wall and chuckles, "Aye, it's definitely not like the rest. But this one is supposed to be in the art museum in Edinburgh. What is it doing here?" Jack takes out his phone, dials, and holds it to his ear. "Amanda found something… Wing four… Bring a cart." He hangs up and turns to face me, a smirk tugging at his lips. "This is one of Alexander Carse's. Or, at least, it's a copy. You're quite the unexpected good luck charm, my wee spitfire."

"Oh, I don't know about that," I purr, taking a step closer, trying to make light of it. There might not be a clue, and I don't want him to get his hopes up.

Jack closes the distance, takes my face in his hands, and kisses me. "You absolutely are." As we hear the cart approaching, we break apart, but his eyes don't leave mine. "Let's load this one up," he tells Cam, pointing at the art without tearing his gaze from me. The intensity of his gaze draws me in like a moth to a flame.

"Fuck me. It's a Carse," Cam says with a gasp.

"Can you two stop eye-fucking long enough to help steady the cart?" Lizzy brazenly asks, reaching for the painting with Cam.

"Right, sorry," I say, pulling the cart closer and holding it in place. A woman a decade younger than me is calling me on my shit—I need to get it together. Jack takes the other side, and even without looking in his direction, I know his eyes are on me.

Lizzy and Cam pull it from the wall and set it onto the cart, securing it. As they wheel it toward the work room, I gasp, forgetting to tell them, "I found initials on it."

Cameron and Jack stop in their tracks and face me. "What? Where?" Cam asks, now looking at the drawing as if it were a 'Where's Waldo.'

I step closer and point to the etched initials in the corner. "Not in the painting. Here."

Jack steps behind me. "Told you, good luck charm." He kisses my neck, the simple gesture causing heat to pool in my belly. I resist reaching behind his neck to pull him closer, no matter how much I desperately want his mouth on me. I don't want to make Lizzy uncomfortable.

"Shite, Barty, we should put your hen in charge," Cam teases. Jack growls but I laugh. "Come on, let's get this examined and a quick bite to eat at the pub. It's going to be a long night."

We continue down the corridor and turn down three others before we're in their workspace. Cam and Jack lift the large piece of art onto their long table and put on gloves. Lizzy and I stand back as they turn it over to remove the frame. A glint of something on the corner of it catches my eye.

I place my hand on Jack's shoulder. "Stop." Neither of them move as I get closer moving around the frame. I try a few angles, but it doesn't reappear. I shake my head and step beck. "Nevermind, I thought I saw... *that.*" There it is. A small, ornate, painted cross glimmers the corner. It reminds me of when my grandmother would have me paint with water on the wood fence in her backyard—nearly invisible.

Cameron steps behind me and follows my line of sight. "Kildalton Cross," he breathes.

"Aren't those the ones you research?" I ask him.

"Aye, but what is it doing behind a knock off rendition of Carse's drawing?"

"Maybe it's not fake," Lizzy offers. "Carse is a farce? Or maybe it is? There could be something behind the paper backing."

"You can't just remove it, right?" I ask as they are about to peel it back. "If this is original work, we should let a professional do it."

"She's right," Jack agrees, and I finally glance up from the art to find his eyes pinning me. The air sucks out of my lungs, as it always does when he looks at me like this. "Cam, Lizzy, why don't we check with the museum that claims to have it? You can go in the morning and see if they have an expert to examine it."

"Good plan," Cam chimes in. "But what if we take a little peek?"

"No," Jack growls. "We shouldn't touch it. If this is real, we need to be careful. To be safe, you two should go and ensure if there's any clues, we have them."

Cam rolls his eyes. "Fine. You're no fun."

Cameron and Lizzy make arrangements to transport it to Edinburgh tomorrow afternoon while we eat dinner. Jack and I agree to stay behind for him to continue his dungeon excavation. I'm pretty sure Jack only wants an excuse to spend some time alone with me—we've had to be quiet the last week with Cam and Lizzy here. It'll only get worse when the rest of his crew arrives next week.

The pub Cam suggested is the same one we went to a couple nights ago. Cam offers to take Lizzy, giving Jack and I time together. I can tell Lizzy is a little stir crazy here; we're both from big cities, and the quiet is almost too much sometimes.

As soon as Cam and Lizzy leave, Jack doesn't waste a moment before wrapping me in his arms and kissing me as if he hasn't all day—even if he has dozens of times. "Come on, there's something I want to show you."

34

JACK

"Are you sure this is safe?" Amanda glances around as we walk into one of the hidden passageways, stopping at a set of stairs.

"I mapped it out a month ago. Do you trust me?"

She chews on her lip. "This looks like I'm going to need a torch... or a few witches to de-haunt this place."

"Come on." I tilt my head toward the dark stairwell. I don't want to divulge that I have a surprise for her that I set up late last night, but I may have to.

Amanda takes my hand and lets me lead her downstairs. "You know this is how horror books and movies start. Or worse, one of those mystery shows!" She begins speaking in her narration voice, *"The author trusted the hot man, following him to his sex dungeon, where she was tortured for eight years..."*

"If it's a sex dungeon, was she really tortured?"

"Good point." She tries again, *"He seemed so sweet and innocent, until she found his collection of floggers and ball gags."*

"How is that better?" I laugh.

"He devoured her snatch for three hours…"

"Three? That's all? Amature."

"They found her laid out on the bed, begging to come again…"

I press her against the stone, leaning in with my hand above her head to brace myself against it. With my flashlight lowered, I can't see her face, but I can feel her uneven, heavy breaths. "I'm beginning to think you're making a wishlist for tonight." I brush a kiss against her neck as her hands travel down my torso, landing on my belt. "If you want my face between your legs for three hours, I'll need your thighs spread wide so I can properly devour that delicious cunt of yours. And I'm sure as hell not fucking you in a dark stairwell."

"What if I want you to touch me here?"

"You can wait." I nip at her ear and trail kisses along her jaw and cheek until I find her lips. She moans into my mouth at the contact, and it takes everything in me to not strip her down right now and bury myself inside her. I selfishly taste and tease her, loving every nip and lick she returns. I reluctantly pull back, knowing exactly how this will end if we remain on the stairs.

My spitfire sighs, though it's more of a whine. "Then, lead the way to my impending doom that will land me a TV show deal."

"You really don't trust me, do you?" I chuckle, taking her hand and leading her down the final ten steps.

"Think about it. *Hot Scottish man shows up in a bar. Spends a night exploring New York. Gives his woman endless orgasms. Disappears for half a year, but shows up at her friend's wedding in a sexy kilt.* It's begging to be made into a made-for-TV movie."

"Sexy kilt?"

"Yeah. Were you wearing anything underneath?" she playfully asks.

"You'll have to find out for yourself the next time I wear it."

"When will that be?"

"A wedding," I reply, but what I want to say is '*our wedding*.' The thought has crossed my mind too many times to count. I can't imagine myself ever being with anyone but Amanda and, one day, I will absolutely marry my spitfire—if she'll have me.

We continue for a moment until we reach the door of the wine cellar, though I wouldn't trust a single bottle in the room. I take out my lighter to light the candles I set up. The wine ranks are a rich mahogany and the room is stunning as candlelight bounces off the glass.

"Jack, what is this?" she breathes.

I continue lighting them until the room is bright enough to see her, but still keeps its charm. I take out my phone and play the song that we danced under the stars to, "Hope I Don't Fall In Love With You," by Tom Waits.

"Dance with me, spitfire?"

Amanda slides her hands around my neck. "But you hate dancing."

"Aye, but I like dancing with you."

I hold her close as we sway to the music. She huffs a small laugh at the lyrics of the song. "So, you hope we don't fall in love?"

"Too late for me." I kiss just below her ear and whisper, "I'm more than in love with you, my wee spitfire."

"Jack…" Her voice is laced with silent apologies.

"I don't expect you to tell me you love me, but I refuse to hide how I feel about you. All I ask is for you to let me love you."

Amanda pulls back, her eyes darting between mine. She lets out a shaky breath and breathes a simple, "Ok."

We stare at each other as silence passes between us. The music fades away, and all I can think is I'm the luckiest man alive to have met Amanda, and I intend to spend the rest of my life loving her.

"I'll have you know, I—" Whatever Amanda was going to say is cut short by the door of the cellar closing. It makes both of us jump. I let go of her to open it but it's stuck. "Very funny, Jack," she teases.

I glance over my shoulder to find her arms crossed and her eyebrow raised at me. I shake my head to let her know I'm not joking. "It's jammed."

Amanda rolls her eyes, crossing the room to stand next to me. She twists the knob but it doesn't turn. "Shit! It's not jammed, it's locked. But… how is it locked? The keyhole is on the inside."

There's a door on the other side of the cellar, we try to open it but it's locked from the inside as well. "Fuck, I'm sorry. I was trying to be romantic."

"Oh, Jack," she sighs. "It was… until we got stuck in a wine cellar with"—she takes out her phone—"zero bars of reception."

I tighten my bun. "Cam knows we're down here. He'll find us."

"Yeah," she scoffs. "Except he's probably fucking Lizzy. We'll see him in three to five business days when he realises we're missing. By then, I will have consumed forty bottles of wine and probably turned into a cannibal."

I can't help but laugh. "We won't be stuck for long." I look around for something I can turn into a makeshift key, finding nothing. I let out a defeated sigh. "I'm sorry."

Amanda wraps her arms around my middle, and laughs. "Apology not accepted until you get us out of here."

35

AMANDA

I only last ten minutes before I start pacing. Jack is rummaging through every drawer, looking for something, anything, that we can jam into the lock. I could use a video tutorial for turning a hair pin into a key right about now.

Jack's hand covers mine that's fidgeting with my necklace. "It'll be ok. We'll find a way out of here."

I glance down at my pendant. "Wait. Would this work?"

"Maybe, but we're not using it. That's your nan's; we'll find something else." He slides his fingers up from my collarbone, until they're cupping my neck and he sweeps his thumb along my jaw. "I'm sorry."

I lift on my toes and kiss him softly. "It's not your fault. I just… I don't do well in small spaces."

Reaching behind my neck, I unclasp my necklace and step out of Jack's hold. My necklace is sturdy enough, but I won't twist it too much for it to possibly break. Jack beats me to the door.

"No, you can't use that. It's irreplaceable," Jack growls.

"I'll be careful."

He envelops my hands with both of his and laughs, "You're such a stubborn lass. If you insist on using it, let me?"

I nod and hand him my necklace. Jack kneels on one knee to examine the hole, then carefully slides the key in, but doesn't turn. With a deep sigh, he finally turns it and the door clicks open easily. He looks up at me with shock and excitement as he opens the heavy door. His elated expression fades and his brows pinch together.

"That shouldn't have worked." He shakes his head as he stands. "This door shouldn't have locked in the first place. I've opened and closed it dozens of times, but this key… this key shouldn't have worked."

"Told you I should've had witches de-haunt this place," I tease. "Don't read into it, we could've jabbed anything in that hole and it would have opened." I snicker to myself at how that came out.

Jack slides the necklace around my neck, clasping it in the back. "I think it's time you take one of those DNA tests, sprite. There are too many coincidences. What if… what if you're—"

"I'll stop you right there. Do you know how common my last name is? What next? I'm related to a fictional wizard in a middle-grade book?" I laugh, shaking my head. "While, yes, I need to do one at some point, there's no way I'm related to the same family you've been researching."

"You're right. But I quite like the idea that fate brought you here." A small smirk pulls at the corner of his lips.

I glide my hands into his hair, bring his lips to mine, and mutter, "It did."

We blow out the candles and make our way upstairs. Fate may not have brought me here to find some long lost family heirlooms, but it definitely brought me to Jack.

36

JACK

I can't shake the idea that Amanda could be the last living relative of the Black family. The key was the perfect fit, sliding in with no resistance and turning with little force. Regardless, when we get back home, I'd like her to look into her family tree, since she knows so little about them.

Back in our room, I suggest we take a quick shower and go out for dinner. Cam and Lizzy should still be at the pub, but we can find somewhere else to eat. I can tell he likes her; there's no reason to interrupt him trying to woo the lass.

I start the shower—extra hot for Amanda. Once the temperature is perfect for her, I step in. "Come on, spit-fire," I call. "We don't have long before the water is cold." While I had plumbing installed for us, the water heater is small. We have ten minutes before it's frigid.

Amanda opens the shower door with a bottle of shampoo and a razor. My eyes narrow as I wipe the water off my face. "You better not let that blade anywhere near that cunt of yours, spitfire. I don't want to tame a hairless beast." She laughs and kisses me. "I'm serious. I want you feisty and wild. A real man isn't afraid of a little winter bush."

"Well, *you* better shave. I want my mouth around that thick cock of yours, but I refuse to pick pubes out of my teeth. In fact"—a devilish smirk tugs at her lips—"why don't I shave you?"

"You're not getting anywhere near my cock with that." I snatch it out of her hand. "If you insist on shaving, I'll do the honours, but we're starting with you. I'll shave your legs, but you're not shaving your cunt on my watch."

"You don't trust me to shave your balls?"

"I trust you with my life, lass."

Amanda swallows hard but slides her hands up my chest until they're around my neck and our bodies are flush. Our lips mere inches apart, I can hardly resist tasting her. There's fear in her eyes I haven't seen in a while. She's like a cornered hare; I'm afraid if I move too quickly, she'll run again.

The steam envelops us and when she kisses me, I can't help myself. I throw down the blade, reach down to grip her thighs, and pull them around me. Her eyes now wild, she surprises me, admitting for the first time, "I love you, Jack." My heart stops, until she adds, "Let me shave your balls."

Amanda's admission leaves me speechless but desperate to claim her. I press her against the shower wall and roughly kiss her, afraid she'll take back the words that mean more to me than she realises.

Her fingers sink into my back as she grips me tighter. "I'm not just saying it so you'll let me shave your taint. I love you," she pants against my lips and I chuckle against hers. My heart swells, overcome with the need to feel her closer.

"I love you, my wee spitfire. More than I've loved anyone. If you really want to shave me, go ahead," I laugh, refusing to pull my lips from hers. She stills in my arms and I reluctantly break away. "What's wrong? Cold feet," I jest.

"No." She offers a sad smile. "You were married before."

I release her thighs and slide her down my body, taking her face in my hands. "I thought I loved her, but it was nothing compared to how I feel about you."

"The other day, when she was here, you weren't tempted to pick up where you left off?"

I tuck her wet hair behind her ears and off her shoulders. Cupping her neck, I keep my thumbs on her cheeks and kiss her forehead. "I don't want her. I want the woman who makes me second guess things, has me looking at things from another angle, forces me to fight with her even though she knows I'll give in… I want *you*. No one else."

She covers my hands with hers. "I don't deserve you."

"It's me who doesn't deserve you."

"What will happen when your project's over and I go back to New York?" Her question is heavy and has been weighing on me for weeks.

I opt for the safe answer. "We'll figure it out."

Chewing on her lip, she says softly, "I have to choose between you and my life back home."

"I'll move to New York, if that's what you want. I love you with all of my being, Amanda. You don't have to decide where we live right now but"—I swallow hard —"choose *me*, and I promise I will *always* choose you."

A playful smile dances on her lips. "Already trying to move in with your billionaire girlfriend, eh?"

Worse. I want to live with the woman I plan to spend the rest of my life with.

"No, I'll get my own place, if that's what you want. But if you leave here, you know I'll follow."

Amanda presses a sweet kiss to my chest, but then sinks down onto her knees in front of me. I take her chin between my fingers. "What do you think you're doing, spitfire?"

"Your wee spitfire was promised she could shave your balls." She reaches for the razor and spins it between her fingers with an excited smile. "Are you ready for a little manscaping?"

"It's not a forest down there!"

"True, but it's been too long since you've fucked my mouth. A quick shave never hurt anyone." Amanda winks and drags the razor to the left of my balls up to my shaft.

"Shite, please be careful."

Amanda smiles, biting her lip, as she taps the razor on the shower floor. She does the same with the other side, then makes quick work to rid me of every last hair around my cock. Thankfully, no nicks or cuts. "There. Was that so bad?"

Her hand wraps around the base of my cock and she licks around the tip, making me twitch. In an instant, she slides her tongue along the underside as she takes all of me in her mouth. I hit the back of her throat, making her lightly gag. I grip her hair with one hand and brace myself on the wall with the other, but I don't thrust into her as she takes me deeper. "*Fuck*," I groan. Moving her mouth up and down my shaft, she sucks hard and tugs on my balls.

Damn it, I'm going to come too fast.

As if she can sense it, Amanda relaxes her throat and moans—knowing the vibration will have me undone.

She feels too good, and I can't hold on. "Fuck, I'm going to come." I thrust three times into her mouth and spill my release down her throat, but pull out just enough to fill her mouth. "Don't swallow," I growl as I pull all the way out. "Stand up." She does as I ask, and I help her up the rest of the way. "Let me see."

Amanda opens her mouth, sticking her tongue out for me, smiling with her eyes. With two fingers, I swipe my cum off her tongue, trace them down her lips, chin, and chest, continuing until my hand is between her legs— marking every inch of her as mine.

"Swallow." I watch her throat bob as she does. "This doesn't belong in your mouth." I press my fingers inside her, a gasp escaping her. "It belongs here."

I kiss her neck, then lower to my knees as I drive my fingers deeper and curl them. Her hands tangle in my hair as I trail kisses from her stomach to her perfect pussy. I sit back on my heels, ready to worship her the way she deserves.

"Jack," she breathes.

"Yes?" I purr, lifting her leg over my shoulder and licking up her centre.

"Mine," she attempts to growl, but it comes out more like a moan.

Fuck, I love this woman. I chuckle as my tongue teases around her clit. I continue licking and sucking, knowing it will drive her mad with desire for more. Like clockwork, her nails dig into my scalp as she grinds against my mouth.

"Shit, keep doing that, I'm close." I continue the same pace and pressure until her cum coats my tongue and she screams my name. I want another from her, but the shower will be cold any minute now. Her grip on my hair loosens and I keep my fingers inside her as I slowly lick around her clit.

Amanda's breath begins to steady, though her legs are still quivering. I remove her leg from my shoulder and stand, withdrawing my fingers from her soaked cunt. She winces at the loss of contact. "Open," I command and she wets her lips before doing as I asked. "Taste how good we are together." I glide my fingers along her tongue and she closes her mouth around them, sucking them clean. Sliding my hand to grip her throat, I kiss her hard, tasting both of us. She kisses me back harder as we explore each other's mouths.

When we finally break apart, I tuck her dripping hair behind her ear as she tells me with as much confidence she can muster through her ragged breaths, "You're mine, Jack."

"Aye, I am." I kiss her forehead. "But it's sexier when you growl it."

37

AMANDA

Jack and I quickly wash off before the water gets cold. He wraps me in a towel, then carries me as if I'm a bride crossing a threshold, and sets me on the bed. The towel pools at my hips, my hair still sopping wet. He ties up his hair and drops to his knees, ripping my towel the rest of the way open.

Trailing kisses up my inner thigh, he growls against me, "I want to take from you until you have nothing left to give me. Even then, it won't be enough." He looks up at me through his lashes as he nips at my flesh.

Who is this man? He's like a damn book boyfriend serenading me with his words. In such a short time, he made me fall head-over-heels in love with him. When I think back to my past relationships, nothing comes within a thousand miles of how I feel about Jack. He said we'll figure things out later, but there's no way I can give him up. Hell, I don't even need to be here now, but I never want to leave... or, at least, not leave Scotland. Living in a castle definitely isn't like the fairytales.

Jack teases my pussy with his tongue and fingers, but I don't want his mouth or hand, I need *him*. "Recovered yet?"

"Hmm?" he asks, his tongue remaining firmly pressed against my clit.

"Are you recovered yet?"

"Aye, but I'm not fucking you tonight."

"What?" I ask, a cross between a whine and a whimper.

"I'm not fucking you," he repeats, then proceeds to resume his torturously slow licks—as if I would let that little comment go.

I scoot back a couple inches, just out of reach of his face. "What do you mean you're not fucking me?"

Jack lifts from the floor and rests his knee on the bed, bracing his hands on either side of my head. "What I'm going to do to you is a hell of a lot more than a quick fuck, spitfire." He kisses my neck, drawing my skin into his mouth and sucking hard enough to mark me. His teeth graze me as he pulls back. "You're going to give me all of you."

"And, what? You're going to *make love* to me?" I tease. His eyes are molten; I realize that's exactly what he intends to do. "Oh, fuck. You're totally going to make love to me, aren't you?"

Jack kisses me softly, and with a chuckle, replies, "I'm pretty sure that's what I've done every time I've been inside you—including our night in New York. It's never been shagging, not for me. We haven't been alone here since you arrived and I want to spend the night worshipping all of you. You love control, but tonight, I want you to let me love you. And yes, you'll come over and over until you can't take another. But I want all of you."

"Sorry, I know you're trying to be sweet and romantic, but I'm not following."

"Oh, my wee spitfire," he sighs, eyes pinning me with so much love, but a tinge of sadness. "I love sitting for hours with you in a bookstore, dancing with you under the stars, and watching the sun rise over the city just as much as I love making you come." I look away, unable to look him in the eyes when he's saying things like this, but as he adds, "You're extraordinary, Amanda," I let out a shaky breath and meet his emerald eyes again. He rests his forehead on mine, as if he knows how hard it is for me to give into this. "So, no, I'm not going to fuck you."

"What am I going to do with you, my hot Scot?"

Jack's lips fall to the crook of my neck. "You're going to let me." He peppers kisses down my chest to my peaked nipples, taking one in his mouth and swirling his tongue. His hand glides up my torso until he reaches my other breast and rolls my nipple between his fingers. My hands fly to the duvet, gripping it tightly.

I need him desperately, wrapping my legs around his waist and attempt to pull him to me. He bites my nipple, making me yelp; a dark chuckle rumbles in his chest. His hands travel down to my thighs, spreading me wide.

"I thought I said that you're going to let me?" he teases.

"I need you," I breathe, tangling my fingers in his loosely tied bun.

He kisses lower when there's a knock at the door. We both groan and Jack shouts, "Busy."

"Stop fucking your girlfriend, Barty, this is important," Cameron calls back with a snicker.

Jack groans, pressing a single kiss to my stomach. "Don't move."

I fall back onto the mattress with a sigh as he grabs my wet towel to wrap it around his waist. He opens the door a couple inches. "Someone better be dead or dying, Cam."

"Put some clothes on. We don't have to go to Edinburgh, we don't have the original. Lizzy confirmed with the museum. Since ours is a fake, we want to open it up." There's a brief pause and whispers I can't hear before Jack closes the door.

Jack grabs his boxer briefs from a drawer and pulls them on before returning to me. "I'll need to worship you later, spitfire." He leans over me to kiss my collarbone. "Cam and Lizzy found something."

I sit up. "I heard. Let me get dressed and I'll join you."

He glances down to my legs wide, my wet pussy still on full display, and drags his hand over his face. "Fuck, I'm going to be hard the whole time, thinking about tasting you again."

"Ten minutes?" I offer, lightly licking up lip.

"You have two, sprite."

In an instant, his face is between my legs, and I selfishly let him devour me. His tongue dives inside me, and I wind tighter and tighter, as two of his fingers drive into me, hooking right where I need him. My legs instinctively attempt to close, but he presses one flush against the mattress keeping me spread for him. It feels amazing, but it's not enough.

"I need your cock, Jack." The words tumble from me, making him groan against my pussy. "Please," I beg. Without a reply, he pulls back and flips me. My feet on the floor, bracing myself on the mattress, another whimper escapes me.

Jack slides his boxer briefs down to his knees, then his calloused hands slide up and down my back, landing on my hips and dragging me closer to him. "One minute. You have one minute to come on my cock, spitfire." He thrusts into my wet pussy, making me cry out. "And you said I couldn't make you scream," he teases with a dark chuckle.

"Harder," I demand, not wanting to give in. He drives deeper into me, hard and fast. The punishing pace is almost too much for me to keep my balance.

"Thirty seconds."

I push back into him, chasing my orgasm. I'm afraid if I don't come in half a minute, he'll let me squirm for who the hell knows how long. He takes a fistful of my hair, wrapping it around his hand and tugging my head up an inch. The prickling of my scalp is enough to make me come; my whole body feels like it's on fire. My pussy flutters around his cock as he grits out a few swears, emptying himself inside me. I fall to my elbows as I catch my breath and come down from my high.

Jack sits on the bed, pulling me with him, still deep inside me. I straddle his lap backward, and a combination of both of our releases seeps out of me. He reaches between my legs, swipes the wetness between his fingers and circles my sensitive clit with it. "You still have ten seconds, but I'm not stopping until you come for me again."

He keeps an arm firmly around my middle as he kisses and sucks on my neck, leaving yet another mark. At this rate, I'll be a fucking leopard. I wrap my hand behind his neck to keep him in place, savoring the sting of his teeth grazing the now sensitive spot. His cock hardens inside me and I grind down onto it.

"Your brother can wait," I whisper. "I need you to come inside me again."

I rock back and forth onto his cock as he continues touching me. "Shite, are you planning on a fourth generation of Bartholomew Jacksons?" he teases. I try my best to not laugh, wondering if breeding kinks are hereditary. His cousin was all too happy to knock up my friend, does he want to have kids? I get stuck inside my head, realizing there are big conversations we haven't had, until Jack pulls me tight to him. "It was a joke," he laughs, kissing my neck. "But if you want to practice, you can have my cock any time you like."

I breathe a sigh of relief and rest my head against him. "Make me come, Jack."

He nips at my shoulder. "Make yourself come, spitfire," he retorts.

"Damn it!" I tease, wiggling further onto his cock and clenching my pussy around him. He hisses and growls as I chase my orgasm. I'm close, and while I want to wait for him, he did ask me to make myself come—and I'll be damned if I don't do exactly as he asks. He pinches my clit and nips at my shoulder, enough to make me come undone. "*Jack!*"

"Let go for me. Come all over my cock; show me you're mine."

My orgasm crashes into me and his quickly follows. I feel him come as he moans, and I can't help teasing him with a little squeeze around his cock.

"*Fuuuuck.*"

He can't see my face, so I can't help my silly grin, knowing what I'm doing to him. He thrusts into me, making me yelp, then wraps his arms around me to hold me in place. "We should go see your brother," I say between broken breaths.

"The moment we finish looking into whatever clue they found, you're mine, spitfire." He kisses my shoulder and pulls me off him.

I turn to face him as his cum drips down my leg. His hand glides up my inner thigh, and with his middle and ring finger, presses his release back inside me. Pulling me to him with his fingers hooked in my pussy, I straddle him. "Need another round?" I tease.

"I'll never get enough of you."

Cameron and Lizzy are waiting for us in the workroom, talking excitedly over a laptop. Amanda's hand is firmly in mine; I bring it to my lips and release it, laughing at my brother who is obviously pursuing our junior research assistant.

"What did we miss?" Amanda asks cheerfully.

"Well, while you were getting laid, we figured out the Carse painting is a fake. The museum has the original and tested for authenticity. We took Amanda's suggestion and looked into old maps and it led us to this castle. We're in the right place," Cam says proudly.

"So, what next?" Amanda asks. "Do you open the painting, or…?"

Lizzy adjusts her glasses. "We started without you and found this…" She zooms in on the image on her laptop, then hands me parchment pressed in glass.

THE KEY TO A GOOD DRINK IS AGE.

Frowning as I read aloud, Amanda asks, "What the fuck is that supposed to mean?"

"We found a couple of old maps, and there used to be fruit grown here for wine. So, now we're looking into which varietals were offered. Some wine ages well, others don't," Cam says with a shrug. "For example, the vines grown here were mostly white grapes for Chardonnay or Pinot Grigio. Red could never grow here. But in the collection of imported wines, there were also a few award-winning Merlots."

"Should've been whisky," Amanda grumbles. Cam and I snicker.

Cam continues, "We were going to visit the wine cellar as soon as you were done... *you know*."

"Oh, for fuck's sake, yes, we had sex," Amanda says, rolling her eyes, then clucks her tongue. "You're one to talk."

"Your key," I say quietly, ignoring her admission. "Maybe it opens more than just the one door?"

Amanda narrows her eyes. "It was a coincidence, Jack."

"What key?" Lizzy asks. My voice was apparently not low enough when I asked Amanda.

Amanda pulls her necklace out from her shirt. "My grandmother gave this to me. It opened a cellar door

earlier, and now this one"—she points her thumb at me
—"thinks I'm some sort of heir to the Black family."

Cameron takes a closer look. "When did you receive this
from your nan?"

"I don't know. Ten, fifteen years ago?"

"This is a Kildalton Cross," Cam whispers, then raises
his voice, "Liz, come take a look at this."

Lizzy steps closer. "Shit, this is just like the ones you
dropped off at the museum a couple weeks ago."

"Hold up, what?" Amanda asks with wide eyes. "A
couple weeks ago?"

"I was in San Francisco to drop off a couple pieces
around the time you two were in London," Cameron
replies, but this is the first I'm hearing that he saw her
on that trip. He extended his trip to meet with a staff
member... I let out a full laugh. He pins me with a
warning look, knowing I figured it out. "Maybe Barty is
right and you're a Black after all?"

"You two are mad," Amanda grumbles. "It's all
just a—"

"Amanda," Lizzy says softly, "it's not. Think about it.
What if you are?"

Amanda steps back. "Even if I was part of the family
you're researching, this is a fucking treasure hunt for a
stolen items. It doesn't matter. It doesn't belong to the

Black family, or to me." She pins Cameron with narrowed eyes. "Yeah, I read your articles."

"What does it open?" Cam asks her.

"We got stuck in the wine cellar and needed something to jam into the lock to get out," Amanda replies. "It doesn't actually open anything, it just happened to be small enough to fit."

I pull her to me and whisper beside her ear, "It wasn't jammed into the lock, it was a perfect fit." My words accidentally come out sultry and she shivers.

"Fuck, you two, this is serious!" Lizzy says, hands on her hips.

"Let's head back to the cellar. The obvious answer is her key opens something there," I say, releasing my spitfire from my hold.

"And if it doesn't?" Amanda asks defiantly.

"Then, it doesn't," I assure her.

We make our way to the wine cellar, and the moment we enter both Cam and Lizzy burst into laughter. "What the fuck is this?"

39

AMANDA

A blush creeps up my neck when I spot the candles Jack lit for us earlier. "Probably a seance," I offer.

Lizzy pins me with a knowing smirk but attempts to cover for me. "Yeah, super haunted castle"

The men move further into the cellar, and I whisper to her, "Really? Haunted castle? That's the best you've got?"

She stifles a laugh as the boys light a few of the candles. "What do you expect? This looks like something out of a bad goth music video from the 90s."

"I was thinking early 80s, but I'm with you on that one," I giggle.

"Can I see your necklace again?" Cam's question quickly ends my laughter.

I unclasp it and look at Jack, who nods as I pass it to Cameron. Cameron attempts to use it to open the door opposite the entry of the cellar. "Don't break it." I wince as he jiggles the necklace in the lock, though I was willing to part with it hours ago if it meant I could leave this wine prison. "How old are these bottles?" I ask, swiping dust off one of them with my index finger.

"Old enough to have you praying to the porcelain gods for a night," Lizzy says, checking one of them.

"Such a waste," I grumble.

The boys are unable to open the door, reinforcing my stance that I'm definitely not a member of this Black family. I pull a bottle of wine from the rack and brush some dirt off the label to find it's nearly a hundred and fifty years old. "The key to a good drink is age," I say to myself.

"What's that, lass?" Cameron asks.

"Nothing, I was just thinking about the clue. The key to a good drink is age. What if—"

"The oldest bottle!" Lizzy chimes in.

"That's what I was going to say, but, whatever." I sigh in defeat. Lizzy laughs.

We begin searching for the oldest bottle in the cellar. As I'm reaching for a bottle on the top shelf, Jack walks up to me, wrapping his arms around me from behind. He whispers with a kiss to my neck, "I'll get the ones on the higher shelves."

"1832," Lizzy calls, and we continue to shout out dates that are lower than the one previously mentioned.

"1818," I yell, followed by a, "Kidding, 1816."

Once we've checked every bottle, the oldest is 1770.

"Shit, America wasn't technically America then," I say, mostly to myself.

"Do we open it?" Lizzy excitedly asks.

"I sure as fuck am not drinking a red wine that's over 200 years old," I teasingly tell her.

"We'll start with the label and go from there," Jack insists with an authoritative tone.

Well, shit, so much for a fun treasure hunt.

Jack and Cameron whisper to each other like a couple of school girls, and while I love this for him, this is worse than a cliffhanger at the end of a prequel novella. "Can you peel it off?" I ask impatiently.

Cameron continues examining the bottle as Jack's gaze undresses me—he has the worst possible timing. When his eyes reach mine, he quickly returns his attention to the bottle and clears his throat. "We'll need orange oil, and we'll need to quickly preserve it."

Lizzy rummages through her pack. "Lucky for you, I have both," she tells them, holding up a small droplet bottle and glass.

This girl is getting laid and still managed to pack some essentials. Meanwhile, I'm just here because I wanted to spend time with Jack... and suddenly I'm feeling like I'm not actually needed. The three of them went to school for this, and here I am with the creative writing degree I barely graduated with, and all I have to show for it is writing practically porn on page.

I'm lost in thought when Cameron exclaims, "You're fucking brilliant." I'm not sure who he's referring to but I assume they found something interesting. I try to join in on their excitement, even though I'm not feeling it anymore.

There's a message on the back:

YOU'RE A PAWN IF YOU CROSS THE WRONG BLACK

"What the hell does that mean?" I ask, frowning.

"It means don't piss off Amanda," Lizzy chuckles.

"Ha. Ha. Very funny. I'm serious," I tell her, rolling my eyes.

"Maybe his family?" Cameron asks.

"Or Ewen himself?" Jack wonders.

"Oh, come on!" I sigh. "It's lowercase. It's not a person, it's a thing."

"What would you cross that could be black?" Lizzy asks, pacing, tapping her finger to her lips.

"It mentions pawns. It's probably chess." They all look at me in awe. "Seriously? Am I carrying the whole team here? To think I—" All at once, Jack's lips crash into mine. My muffled protest does nothing as his tongue demands entry I too willingly give. "It was just a—" Despite my protest, he continues his assault on my mouth as if he needs me more than he needs to breathe. "Your brother's right there."

When Jack and I break apart, he shakes his head with a light laugh. "It might not be chess. But, fuck, if it is…." He tightens his bun with a beaming smile. "Shite, you could be saving us weeks of research. You're coming along to all my digs." He kisses me one last time before returning his attention to the bottle and message.

"Oh, look, the romantic suspense author solved another clue!" I sarcastically exclaim.

This whole thing is now feeling ridiculous, as if we're playing a board game and need to guess who unalived who and name the weapon. While I was interested before, I'm now annoyed. I sigh and step out, needing a moment away from my two nerdy friends and equally nerdy boyfriend. I take a seat on the stairwell and no one seems to notice.

The cellar door closes with a thud and I rush to it. Lizzy shrieks from the other side as I grasp at the handle. Jack and Cam yell for me. I grasp for my neck-lace, but realize it's not there, Cam still has it. "Jack," I holler through the thick door, "use my necklace." In under a minute, the door is ajar. I expect Jack but find

Cameron with his hand still on the key pendant in the lock.

"Not of the Black family?" he asks with a smirk.

"It's not like that. If it was supposed to be some sort of skeleton key, it would open that other door, too," I counter. Unlike the person leaving us clues, these men and Lizzy have a wild imagination. "If the clue is chess, we should go upstairs and see if—"

A rumbling that sounds like an earthquake shakes the castle. The cellar door closes again. This time, a steel, wrought-iron gate pulls in front of it. "Jack!" I helplessly scream. I don't have my necklace and the gate is too heavy to lift as I grip it with both hands and heave, to no avail. "There's an iron gate on the outside."

"It's alright. Lizzy got impatient and smashed the bottle. There was a key inside," Cameron yells. Because of course there is; the person leaving us clues is an unin-spired asshole. "It fits in the lock to the other door, but not the one we came in. There's a tunnel. We're going to see if it leads us to anything."

I take it back. Jack, Cameron, and Lizzy are assholes. Who in their right mind goes into some random ass tunnel in the hope of finding lost treasure? Did the key fit? Sure. But does it mean they should've used it? No! This is the equivalent of someone running upstairs in a horror movie. I rub my face in my hands. Dumbasses.

I call out one last time, "Stay put, I'll call for help."

I know there's no point. All three are probably already elbows deep in spiderwebs and loving it. Since I seem to be the only sensible person in the mix, I rush up the stairwell to grab whatever tools I can find and, if I'm lucky, a couple of flashlights. My reception is garbage upstairs, but I'll alert the authorities—some hot Scottish fireman should save the day.

I make it to the last step when a gate crashes down in front of me with a clang.

Mother fucker.

"Help!" I scream to no one.

I'm stuck in a castle dungeon with no food, no water, and no cell reception. My boyfriend is prancing around in some tunnel somewhere with his brother and my friend's sister—who Cam is most definitely fucking. We've been here a week and I'm living in some sort of fucked up adventure romance I never asked for.

This is it. This is how my story ends. Here lies Amanda Black. She leaves behind her collection of smut and dreams of getting a dog one day.

I could be in New York right now. Jackson could have a chai ready and waiting for me.

Fucking hot Scot with his declarations…

I need to find a way out of here, or I'm fucked in the most unliteral sense ever.

40

JACK

"Amanda is on the other side! I won't leave her," I growl at Cameron.

"She'll call someone for help. This is a once in a lifetime opportunity. Look!" He gestures down the small passageway. "This is why we're archaeologists. We weren't meant to teach at a uni, we were meant to discover things like this. There's a fucking tunnel, Jack. A tunnel your lass helped us find. Let's see where it leads."

"It's stupid," Lizzy counters, but then adds, "But I agree. This is the shit we live for. I grew up reading and watching adventure books and movies, which inspired me to study archaeology and anthropology. I'm certainly not meant to spend my life cataloging artefacts. I say we go. Amanda is a grown woman and can fend for herself for a couple of hours." Lizzy marches into the tunnel and Cam follows. I pause for a moment, but they're right, we need to see where this leads. "I mean, your girl will definitely be hangry in an hour, but she'll survive until we return. Pisses me off, she could eat tacos all day and not gain a pound." She sighs. "She'll be fine. Worst case, you'll rescue her, and live happily ever after like the end of one of my sister's fantasy books."

I like the sound of that…

No.

I need to get to Amanda.

"As fun as that sounds, I didn't map this tunnel out. We don't know where it leads and could end up on another side of the castle without a way out," I attempt to reason with them as we walk further into the tunnel.

"Where's your sense of adventure, Barty?" Cam teases but then concedes, "I get it. Your lass is trapped on the other side of the cellar." He lowers his voice so only I can hear, "If Liz was stuck, I'd tear down the door to make sure she was safe."

With Lizzy far enough ahead, I whisper, "You like her, don't you? You're not just…"

"A wee bit," he winces. "I know she's young, but I like spending time with her."

"Guys," Lizzy calls. "Amanda was right." We catch up to her and there's an entire chess board with pieces etched in the stone wall, as if someone abandoned it mid-game. "The clue said 'you're a pawn if you cross the wrong black.' I don't play chess. Any ideas?"

I scan the board and notice the pawn could take the bishop or knight. "Forking."

"I'm sorry, what?" Lizzy laughs.

"Forking," I repeat. "It's when you attack two pieces at once."

"Oh, I totally thought you said 'fucking.' You two with that accent, gets me every time. Forking makes way more sense. So, what now?"

Cam traces the stone knight and bishop, tapping the knight. "This one has a Kildalton Cross. There's a small hole right here that looks a lot like a…" He reaches in his pocket and takes out Amanda's necklace, pressing it into the stone. "She's a Black, Barty. No denying it now," he chuckles, turning the key.

The wall shifts toward us and opens to the left. Lizzy gasps, and Cam can't wipe the smirk off his face. I step into the room, half-expecting to find the missing arte-facts we've been searching for. It's empty except for a small, black-stained wooden box. Cam and I kneel in front of it, carefully unclasping the metal holding it shut. Inside, there's a scroll tied in leather and page that looks as if it was ripped out of a diary or notebook.

"Do you have gloves?" I ask Lizzy. She nods and takes out three sets. We put them on and carefully untie the leather and open the rolled parchment.

It reads:

WORN WITH PRIDE, WHEN LOVE WON'T DIVIDE

Lizzy mutters the words to herself and Cam sits back on his heels, raking his hand through his hair. If Amanda was here, I'm sure she'd have it figured out already. Every clue brings us closer, but I'm beginning to wonder if it'll end in an empty room like this one. We have dozens of men and women coming on-site to help us search this castle and two others; is there any point in them coming?

"What's worn with pride? Maybe a wedding ring?" Lizzy asks.

"You're in Scotland, lass. It could be tartan… A kilt." Cam beams with excitement.

"A wedding?" I offer. "Love won't divide."

"Maybe there was a big wedding? Or it could be as simple as finding something here with the family tartan or something?" Lizzy shrugs. "It feels a little anti-climactic."

"Aye," Cam huffs. "What's written on the other paper?"

"It's from Ewen's journals; it's his handwriting."

Cam eyes widen. "Shite. We should look for a way out of here and find your lass. I want to examine it."

As they step out of the room, a glimmer of light bouncing in the corner catches my attention. It's small, no bigger than a coin. As I approach and lean over to expect it to be a gold piece, I find it's a piece of broken glass with an etching. I shine my light on it.

AMB

"Fuck," I mutter. Cam and Lizzy look over my shoulder. "Those are Amanda's initials."

41

AMANDA

Stuck in a fucking castle… Well, this is certainly going in a book.

Sitting on the steps of the stairwell, I rest the back of my head against the wall. I'm afraid to go exploring, I'll probably get lost. Staying here is equally useless, though. I grab my flashlight and make my way back down the stairs. I check the door to the cellar and it's still covered in iron.

I think back to the morning after the gala; this little adventure sounded like it would be a great inspiration for a book. Instead, I'm stuck in a castle with very little adventuring happening. I'm dirty, starving, and annoyed. I'm not cut out for this—I'm an author, not an archaeologist.

I bet Blair was better at this fortune and glory questing…

I shake the thought away and continue down one of the corridors. While I might not have cell reception down here, I'm tracking my movements in my notes app.

Right turn.
Twenty steps.
Left turn.
Eleven steps.
Scary ass skeleton on the right.
Ten steps.
Gross dead rat.
Right turn.

Dead end. There's a door with a thick circular handle. I stuff my phone in my back pocket and use both hands to pull it open. Surprisingly, it's not locked. I take out my phone again.

Unlocked door.
Seven steps.
Left turn.
Four stairs.
Leather whip.

Whip?

What the hell? Is this some kind of BDSM dungeon? I pick it up and it's definitely a bullwhip. It's not that old and in surprisingly good condition. I check the handle.

BWJ

Jack? He must've been surveying this space and dropped it. I coil it up and put it on my shoulder like a purse strap.

This will come in handy later…

Twenty steps.
Right turn.
Ten steps.
Six stairs.

There are voices echoing the halls. I call out, "Jack? Cam?" I continue down the corridor and count each step to myself.

Seven steps.

"Lizzy?"

"Amanda?" Jack yells. "Where are you?"

"I don't know!"

"Stay there. Keep talking and we'll find you!" Cam hollers.

"You know I suck at following directions," I laugh to myself.

"Amanda, you need to keep talking so we can follow your voice," Lizzy says, but her voice sounds more distant. They're moving away from me.

Fuck. I try not to panic. "Here. I'm here. Not sure what you want me to say. Should I start reciting poetry? I don't have a good singing voice, or I'd offer you a song. Jack, did you know you left your whip down here? Why do you need a whip? Those cow-sheep things don't deserve that, you know. They're adorable. I'm not into being whipped, in case you were wondering. Maybe a paddle. I think I could handle a paddle."

Jack comes into view and I run to him in relief, wrapping my arms around his neck and climbing him like a tree. He holds me close, kisses my shoulder and whispers, "Fuck, spitfire, I was so worried about you."

"Sure, you totally were," I say sarcastically, confident he was giddy over finding a secret tunnel. "Did you find your treasure?"

He doesn't let go of me. "No, but I found you."

"We found another clue," Lizzy says from behind him. I glance up to see Cam unable to take his eyes off her—she's so fucking oblivious. I stifle a laugh and she adds, "Your initials are in a piece of glass and there was a small scroll with 'worn with pride, when love won't divide' written on it."

I slide down Jack's body but he still keeps me flush with him as my feet hit the floor. "Sounds like some sort of slogan," I laugh.

"We think it might be a wedding. Maybe a tartan or kilt," Jack says, his eyes dark. If Cam and Lizzy weren't here, he'd have me naked in seconds. "As soon as we're out of here, we'll research it."

Cameron hands me my necklace and Jack clasps it around my neck. "It opened up another door, Amanda. There's no denying that the necklace is from the Black family," Jack says softly.

"There's no way I'm related," I insist. "My family isn't even Scottish—that I know of."

"What's your nan's name?" he asks.

"Fiona, why?"

Jack and Cameron look at each other, eyes wide. When Jack's return to me, he tells me, "She was the last living Black... I suspect not anymore, though."

I step out of his hold. "No, there's no way."

Jack sighs. "Black was her maiden name, wasn't it?" I nod. "What doesn't make sense is she didn't have any children. At least not any that were on public record."

"See, I told you! It can't be the same Fiona Black." I triumphantly exclaim.

"While I love this little revelation, can we maybe get out of here?" Lizzy asks, chewing on her lip.

Jack chuckles and kisses my forehead. "Come on, spit-fire. We'll figure it all out upstairs."

Cam and Jack lead the way back to the stairwell that's blocked at the top. We'll need to find a way to open it, but he insists there's another way out down another corridor if we can't. As we walk past the cellar, he asks, "A paddle, huh?"

"Oh, right, your whip." I hand it to him. "Not really for me. I'm always down to try anything but I think that's more Layla's thing."

"I didn't need to know that," he laughs.

I kiss his cheek and whisper, "I prefer chapter seven."

42

JACK

The top of the stairs is still blocked, so we take a side passage that, thankfully, is free of iron gates.

In our workroom, Lizzy is pressing the new clue in glass to preserve it while Cam is examining the broken piece with Amanda's initials. I pull up the Black family genealogy in hopes of finding out more about Amanda's nan. I found a picture of her and Amanda confirmed it's the same woman. What we can't figure out is why her mother isn't listed anywhere; it's like she never existed at all. I place an order for a DNA test to see if it will give us any answers.

Amanda rests her head on my shoulder and yawns, but insists, "I'm fine. Just need a little nap."

"It's late." I kiss the top of her head. "Go shower and rest. I won't be working much longer."

She sighs but doesn't fight me, kissing me on the cheek as she stands and leaves.

I scour document after document and stumble across adoption paperwork for an Amanda Black, who would be around my wee spitfire's age. The parent information is censored—another dead end. We've never talked about our families, so I'm not sure if she's adopted. If she was, and doesn't know it, I don't want to accidentally drop this on her now. I'll wait until the morning to show her. She's exhausted after the day we've had.

Lizzy's phone buzzes on the table, but she ignores it. It buzzes again and she turns it over. "It's my mom, I'm going to step out for a minute."

Cam and I return to our research, but a few minutes later, Lizzy rushes back into the room, her face as white as a ghost.

"What's wrong?" Cameron asks her.

"I need to find Amanda, is she in your room?"

"Aye," I reply. "Everything ok with your mum?"

"She, uh... she's fine." Lizzy swallows hard. "Amanda's book. My mom said it released early, but published under a Blair Jackson. That's your ex-wife, right?"

"What the fuck?" Cam says through a cough.

I don't answer Lizzy, I rush out of the workroom to find Amanda. Lizzy follows, saying something but I don't hear it. My ears are ringing and the anger coursing through my veins makes me want to punch a wall.

The shower is running, so Lizzy waits outside as I enter the bathroom. "Amanda?"

She opens the shower door. "Yeah?"

"You have to get out, love. Lizzy has some news about your book."

"Based on that frown, I'm guessing I'm not a number one best seller?" Amanda reaches between my brows to swipe away the creases.

I take her hand and kiss her palm. "No, it's Blair." I shut off the water and grab a towel for her. "Come on."

"Blair?" Amanda steps out, her brow furrowing in confusion, and I wrap her in the towel, holding her against me. "What's going on?"

"I don't know, something about her publishing your book." I release her to dry off.

"What? How could she…" Amanda looks off in thought then returns her gaze to me. "Where's Lizzy?"

My anger about Blair dissipates as Amanda stands before me naked. Water drips down her body, and after the day we've had, all I want to do is trace the droplets with my tongue.

Fuck, what's wrong with me? Her book was stolen and I'm seconds away from hauling her over my shoulder. I want to steal her away and make love to my spitfire.

Amanda's eerily quiet, either piecing this together or still processing it. Once she's dried off and dressed, we meet

Lizzy in our room. She explains to Amanda that Blair published the manuscript as her own and that Amanda needs to call her publisher. Since Lizzy's mother owns the company, with Ben and Julian as investors, I'm hoping that between all of them, someone can right this.

Amanda's fist is balled at her side the entire time Lizzy speaks. I keep her hand tightly mine, swiping my thumb against her knuckles, but it does little to calm either of us.

"My aunt is a corporate lawyer and knows a lot about copyright law, if you need to talk to someone?" Lizzy offers.

"Yeah, I need to figure out how to take it down," Amanda says evenly. Her grip on my hand tightens. "I need to go back home to sort it out."

No.

My heart stops, and it's as if all of the air has left my lungs. "I'll come with you."

"You have to finish your quest for fortune and glory," Amanda says teasingly, but her eyes remain filled with anger. She cups my cheek, and I cover her hand with mine. "Stay. I need to go destroy your ex-wife for copyright infringement... and for not loving you the way you deserve. But mostly for stealing my book. She shouldn't have fucked with what's mine."

I kiss her palm, hope filling my chest that she'll return to me if I stay. "Alright, spitfire, I'll stay. When do you want to leave? I'll drive you."

"No, that's stupid. You're not going to waste an entire day driving round trip. I'll leave in the morning. Maybe Cameron can lend me his truck."

"Hey, guys. So... I'm still here," Lizzy chimes in, raising her hand. Amanda and I laugh. "I'll probably go with you, if that's ok?"

"Sure," Amanda replies with a sigh. "This is so fucked up."

There's a chance Lizzy's a wee bit like my spitfire and is running from my brother, but I offer anyway, "You're welcome to stay on with Cam and I."

"Are you sure?" she asks with a grimace. "I came here with Amanda to be some sort of cockblock, but *clearly* that's not really an issue anymore. I'd love to stay on and figure out what the next clue is." I glance at Amanda. She's pressing her lips together to stifle a laugh.

"Absolutely," I reply. "Why don't we clean everything up in the workroom and get an early start tomorrow?"

Lizzy nods, wishes us good night, and leaves our room. As soon as the door is shut, I wrap Amanda in my arms and she returns the embrace. "I'm so sorry," I whisper.

She looks up at me, resting her chin on my chest. "I'll call Ben in the morning. I only had to use half a billion to cover Blair's investment, so I still have a billion in the bank. That should be more than enough to publicly destroy her. I'm sure Ben will throw in some coin to make it happen."

I shake my head. "She's not worth it. Take back your book and let her go. She was trying to steal my research and have her name attached to this place. Seems like she set her sights on you instead, but no good can come from letting her get to you."

She hums thoughtfully, then says, "In the contract, it mentions preservation and renovations. Is it all covered? I don't want to spend a dime of Ben's money if you need it."

"I'll be alright, lass." I hold her tighter and sigh. "I'm more worried about you and your book." Amanda lifts onto her toes and kisses me. "Go make a couple calls and book your flight for tomorrow. I'll wrap everything up with Cameron and will be back before you know it."

I leave her to make her arrangements and return to the workroom, walking in on Cameron obviously about to kiss Lizzy. I slowly back out of the room but my boots on the stone floor give me away. Lizzy steps back from Cam and I can't help but laugh as both of them shoot me a glance of guilt.

"Can you two make sure everything is prepped for tomorrow?" I ask.

"Absolutely, Barty," he says with a wink.

"I should head to bed," Lizzy says, slinking toward the door. "I already cleared my station to get an early start tomorrow." She rushes out of the room, and my brother can't wipe the ridiculous grin from his face.

I follow Lizzy, needing to make sure my spitfire is alright. She was too collected, too quiet, when I left her. Cam calls after me as I'm a foot out the door. "I know you're going to follow Amanda home."

I pause and turn with a smirk. He's right. If she decides to stay there, I'll move thousands of miles to be with her. The moment this project is complete, I'll be wherever she is.

She's home.

43

AMANDA

This is worse than when Becca and Julian were outed by his agent to the media. It's worse than Layla and I dealing with a shady book publisher. This is worse than…well, most things. This is someone stealing something that's *mine*. I managed to—for the most part— keep my cool around Jack, but now that he's not here, I allow myself to stew in my rage.

I book an early afternoon flight, giving me enough time to drive to the airport. Being in the middle of nowhere, I can't exactly call a rideshare to pick me up, and I don't want Jack driving me. Either he'll want to pull over for a quickie, resulting in me missing my flight, or spending more time with him will make me second guess leaving. He's right, I should let this go, and maybe in time, I will. For now, I need to get my book pulled from all distribution sites and lawyer up.

Jack returns to the room with a bottle of whiskey and two glasses. "Have a drink with me?"

"Sure. I don't normally drink whiskey by itself, but *when in Scotland...*" I'm careful to keep my tone light. If this is my last night here for a while, I don't want to spend it in a shitty mood, or sad that I have to leave.

He pours a little into mine, and a bit more for himself. I clink my glass to his and take a sip, coughing as it burns my throat. He laughs into his glass while I pick up my phone, scrolling my music. I land on the song "Until I Found You" by Stephen Sanchez and press play.

I set down my whiskey and offer my hand. "Dance with me?"

"Always."

With a small smile, Jack removes his glasses and sets them on the table. He then takes my hand, tucking it against his chest and wrapping his other hand to my lower back. We hardly move an inch in either direction, but I don't care. I can't tear my eyes away from his beautiful green ones. Almost a year ago, this man changed my life, making me fall for a complete stranger in one night. To think I almost walked away from him, because of someone who is the furthest thing from a friend. I was a fucking idiot.

A stray tear leaves my eye. *So much for keeping things light.* Jack doesn't brush it away, instead kissing the wet trail it left behind on my cheek. When he pulls back, his eyes are glassy and it's enough for mine to well with more tears I can't keep from falling. I rest my forehead on his chest and try to keep my breath steady.

His lips pressed to the top of my head, he whispers, "I love you, my wee spitfire."

I shamelessly dry my wet eyes on his shirt and chuckle, "I'm not an easy person to love."

"Doesn't matter. You're mine."

He tilts my chin and kisses me. Unlike his other kisses, it's tender and sweet. There's no way I'll be able to stay away from him for long. The minute things are sorted back home, I'm running right back into his arms, if he'll still have me.

The song ends and I pull back to look at him. "I love you, Jack." I link my arms around his neck but stifle a yawn, not wanting to kill the moment.

"I'm going to take a quick shower." He kisses my fore-head, and I sigh against him. "Go rest."

Jack slides his hands up to my hands and pulls them down to kiss the inside of my wrists, one at a time. Without a word, he tugs back the covers, finishes his whiskey, and leaves to take a shower. I strip out of my clothes and slide into bed. The moment my head hits the pillow, my eyes are heavy and I have to fight to stay awake.

I fail and wake up to a dip in the mattress, and smile to myself as he climbs into bed behind me. He pulls me close and peppers soft kisses on my shoulder. I can't help pressing my ass against his hard cock, loving the low growl that comes from him every time I do it.

I turn my head enough for my lips to reach his as he caresses my thigh. He pulls my leg up and over his and whispers, "I thought you were asleep."

"I'll sleep better if I come."

Jack's fingers trail up my thigh until they reach my clit. Tracing slow circles, eliciting a moan from me, he murmurs against my lips, "I'm going to miss playing with this pretty cunt every night." He pauses long enough to line up his cock with my wet pussy, teasing my entrance before pushing inside. He remains still, deep inside me, and continues circling my clit. "I'm going to finish what I started earlier tonight."

I snake my hand around his neck, needing his mouth on me. As his lips brush my neck, he doesn't mark me like he usually does. Instead, he kisses from my ear, down my neck and collarbone, finally landing on my shoulder. He begins slow thrusts, pushing deep inside me as the pressure on my clit intensifies. I swallow hard, knowing exactly what he's doing. This isn't hot sex in a hotel room; he's claiming me as his in a different way. I give in, and let him love me.

He continues the same pace and pressure, leaving me panting. With every kiss, every thrust, I wind tighter and tighter. "I'm close," I whimper into the darkness.

"Not yet," he says against my neck. "I want to feel you come around my cock as you take all of me."

"It's too much."

"Tell me to stop and I will. But I'm staying inside you until you say the word." He continues his slow thrusts and kisses my neck harder, drawing the skin into his mouth and sucking enough to mark me. His teeth graze the mark he left, forcing my orgasm to crash into me. I cry out his name and he chuckles darkly, "I thought I told you to wait."

My pussy pulses around his cock as he quickens his thrusts. It prolongs my high, making my vision blur and my body quiver. With a final push, he holds himself inside me, wrapping his arm around my middle to keep me close. He growls "mine" when he comes, and I feel the rumble along my spine.

When I finally catch my breath, I huff a small laugh. "I think that's my line."

"No, my wee spitfire." Jack kisses the spot he marked me and pulls me tighter. "You're mine as much as I'm yours."

With him still inside me, every ounce of anger I felt earlier has melted away, and I drift off asleep with the man I've fallen hopelessly in love with.

Waking up wrapped in Jack's arms makes leaving today even more difficult. Once my eyes adjust to the light peeking through the curtains, I reach for my phone to check the time, spotting a few missed text messages in a group chat with Layla and Becca.

BECCA

Grab your pitchforks ladies!

LAYLA

Can't I just have Ben destroy her? I'm pretty comfy in bed right now.

BECCA

Amanda - where are you?!

LAYLA

It's 4am here, Becs.

BECCA

Right, sorry! She's probably getting serviced by your husband's cousin as a wakeup call.

LAYLA

What?

Since when?

BECCA

Since the gala, I think.

LAYLA

Amanda! You little slut! Why did no one tell me?

BECCA

You were busy.

LAYLA

I was not! Why didn't Ben tell me?

You all suck.

I bite my lip to keep from laughing, and reply.

No wakeup call. Sorry to disappoint.

BECCA

Where have you been?

What's the deal with Blair Jackson?

Who keeps their ex-husband's name? That's fucked up.

Also, why does this book read like it's unedited?

Shit, Becs. Have enough questions? Blair was an alpha reader, she had my rough draft.

LAYLA

If you two ever dare to steal my books...

Yeah, because your pirate smut would go over amazing with my readers. Hard pass.

But you still need to send me your new book you're working on. I can't wait to read it!

BECCA

Can we just video chat? I need to know what's going on with this bitch.

I press the video button and my friend's faces appear on my screen. "Hey, guys."

"Are you naked?" Becca asks, pulling the phone closer to her face to double check.

I glance down. and I'm only covered by Jack's arm over my tits. "Sort of." I shimmy the sheet up. "Better?"

"You have great titties. Just let them breathe," Layla laughs.

"Shh, you'll wake Jack." At the sound of his name, he pulls down the sheet and returns his arm to my breasts. "Jack," I whisper, "I'm on a call. I kind of need to cover up."

He groans and nips at my shoulder. "It's too early, sprite. Tell the hens you'll call back later."

"Hi Jack," Layla sings. "Did we interrupt your *wakeup call?*"

"Guys, stop! I only have a few minutes," I tell them.

"Two minutes," he grumbles.

I quickly tell my friends about Blair and how I'm going back to New York to sort things out and meet with my publisher. Becca and Layla attempted to pry information out of their husbands, but Ben and Julian insisted they couldn't say anything. As much as I don't mind my friends knowing, I appreciate the confidentiality. Jack begins to get a bit growly, nipping at my shoulder, so I hang up and turn in his arms.

"Sorry about that," I say, toying with his beard.

"I selfishly want you to myself this morning. Hope that's alright?" he asks, pulling me closer.

"I'm all yours." I kiss him softly but he still lets out a low growl, which I feel everywhere.

"What time do you have to leave?"

"About an hour. I need to see if Cam will let me take his truck."

"Do you need your suitcase?"

"Yes," I say, playfully smacking his chest. "What kind of question is that?"

"I could take you on my motorbike. You'll get there faster, but you won't be able to bring luggage," he says through a yawn.

"Are you going to wrap me in bubble wrap first?" I tease.

"Of course." Jack kisses me, and I sigh against his lips. "I have to finish a few things and I want to show you something before we go."

"Is it your cock? Because, spoiler, I've seen it plenty. Though, I could use another peek for the road."

"Fuck," he chuckles. "I'm going to miss you."

"Don't," I warn.

"I know... but I will." He tucks a few stray hairs off my face, his eyes soft. "I ordered you a DNA test but I'll have it routed to New York. I found a few documents last night, including one that shows there was an Amanda Black adopted around the time you were born."

"Yeah, it's probably me," I reply. "My grandmother had to adopt me when my mother died."

"It doesn't list who the parents were, but your nan doesn't have any record of children. Do you have any pictures of your mother?"

I think for a moment, not recalling a single photo album or picture of my mother. My grandmother mentioned that there was a flood and she lost most of them, but *all of them?* I shake my head. "No, I don't. When I get home, I'll take a look. I have a box of her things, there might be something in it."

"I hope you do." He sits up. "Come on. I'll make you breakfast, then I'll show you what I found."

I secretly hoped for a 'wakeup call' like Layla suggested, but with my stomach grumbling, I'll settle for my hot boyfriend making me breakfast.

44

JACK

After a quick bite and tea, Amanda packs up a few things she'll need when she's home. I don't really have the time to take her to the airport, but if her luggage is here, it'll increase the chances of her coming back. We look through the adoption paperwork I found, and it is indeed hers. I make a copy to take with her. There's a chance she can access more than I can, being that it's her own information.

While I don't have bubble wrap, I do have several layers of leather I can wrap her in. The drive to Edinburgh should be around four hours on my bike, giving me an hour with her before she has to check in at the airport. I'll take every moment I have with her until she has to leave.

The roads are clear, despite the light dusting of snow in some parts. We've had a fairly dry winter, which I'm thankful for. The last thing we need is to get stranded on the side of the road, like I was when Ben got married.

After crossing the Long Loch Bridge, we pull over at the viewing area for Eilean Donan Castle to stretch our legs for a minute. Together, we find a quiet spot to sit and look out onto the water. I pull her onto my lap and keep her close, dreading the ticking clock until she's gone.

"That's the castle I was supposed to tour. The one I bid on at the gala," she chuckles.

"When you come back, we'll go," I offer.

"I thought it would be bigger."

"It's plenty big, sprite."

Amanda shivers, and I lift her off my lap to retrieve the small blanket I have tucked in the side of my bike. I wrap it around her and rest my forehead on hers. "Thank you," she whispers.

We look out onto the water, appreciating the castle in the distance for a while longer, while she tells me about an idea she has for an adventure romance book. She insists it won't be about me, but from the sounds of it, she's definitely including some facts with her fiction. I wouldn't mind if she did, but I remind her that the night we had in New York is ours alone.

The rest of the ride to Edinburgh is uneventful; the roads clear of hazards we are able to make good time. I'll miss her arms wrapped around me on the ride back. Before taking her to the airport, we stop at a wee book-shop. We don't have time to browse, but we pick out a book for each other. Even though I have a copy, she choses *Maybe in Fifty* and signs it:

NO NEED TO WAIT FIFTY, WE FOUND EACH OTHER.
XO, YOUR WEE SPITFIRE
P.S. DON'T SELL THIS, IT'S NOT WORTH ANYTHING
WITHOUT A REAL SIGNATURE.

After the bookshop, we grab a quick bite to eat and we're off to the airport. I park my bike so I can walk her in. There are a few men in line wearing kilts, all different tartans.

Amanda smiles and says, "For the record, you look way hotter in a kilt than they do." I mirror her smile and shake my head at her ridiculous comment. "When you get back, you should look into the wedding theory. There could be a textile somewhere in the castle."

"Cameron is researching it today."

"I'm pretty sure there's exactly zero research going on there today. He's definitely too busy fucking Lizzy," Amanda says with a quirked eyebrow.

"Aye, he's a wee bit smitten."

She checks the time. "Fuck, I need to go."

"I know," I concede. I slide my hand up to her neck and pull her lips to mine. Her fingers tangle in my hair as she kisses me like it's our last. I refuse to believe that's the case. My chest tightens as we break apart. "I don't know how to say goodbye to you."

"Good, because we aren't saying goodbye," she says with a small smirk, though her eyes are etched with everything but her usual joy.

I glance up at the ticket counter, the line growing with passengers. "Are you flying first class?"

"No, but I don't have to check my bag and my ticket is linked on my phone, so I can go straight to security." Amanda reaches behind her neck to unclasp her necklace, takes it off, and offers it to me. "You might need this."

My hand covers hers. "No, it's your nan's."

She turns my hand over and places it in my palm, her hand firm against mine. "Collateral. Now I have to come back for it." I chuckle and take her in my arms one last time. "No goodbyes, but I need to go." She presses a sweet kiss to my lips. I shut my eyes tight, wanting to memorise the feeling of her against me. "I love you."

"I love you, too, spitfire."

Amanda steps out of my hold, and I watch her walk away. As soon as she's out of sight, I look back to the ticket counter, the line dwindling. Without a second thought, I do the one thing that feels right.

45

AMANDA

The entire flight, I'm an emotional wreck. Between leaving Jack at the airport, the bullshit with Blair, and getting stuck in the castle last night, my life is crumbling around me.

I take out my journal and begin recounting everything that happened at the castle. I haven't written in a few days and missed the feel of the ink gliding across the paper. Since this is for my eyes only, I write everything, including last night's vanilla sex. Part of me wishes Jack had used that whip after all, but we both needed the emotional connection and it was absolutely perfect. I know I'm a stubborn woman and fought loving him, but now that I've given in... I can't imagine any other ending. Trying to not fall was all for naught—he claimed every part of me as his.

Landing in New York, I stuff my journal in my bag and disembark. The time difference is going to fuck with me, so I'm grateful I'm not meeting with a lawyer until tomorrow morning. I want nothing more than to get home, shower, pop a melatonin, and crawl into bed.

Between the time it takes to get through customs and the rideshare home, it's nearly 10pm before I walk through my front door. I've only been away for a little while, but it feels like ages. I turn on the heat and toss my bag onto my couch. I don't have my grandmother's necklace, so I pull out her plaid blanket from my linen closet, and wrap myself in it. Curling up in my reading chair, I unlock my phone and find a new message from Jack. I was able to text him on the plane with the in-flight wifi, but he was asleep most of the time I was over the Atlantic.

JACK

Good morning, my wee spitfire.

Did you sleep ok?

You know I didn't.

It's late there, you should get some rest.
I'm working down in the tunnel today
with Cam while Lizzy researches clans.
Call me when you get up?

Of course.

I love you.

Not as much as I love you.

It's not a competition, you know.

Aye, but it's still true. Sleep well, sprite.

xo

My eyes are heavy, so I listen to my sweet boyfriend and get ready for bed. Sliding into the cold sheets without him is harder than I thought it would be. As soon as I get everything figured out with Blair, I'm on the first flight to Scotland.

Just like Jack, I hardly sleep, even with my trusty melatonin. True to my word, I call him as soon as I get up. He didn't find anything new in the castle, but Lizzy made headway with researching clans. Tomorrow, they'll scour the bedrooms and various common spaces for any trace of the family's tartan.

I stop at my favorite coffee shop to see Jackson before meeting with Lizzy's aunt. Instead of ordering my usual chai, I opt for an English breakfast tea with milk… and sugar, even if it would offend my hot Scot.

The office is a twenty minute walk, so I stroll down the street, tea in hand, filling my lungs with the cold winter air. It calms my nerves and gives me time to take in the city I love so much. The only thing missing… is Jack.

Once at the highrise, I check in with security and make my way to the twelfth floor. A secretary greets me as I exit the elevator and guides me into one of the meeting rooms, offering me water. As she leaves, I sink into the leather chair and blow out a long breath. A few minutes later, Melanie enters.

"Ms. Black. Hope you weren't waiting long." She offers her hand and I take it.

"No, not at all, Ms. Barlowe."

"Please, call me Melanie." *Well, shit, I feel like I should have her call me Amanda now...* "I'm not sure how I turned into a fixer for billionaires, but let's dive right in. Blair Jackson published your work under her name with no citation. She applied for and was granted copyright here in the US. At this point, we'll need to track your work in progress back to the date of origination to prove it's plagiarized work."

"It didn't even make it to my developmental or line editors. It was probably riddled with typos and using the word 'that' seven hundred times." I chuckle to myself. "Apparently, it's my favorite, and my editor slashes it almost every time. I read the book on the plane. Blair didn't change anything about the book and it was left on a shitty cliffhanger, since I wasn't done with it."

"You have the financial means to do whatever you want here. Do you want it taken down? Lawsuit? We can do pretty much anything to destroy her." Melanie has a tiny smirk tugging at her lips. While I know she's ruthless, based on what Lizzy had told me, I think she might enjoy the idea of taking Blair down much as I do.

Jack's words ring in my ear. *She's not worth it. Take back your book and let her go.*

"What is her current sales ranking?" I ask.

"Not even grazing the top five thousand. Reviews are coming in, it doesn't look good. Even if we pull it, you won't be able to republish it without readers thinking it's a cleaned up version of her book." She winces and offers an apologetic shrug.

"Leave it," I say evenly. "Let her bathe in the one-star reviews. I'll publish something else."

"I was hoping you'd say that. Do you have something ready? We can reach out to your publisher and see about expediting things."

A sly smile spreads across my face. "Oh, I have a story alright. I'll meet with my editor as soon as we're done."

"Great, less work for me," she laughs. "We can still slap her with a lawsuit if you're feeling feisty. Up to you."

"No point. I have something she'll never have. That's enough for me. But I'm wondering if there's something else you can help me with, or maybe point me in the right direction?" I take out the scanned copy of my adoption paperwork. "My mother died when I was born and my grandmother raised me. Her name is censored and there's no father listed. There's a small—and I mean *small*—chance that I might be related to the family Jack is researching. Even if I'm not, I want to know about my family."

"We can petition for the record. If your mother is dead, they'll likely release the information. Adoption is more complicated than you'd think. My friend, Riley, adopted two older children who are all grown up now, and none of them have access to their parent's information. Most people don't want it, and those that do almost always end up at a dead end."

"Jack wants me to take a DNA test, so I'll be doing that tomorrow when it arrives. I don't have any living family, so any answers would be helpful."

Melanie nods thoughtfully. "Absolutely. I'll see what I can do on my end. I might need you to sign paperwork. I'll draft it up before you leave. In the meantime, feel free to use this room as an office for as long as you need to make arrangements with Alexander Publishing." We both stand and shake hands before she leaves me in the meeting room alone with my thoughts.

My anger over this has subsided, and I'm grateful that I'll be able to return to Scotland sooner than expected. I take out my journal and phone. As the phone rings, I sift through the pages, reminiscing about my time with Jack until I find my most recent entry including Blair's betrayal. The assistant answers, and because my agent isn't in office, she transfers me directly to Lizzy's mom.

"Emma Alexander," she answers brightly.

"Hi, it's Amanda Storm. I have a favor to ask…"

46

JACK

After another sleepless night, I drag myself out of bed to the sound of Cameron and Lizzy arguing. I follow their voices to our work room, finding Lizzy with her hands crossed over her chest and Cam's on his hips.

"What's going on here?" I ask, dragging my hands down my face to wake myself up.

Lizzy's eyes narrow at Cam. "Your brother doesn't believe me that Amanda's not a Black."

"How the hell else do you explain it, Liz? And what of the initials etched in glass? She. Is. A. Black," he growls.

"You won't give me a chance to explain!"

"Alright, since he won't listen, explain to me why you think she's not a Black," I announce, ignoring Cam's huff and roll of his eyes.

Lizzy marches over to her computer, pulling up her research from yesterday. "Her grandmother was the last

Black, but look at this?" Lizzy points to an excerpt from the torn page of Ewen's journals. "Ewen had an affair. I followed the lineage and she's not just a Black, she's a *Blackwood.* The timing lines up to when her mother died."

"Why would her nan adopt her, if she wasn't a Black?" I ask.

"Her grandmother must have known who she was. If I'm right, Amanda is heir to *three* castles in Scotland. Greedy bitch," she grumbles. "They were one of the most wealthy families here in Scotland. She didn't need Ben and Julian's money, she's a billionaire without it."

"If you're right. We won't know anything until we get her DNA results back."

"Look, the woman he had an affair with, her name was Alice Marianne Blackwood." Lizzy traces their family tree. I lean forward to watch more closely. "She had a son, Archie Matthew Blackwood. Every generation, someone had the initials AMB."

"Should've listened to your lass, Cam," I tease. "This is brilliant, Lizzy." I check the time; it's still the middle of the night for Amanda. "I'll call her in the morning and let her know what I found. In the meantime, any movement on the clue?"

"Aye, but you're not going to like it," Cam says, rubbing the back of his neck.

"Fuck, I knew it," I say, defeated.

"You were right about the wedding and tartan, but the tartan isn't the Black's, it's the Blackwood's," Lizzy adds.

"So, it's hidden in another castle?"

Cam lays out a map of the castle. "No, it's probably here, we just need to figure out where."

Lizzy pulls up the crest for the Blackwood's, and inscribed in Gaelic are the words 'Never Hidden.'

"What the hell does that mean?" I snap.

"They're here," Lizzy mutters, looking off in thought. A second later, she pops up from her seat. "Follow me." Cam and I leave with her out of the work room. She leads us to the music room and takes a picture of one of the paintings with her phone. A moment of typing later, she shows us her screen. "Fuck, yes! I was right! Missing, presumed stolen."

I look around. "If everything has been hidden in plain sight, why would someone send us from castle to castle to find it?"

"The paintings aren't the treasure," Lizzy says with a wide smile. "Amanda is. She's the secret they were keeping. All of this? It was always here but people were probably too lazy to look into it. Whoever did the initial assessment wasn't cross referencing the database."

Cam claps me on the back. "We'll bring the crew in early to catalogue everything properly. I know what you're thinking... Go get your spitfire, Barty."

"I already have a ticket," I take out my phone and show Cam and Lizzy my flight for tomorrow afternoon.

"I fucking knew it," Cam jokes.

Lizzy bites her lip to hide her amusement. "A certain cousin in England might have a way you can get there faster."

47

AMANDA

I wake up to a knock at my door. I fell asleep earlier than normal last night; the weight of everything happening has me emotionally drained. I check the time, it can't be later than 10am…

"2pm?" I shriek. I scramble to put on a pair of leggings and my NYU sweatshirt, sans bra. "Coming!" Rushing to my door, I grumble, "So help me, if it's someone trying to sell me something."

I check the peephole and gasp; I can't unlock it fast enough. I fling open the door with a wide smile.

"What's a pretty lass like yourself doing in a place like this?" I run into Jack's arms, wrapping legs around him and burying my face in the crook of his neck. "Aren't you going to invite me in?" I hold him tighter, and he carries me inside.

"What are you doing here?"

Jack sets me down, but I keep my arms linked behind his neck. "I'm here because you're here."

"No." I shake my head. "You're supposed to be dirty in some tunnel, digging up treasure. Why are you here?"

"They're artifacts, not treasure," he chuckles, but his face falls when something behind me catches his eye. His brows pinch and he pulls my arms down from his neck. I follow his line of sight, frowning in confusion. "Where did you get this?" he asks, holding up my grandmother's blanket. "Fuck, the little lass was right," he mutters.

"It was my grandmother's, why?"

Jack takes out his phone and shows me a crest and a plaid that's similar to the blanket. "Blackwood family's tartan. There's so much I need to tell you." He sits on the couch and pats the cushion next to him for me to join him. When I do, he takes my hand in his and kisses the back of mine. "Lizzy found information in one of the journals and traced the lineage of the Blackwood family. The missing items we were looking for? It wasn't paintings, books, or jewelry. It was the secret that Ewen's affair with a Blackwood lass led to a wee bairn. Several generations later, including a certain great uncle worth millions, and we think you're the last Blackwood."

"What? That doesn't make any sense." I stand and begin pacing, absorbing everything he just told me. "Why would my grandmother have that blanket of another family's tartan?"

"I don't know. My guess is to give you something that shares a secret about who you are... Sound familiar?" he teases.

I chuckle. "She didn't leave me a book she wrote, in hopes that I'd figure out she wrote it." I pause, my laugh ceasing. "Did she?" I rush down the hall to my bedroom and quickly slide my closet open to retrieve the box of my grandmother's things. For years, I let them collect dust, never bothering to open it. I sit on the floor with it, taking out old books, an expired coupon for a restaurant that's no longer in business, pictures of the two of us, a glass vase with my initials etched in the bottom, and a small notebook.

I thumb through the books, but nothing looks to be annotated. I then open the notebook and find it's a diary. There's a letter folded inside. I look up, realizing I left Jack in my living room, but he's sitting across from me patiently.

My dearest Amanda,

I may not have given birth to you, but I love you like my own daughter. If you're reading this, either your curiosity got the best of you yet again, or I'm no longer with you. I hope, for both our sakes, you're just being your beautiful, inquisitive self.

In this diary, you'll find everything I know about your family. Your mother was one of the strongest women I've ever had the pleasure of knowing. She had a brother, Arthur, who passed away before she was born, leaving her to be the sole heir to the Blackwood fortune.

While your mother wasn't my daughter, she was my family. Generations ago, Ewen Black had an affair with Alice Blackwood, resulting in a child. That child is what joined her family with mine. Both families have kept it a secret for hundreds of years. You, Amanda, are the last of the Blackwood family, and therefore also the last Black.

Being the skeptical, stubborn woman you are, I know you will do your own research. When you accept the truth, return to Scotland. Ewen left you dozens of clues, unless a researcher has figured it out before you see this. If you're like me, and you like the spoiler of skipping to the ending of a book, start at Swarthmore Castle, it'll save you time.

If you're reading this when I'm no longer with you, I hope you find all the love you deserve, maybe even a nice Scottish man to carry on the Black and Blackwood lines.

I love you, my darling, to the moon and back.

Now, go take back what's yours.

Love,

Grandma Fiona

Tears paint my cheeks and Jack brushes them away. "Guess I don't need that DNA test," I jest through broken sobs.

"What does it say?" he quietly asks.

I hand him her letter. I'm about to get up while he reads it, but he pulls me into his lap. I begin reading her diary until he finishes. She wrote about my family, my mother, and how apparently I'm supposed to inherit a castle… *or three.*

"She's right, you know," Jack says as he folds up the letter and hands it back to me. "It's yours."

"I don't want it." I shake my head. "I don't need fortune and glory."

"What do you want?"

"I already have everything I want."

48

JACK

I'm jet lagged and Amanda is emotionally drained, so we clean everything up and climb into bed. She tucks into my side, an arm and a leg slung over me. "I can't believe you're here," she whispers.

"Ben chartered a plane, but I was planning on coming tomorrow." I show her the plane ticket I cancelled.

"Such a hopeless romantic, chasing after the girl who got away," she teases.

"Cam and Lizzy are cataloguing, and our crew will begin coming in tomorrow. I'll need to go back soon," I sigh, kissing the top of her head. "But I needed to see you."

"Couldn't stay away from your hot billionaire girlfriend, eh?"

Tempted to tell her I can't stay away from the woman I want to spend forever with, I opt for a safer option, "I couldn't stay away from the woman I'm in love with." I tilt her chin and press a soft kiss to her lips. "You're more than a girlfriend, spitfire."

"Oh no. Is prematurely proposing a family thing?" She winces. "I love you, Jack, but please don't be ridiculous and plan some over the top engagement-turned-wedding for me."

I cough a laugh. "No, I'm not Ben. I will absolutely marry you one day, but I want time with you when we're not unearthing a family mystery or dealing with my ex-wife stealing your book."

She breathes an exaggerated sigh of relief. "Phew, ok, so I'll just expect a proposal in ten business days."

"Why ten?"

Amanda bites her lip and sits up to rest her chin on my chest. "I forgot to tell you. I'm publishing. I should have editor notes by then."

"You got your book back? That's amazing news!"

"Nope," she replies, popping the 'p.' "Better. She can have my unedited romantic suspense story. She made her bed, she can lie in it. I'm publishing a sexy as fuck story, though. Think: adventure romance meets spicy rom-com."

"Let me guess, someone gets stuck in a castle?"

"No…" She bites back a smile, and I raise an eyebrow. "Ok, fine, yes, they get stuck in a castle. But I'm making the sex so much hotter."

I choke on my own air. "Excuse me?"

"What? Don't worry, she'll still suffocate him with her pussy. I write men who like to eat."

I sit up and pin her beneath me. "Don't make me go to the store for a can of squirty cream. You may prefer chapter seven, but I have no problem with chapter fourteen."

"You wouldn't dare," she huffs, narrowing her eyes. "But can I take a moment to enjoy the fact that you just called whipped cream 'squirty cream.' That sounds like a bad erotica title."

"Or the title of your next book, *Amanda Gray*." I kiss her neck and press my already hard length against her centre. She stifles a moan at the contact, and I can't help teasing her further. "So, tell me, what could be 'so much hotter' than when I make you come eight times in a single night?"

"You'll have to wait until we're home to find out."

49

JACK

SIX MONTHS LATER

With Swarthmore Castle nearly renovated, we're only four months out from the museum opening. A dozen researchers, in addition to Cameron, Lizzy, and I, finished cataloguing the remaining art and other arte-facts two weeks ago. There are no additional clues from what we can tell; Lizzy was right, my spitfire was the treasure.

Amanda is in Edinburgh for a book signing. I told her I wouldn't be able to attend but I plan on surprising her and spending the weekend home. It'll also give me a chance to visit with my family. As much as I love working in Skye, I haven't seen my parents in months and they haven't met Amanda yet.

Her signing is in two hours, leaving me enough time to stop at my parent's place in Craigentinny before seeing her. My mum answers the door before I reach it, with a beaming smile. "Come in, come in!" She looks behind me. "Where's Amanda?"

"I'll bring her by tomorrow. I have something important I need to pick up," I tell her as I walk inside and give her a knowing look.

"Jack," she gasps. "You need me mum's ring?" Her hand clutches her chest and she begins speaking in Gaelic—which she only does when she's excited. Mine is rusty but I make out that she said she thought this day would never come.

"Mum, relax, I'm not planning on asking any time soon. I just want it for the right moment." Amanda's special and deserves a perfect proposal, even if I would've asked her no less than a hundred times before today.

"Yes, yes, of course." She steps out of the room to fetch it.

Ben bought his own ring for Layla, and Blair insisted on something modern, which left this ring to Cameron. I talked to him last week about it, and with his blessing, I'm going to give it to the most extraordinary woman I've ever known.

Mum returns and opens the small jewellery box as she hands it to me. "You're going to ask her soon, I can tell."

"Aye, you're right. It will be sooner than later."

"That ring will be on your lass tomorrow," she deadpans.

My face falls as I admit, "No, she's not ready." I take one last look at my nan's ring and tuck it into my pocket. "We'll stop by for tea tomorrow."

She takes my face in my hands and pulls me closer, narrowing her eyes. "You're a braw man, Jack. Ask the lass when you're ready." I nod in thanks. She lets go of my face and rights her posture. "Tea it is."

I hug her tightly, we say our goodbyes, and I make my way to Amanda's signing. When I arrive there are no less than fifty people waiting outside the bookshop. I wait in line with them, hoping Amanda won't see me too soon—my plan is to blend into the crowd. I take a seat next to two women who are talking about her book.

"Can you imagine? If a man put his cock in me *on accident*, I would be tossing him on the bed and finishing the job," one says. I do my best not to laugh but I can't help the smirk pulling at my lips.

"Do you think he's real?" the other asks.

"No, there's no reason an artist would be hunting a missing treasure."

I'm grateful that Amanda changed her story to make me an artist and her a self-made billionaire. It still made for a fun novel, but keeps our lives semi-private. As promised, she omitted New York, and had the main characters meet at a gala.

The room fills with excited readers and Amanda takes the podium for a reading before she'll sign copies of her book. "Welcome everyone," she says with a bright smile. "Tonight, I'll be reading an excerpt from my recent release, *The Ruined Spitfire*. I started writing this bo—" She spots me and lightly licks her upper lip with a chuckle, then returns to her audience. "I started writing this book when I heard a story about a hot Scot falling for a woman he hardly knew." She clears her throat, opens her book and begins reading.

A few minutes later, she's reading a passage I'm not familiar with.

"This tall, beautiful man can't take his eyes off me. Worse, I can't look away. Something about his emerald eyes has heat pooling in my belly. One thing is certain, I'm going to spend the rest of my life with this man, if only he'd ask."

There are murmurs around the room. I tilt my head to catch some of it. They are all saying the same thing; the last part wasn't in her book.

Amanda clears her throat. "The last paragraph is part of an extended epilogue I will be posting on my website later this week. Just know, she doesn't wait for him to ask her."

What is that supposed to mean?

There's a round of applause, and I couldn't be more proud of my spitfire; her book reached number one on her release day. We celebrated over a whisky sour and whisky in New York, at the same hotel bar we met when her last release didn't do as well as she'd hoped.

When Amanda is done with closing remarks, she steps away from the podium and settles into a chair at her prepared table as readers line up. I stand and find the romance section of the bookshop to pick up a copy of one of her books. I'm about to pull her new title from the shelf when I see Maybe in Fifty. I tuck it under my arm and make my way to the cashier. Once I've paid, I join the line of readers.

I wait in line for over an hour and when I make my way to the front, I hand her my book and it takes everything in me to not lean over the table to kiss her. She does her best to not smile but fails miserably. "I believe you have several copies of this title."

"Aye. One of my favourites."

She bites back a smile. "Who should I make this out to?"

"Surprise me."

Amanda scribbles a message and signs the book. She hands it to me, but as I take it, she doesn't let go of it. "Don't read it until later. I'll be done in thirty minutes." She releases the book, and I step out of the way so the next reader can have theirs signed.

As much as I want to read her message, whatever she wrote is important to her, so I resist the temptation. I leave the bookshop and walk down to a small cafe that's still open. It's the same one we visited when she was in Leith for the first time. I order a black coffee and a black tea, adding sugar despite my disgust. When I return to the bookshop, there's only two readers left in line. I watch as Amanda attempts to give them her undivided attention, but still glances over at me every so often.

Once she's done with her signing, I hand her the tea and help box up her bookmarks and other collateral materials. As she sips her tea, she asks, "Did you read it?"

"You asked me not to." I reply with a shrug as I continue placing items in her box.

Her hand covers mine as I reach for the pens. "Come with me."

Amanda interlaces our fingers and leads me to the romance section, glances around as if she's on a heist, then says, "Ok, read it."

I open the book and the message reads:

MY HOT SCOT,
I AM NOT WAITING FIFTY FOR YOU TO ASK.
MARRY ME?
XO, YOUR WEE SPITFIRE

My heart stops. I glance up only to find her on one knee in front of me, a jewellery box open with a simple white gold band. I drop to my knee and glide my hand into her hair, bringing her lips to mine. I don't stop kissing her while I pull out my nan's ring from my pocket.

"Is that a yes?" she asks.

I pull back enough to look into her eyes. "You couldn't wait until tonight?" I open my jewellery box to reveal my nan's ring. "Will you marry me, spitfire?"

"Oh, come on! Way to ruin my grand gesture," she laughs. I remove the ring, and as I slip it onto her finger, she gasps. "It's stunning. Wait, this isn't part of the Swarthmore Castle treasure, right?"

"No," I chuckle. "It was my nan's. Is that a yes?" I echo her question.

"I don't know, I asked you first."

"I asked you second," I counter.

"Semantics. Will you marry me, Jack?"

"Yes, sprite, I'll marry you." I kiss her. This time, I don't care that it's not innocent enough for a bookshop. I taste and tease her mouth until she moans into mine.

"I love you," she mutters against my lips.

"I love you more, my wee spitfire."

"Damn it, Jack! Can't you just be mine and not one-up me?"

I press a final kiss to her lips and tell her, "Where is the fun in that? I will always be yours, Amanda, and for the rest of our lives, you'll be mine."

EPILOGUE
JACK

One Month Later

The sun rises over the horizon, painting the sky a beautiful orange and yellow, just as it did when I met my wee spitfire. Today, I'm not just claiming her as mine, I'm making this incredible woman my wife.

Amanda wanted to elope, and I don't blame her. She doesn't have any living relatives, whereas I have a close family. While this is my second marriage, I would never be able to live with myself if I didn't invite them.

Amanda worked with Lizzy's uncle—who is an interesting bloke—to coordinate a small wedding for us. They arranged everything in one month, but it was the longest month of my life.

I join Amanda on the balcony of our hotel room, and wrap my arms around her from behind. "Mornin'," I whisper against the crook of her neck. There isn't a moment I'm with her when I'm able to keep my hands and mouth to myself.

She turns in my arms and pins me with worried eyes. "Are you sure you still want to do this?"

"Of course, why wouldn't I?" I ask, frowning.

"I don't know," she says quietly.

"If you don't want to, I'll still love you, even if we never get married. Fuck, I'll still love you, even if you leave me. We can call off the wedding and it won't change how I feel about you. As much as I love the idea of calling you my wife, we don't have to get married if you don't want to."

"What if in a year, I'm fluffy from eating too many tacos with Layla? Or what if this was all just some sort of chemical thing, like endorphins or something, from too much sex?" she teases, but there's genuine concern behind her voice.

I rest my forehead on hers. "Eat your tacos. Do—or don't—let me make love to you every night. I want to spend the rest of my life with you. What's this about?"

With a small shrug, she replies, "Cold feet, I guess."

"Let's call off the wedding," I offer, scared for the first time in months that I might lose her.

"No," she says quickly. "I want to marry you. I love you so fucking much. I want to be your wife, and want to spend forever with you. Weddings are just a reminder that I don't have family. I don't have anyone to walk me down the aisle..." She shrugs and shakes her head again, frowning. "I'm just in my head."

"Amanda." Her eyes snap up to me. "Fuck tradition, I'll walk you down the aisle."

"That won't be weird?"

"*I'm* your family now. We decide what we want to do, together."

She chews on her lip, then sighs and asks, "I know I said I wanted to keep my last name, but would it be ok if I changed it?"

"To Blackwood? Of course."

"No." Amanda offers a small smile. "Jackson. I know I'm the last Blackwood, but if we're going to really be a family—" I kiss her to end her explanation. "No more Barty Juniors, though," she chuckles against my lips.

I place my hand on her belly. "When you're ready—*if you're ever ready*—we'll make sure to carry on your name. We don't need a fourth generation of Bartholomew Jacksons, unless you want to torture the bairn."

Amanda wraps her arms around me. "Now that I'm done freaking out... let's go get married." She then says softly, "I love you, Jack... don't you dare try to one-up me this time."

Kissing the top of her head, I do no such thing, and tell her, "Except we both know I love you more, my wee spitfire."

BONUS EPILOGUE

AMANDA

One Year Later

Marriage is not what I expected it to be. Not only am I still hopelessly in love with my husband, he's my best friend, my biggest cheerleader, and as he promised... *my family.*

After everything was inherited, Jack and I have billions, even after donating to charity. I transferred everything from the three castles that were passed down to me and turned them into museums. The donation ended up increasing our wealth, and no matter how much we give away, the number never seems to budge. Worst first-world problem to have in the history of time.

I refuse to live in a large space, so Jack and I have been living in our apartment in Leith. We also have small apartments in Paris and London, as well as my old place in New York. He's had two major projects since Swarthmore Castle, and I've traveled with him for both. I'm an author, I can live anywhere.

Sitting in bed with my laptop perched on my lap, I'm inches away from finishing my book. While my little romantic comedy was a fun little side tour, I'm so much happier writing a political romantic suspense this time.

Wrapping up the epilogue, I can feel Jack's eyes on me. "Almost done," I tell him as I continue to type. He doesn't say anything, and I can still sense him lurking. I glance up from the laptop to find him standing at the foot of the bed, completely naked, holding his... "Oh no. *Oh no, no, no.* Put that thing away."

Jack continues his silence as he slowly strokes it and rounds the side of the bed. "I know you'll love how it feels in your hands. I promise I won't use it on your arse."

"You are not using a *bullwhip* on me, Jack," I growl.

"I won't use it on you. I had other plans," he purrs. I give up on my book for now; this is definitely more exciting. I set my laptop on the bedside table and strip out of my sweatshirt. His gaze falls to my breasts and a rumble comes from his chest. "Are you done writing?"

"No, but I'm curious what your other plans are."

Jack sets down his whip and hands me my laptop. "Finish your book and I'll show you."

"And, what, you're just going to stand there?" I raise an eyebrow but my eyes widen when his darken. He climbs onto the bed and sits next to me. In a swift motion, he lifts me and sets me between his legs with my back flush to his chest. "You think I'll get much done while your cock is pressed against my ass?"

"Write. Or I'll press my cock *in* your arse."

"As if I wouldn't be into it," I grumble.

His hand slips into my leggings and cups my pussy. "What was that?"

"Nothing," I breathe as he slides two fingers inside me.

Jack kisses my shoulder. "You don't get to finish until your book does," he teases.

"Two can play that game, dearest husband."

I take off my leggings and panties, tossing them to the floor. Reaching into the nightstand, I remove a bottle of lube, squirting a dollop onto my hand to coat his cock.

"What are you up to, spitfire?"

I flash him a devilish grin and return to my position in front of him, this time lifting up enough to line his cock up with my ass. Sitting an inch onto him and stopping, I look over my shoulder and ask, "How long do you think you can last without coming?"

"Fuck, sprite," he groans as I lower myself another inch, then another. He holds onto my hips to slowly guide me the rest of the way down. I'm deliciously stretched and have to resist fucking him. Most of the time, he breaks me and I give in. Tonight, I'm pretty sure he'll be the one to cave.

"I know you love my cock in your tight arse, but you need to finish writing."

"Oh, I intend to." I wiggle further onto his cock, making him grit out a couple of swears. I smile to myself as I bring my laptop back in front of me to finish the last paragraph, clenching my ass every so often, just to fuck with him.

Jack reaches between my legs and circles my clit, making it harder for me to concentrate. My words read like a drunk person wrote them and I'm pretty sure I changed point of view at least once. Also, the last two sentences are suddenly in third person. Why he thought this was a good idea is beyond me; I'll have to do a massive edit in the morning. Then again, I'm also an idiot for thinking I can write with his cock in my ass.

"How is your book coming along, sprite?" he grits out.

"It's great," I pant. "Best I've written."

He chuckles darkly and nips at my shoulder. "Why is there a missing dialogue tag? You also switched tenses."

Fuck, this is worse than I thought.

"Will you please just let me come so I can finish my book?"

"Finish your book and I'll let you come," he counters, kissing my neck. "I have big plans for you tonight."

"Fine, I'll do it myself."

I swat his hand away from my clit and press two fingers inside me to wet them. I drag them up to circle my clit. I need to move fast; it's only a matter of time before he stops me. He shifts behind me to reach into the drawer of the bedside table and pull out my vibrator.

"This cunt is mine tonight. You come when I let you, my beautiful wife." He turns it on and slides it between my hand and clit. "You can touch yourself when I'm gone next week. Until then, you're mine."

I fucking love when he gets all growly like this. He presses the vibrator inside me. The fullness makes my ass clench around his cock; he hisses at the sensation. Anxious to find out what he has planned, I grind down onto him and chase my orgasm.

Jack pulls the vibrator out of me, turns it off, and tosses it aside. Not a second later, I'm lifted off his cock and set on the bed next to him. I wasn't close, but I'm gasping to catch my breath. He moves off the bed and fetches his whip.

"Oh, fuck," I mutter.

"Oh, fuck, is right." He climbs back onto the bed, this time nearly straddling me. "Tell me if it's too much."

Pinning my hands above me at the top of the head-board, he wraps the leather around both of my wrists and binds them. He secures them to the headboard and, all at once, I'm wet and desperate to see how this plays out.

Jack slides off the bed and walks into the bathroom. "Jack," I call. "Are you seriously going to just leave me here?" The water to the faucet turns on and I ask, "What are you doing? Washing your dick off in the sink?" The sound of the faucet stops and he returns to the room a moment later.

"So fucking beautiful all tied up for me." His eyes are dark, full of lust, as his gaze rakes my body. "Consider this my new take on chapter seven."

My husband's gone mad. It's going to be so fucking messy; we usually do it in the shower. I don't know if I have a clean duvet handy. He climbs onto the bed and spreads my legs wide.

"I've been craving the taste of you all day," he groans and licks up my center, swirling his tongue around my clit. His eyes stay fixed on mine as he slowly presses three fingers inside me, making me cry out. He chuckles against my clit. I pointlessly tug at my restraints. It's almost too much.

"Please, Jack," I beg, desperate to have him inside me.

He withdraws his fingers and presses a single kiss above my pussy before trailing his lips up my body. "You need my cock?"

"Yes," I breathe. "Are you sure we shouldn't move this to the shower?"

Jack grazes his teeth against one of my nipples. "I'm sure, my love." He licks and sucks on the other, then moves up to my neck. The sting of him marking me makes me moan and writhe beneath him. I wrap my legs around him, needing more.

He reaches between us and lines up his cock before pushing inside. Kissing me deeply, he begins moving in and out of me, hard but not fast. He keeps a perfect pace, winding me tighter. I want to touch him, rake my nails down his back, push him off so I can straddle his face... I'm helpless, but I love every second of it.

My hips buck while I try to maintain any semblance of control. He laughs against my lips, "I love that you need more, but you're going to be a good lass and wait for me."

He angles my hips to take him deep, then reaches between us to circle his thumb on my clit. My breath is ragged and my body is begging for release; he winds me tighter and tighter until my orgasm is almost in reach. His thrusts become harder; he's close too. Our kisses are urgent, fevered. The need to be closer to him is unbearable.

"Let go. Come for me so I can worship your perfect cunt with my face between your legs, and claim every inch of you for the rest of the night," he growls.

Jack's words are my undoing, but they're his as well. I feel him fill me as my pussy pulses around his cock. His mouth travels down my body until his tongue is firmly on my sensitive clit. I cry out as he presses two fingers in my pussy, coating them with a mix of both of us. He swirls his fingers inside me, then drags them up to my clit, circling it twice before trails them up my body. He traces his wet fingers around each of my nipples, then returns his fingers between my legs. Only this time, when he pulls his fingers out of me, he sucks them clean and drives his tongue into my mouth to taste both of us. I kiss him back harder, matching every swipe of his tongue.

He reaches up to my bound hands and carefully removes the leather. The moment my wrists are free, he pulls me onto him, taking me in his arms, and practically refuses to stop kissing me.

"Mine," I growl into his mouth.

He smiles against my lips and whispers, "Yours."

SIP HAPPENS SNEAK PEEK
LIZZY

There's a knock on my open office door. I glance up and my breath catches as a ruggedly handsome man walks in. He's easily 6'3", with bright green eyes and a megawatt smile that's impossible to ignore. I close my gaping mouth and he asks, "Is this Elizabeth Alexander's office?"

Uh, yeah, it's on the door…

"Yes, that's me," I reply brightly.

"I was told you did all the displays for the Kildalton Crosses I brought my last time here."

Fuck, his accent is hot. Not just his accent, though, this man has to be some sort of model or something. Wait, what did he say? Something about Kildalton Crosses? Shit, ok, play it cool like you were listening to what this sexy Scottish man was saying.

"Yes," I say, unsure if I'm agreeing to something or not. It takes me a moment to process, but I finally put it together. "You're Cameron Jackson."

"Aye, that's me."

"I did the displays for the collection."

His brows pinch together. "I believe that's what I said... I'm sorry, have we met?"

"No, I think I'd remember meeting a hot Scottish archaeologist in my museum before." *Fuck, I just said that out loud.* My eyes wide, my hand flies to my mouth. "I'm so sorry, what I meant to say is: I think I'd remember meeting you."

"You think I'm hot, lass?"

Yes. "Doesn't matter. My apologies, that was completely unprofessional of me, especially since I'll be on your brother's excavation site when it starts."

Cameron's eyebrows playfully raise once. "Is that so? Well, for now, I have additional items for the collection."

"Wonderful. I'll catalog and add them to the current exhibit."

He rubs the back of his neck, looks up at me through his lashes, and offers me a boyish grin. For a man who is easily ten years older than me, he's really laying the charm on thick. "There are a lot of pieces. Perhaps we should discuss over a pint?"

"A pint?"

"Aye, unless…" His eyes widen and he pauses.

"Unless what?"

"Can you drink here? Are you of age?"

Of age? What is this? Regency Era England? "Yes, I'm *of age*. I was just confused about why you would want to have a drink with me."

"It's settled. I'll be back at 4:30 when the museum closes, and will wait until you're off work."

Before I can protest, he's out of my office, leaving me completely in shock. *What the hell just happened?*

LOVED UNEXPECTEDLY RUINED?

I hope you loved reading Amanda and Jack's story as much as I loved writing it! While their story is complete, Lizzy and Cameron are getting a wee novella: *Sip Happens*, a crossover between the Top Shelf Romances series and the Love At All Cost series.

Wherever you feel most comfortable, please consider leaving a review on Goodreads, Amazon, or social media! Your honest review means the world to me.

To keep up with all of my upcoming releases, be sure to follow me over on Amazon!

xoxo,
Irene

ACKNOWLEDGMENTS

First, I would like to thank my amazing 'Big Fucking Deal' women: Jodi, Eliza, Maia, and Kelsey — I couldn't do this without you!

To my alpha and beta readers Dani, Eliza, Kendra, Amanda, Whisper, and Effie — You ladies are amazing! I'm so grateful for all of your help with this book.

To my ARC readers — Thanks for taking a chance on me! I know my books aren't your typical spicy romcom, so thank you for jumping in with two feet with this novel. I am so blessed to have all of you reading and reviewing my work before launch.

To my incredible line editor H.M. Darling — Without you, my books would be trash! I can't thank you enough for helping make my books amazing!

Finally, thank you to all of my author friends for not letting my imposter syndrome take over, my "real life" friends for believing in me, and my family for putting up with my silly little dream of becoming a published author.

xoxo,

Irene

ABOUT THE AUTHOR

Irene Bahrd is a Gryffindor Capricorn and one of the most avid readers you'll ever meet.

She started her writing journey as a dare from a friend, after recounting dating stories from her early twenties. They inspired her to write spicy parody and romantic comedy novels that feature a variety of book boyfriends —from growly alpha heroes to cinnamon roll golden retrievers.

Her favorite genres to read include fantasy romance and contemporary dark romance. You'll find some of her favorite books and authors referenced by characters in her own books.

Irene can be found on Instagram and TikTok under @irenebahrdauthor

ALSO BY IRENE BAHRD

<u>Love at all Cost Series</u>

A Voice Without Reason

Not Her Villain

Maybe in Fifty *(Prequel Novella to Unexpectedly Ruined)*

Unexpectedly Ruined

<u>Stand-Alones</u>

Never Yours

Flexible Standards

Undeclared Heir

Arranged Vacancy

The Al Dente Diet *(Collaboration with J.L. Quick)*

<u>Top Shelf Romances Series</u>

Mine with Extra Lime

Falling the Old Fashioned Way

Royally on the Rocks

Trouble with a Twist

<u>Top Shelf Novella Series</u>

Wine About It

Rosé to the Occasion

Mule Tide Cheer

Sip Happens

Printed in Great Britain
by Amazon

36780802R00208